Fiona McFarlane's stories have been published in various magazines and anthologies including the *New Yorker*, *Best Australian Stories* and *Zoetrope: All-Story*. Her first novel, *The Night Guest* (Sceptre, 2014), was shortlisted for the *Guardian* First Book Award, the Miles Franklin Award and a *Los Angeles Times* Book Prize among others, and won several prizes in Australia including the inaugural Voss Literary Prize and a New South Wales Premier's Literary Award. She lives in Sydney.

the

HIGH

PLACES

FIONA
McFARLANE

SCEPTRE

First published in Australia in 2016 by Penguin Random House Australia

First published in Great Britain in 2016 by Sceptre
An imprint of Hodder & Stoughton
An Hachette UK company

First published in paperback in 2017

1

'Art Appreciation' originally appeared in the *New Yorker*; 'The Movie People' in
Best Australian Stories 2010 and *Something Special, Something Rare*; 'Those
Americans Falling from the Sky' and 'Mycenae' in *Zoetrope: All-Story*; 'Exotic
Animal Medicine' in the *Missouri Review* and *New Australian Stories 2*.

A CIP catalogue record for this title is available from the British Library

ISBN 978 1 444 77673 7

Typeset in Adobe Caslon Pro

Printed and bound by Clays Ltd, St Ives plc

Hodder & Stoughton policy is to use papers that are natural, renewable and
recyclable products and made from wood grown in sustainable forests. The
logging and manufacturing processes are expected to conform to the
environmental regulations of the country of origin.

Hodder & Stoughton Ltd
Carmelite House
50 Victoria Embankment
London EC4Y 0DZ

www.sceptrebooks.com

For Emma

Contents

Exotic Animal
Medicine

The wife was driving on the night they hit Mr Ronald.

'My first drive since getting married,' she said.

'First this, first that,' said her husband. He looked at her, sitting high in the seat: her hair looked flimsy and blonde. It was ten o'clock and only just dark. These were the days for marrying – the long days, and the summer. It hadn't rained.

'You've got to be thankful for the weather,' the registrar had said to the husband. The husband was thankful for the weather and for everything else. He carried his shoulders inside a narrow suit and his wife wore a blue dress. They came out of the registry office into the pale summer and St Mary's rang the hour.

'Listen!' said the wife. 'Just like we've been married in a church.'

It was midday, and because they were in Cambridge the college bells also rang.

'Like we've been married in every church,' said the husband.

Their witnesses – two friends – took photographs. The four of them went to a pub on the river to celebrate among the tourists and the students who'd just finished exams. The tourists pressed around them, clumsy at the bar; the students slipped through and were served first. The bride and groom were rocked from side to side in the crush. They co-operated with the crowd and liquid spilled over their glasses.

They began to drink.

Their friend Robbie swayed above their table. He motioned over their heads with his benevolent arms.

'I suppose I'm best man,' he said. 'By default. So, a toast: to David and Sarah. To Sarah and David. I'll make a statement about love. I'll say a few words.'

'You've already said more than enough,' said the other witness, Clare.

'Not nearly enough,' said Robbie, and sat down.

By now it was four in the afternoon and the June town was keeping quiet. The lawns maintained their perfect green. The river lay straight like a track for trains. David and Sarah and Clare and Robbie walked along it to find another pub, and beside them swans idled on the brown water, ducks chased punts for food, geese slid against the wet banks. Tinfoil barbecues were lit on Jesus Green, one by one, and the smoke hung in morose columns above each group, never thick enough to form a cloud. The husband and wife and their friends picked their way among the barbecues. They encountered dogs, friendly and wayward.

'Stay well today, canines,' said David. 'Stay happy and healthy.'

Sarah was on call that night.

'I'm not worried about them,' said Sarah. 'It's the Queen of Sheba I'm worried about. But he'll be good.'

(At the surgery, the Queen of Sheba lifted his haunches and lowered his head to stretch his grey back. He walked figure eights in his cage, the way a tiger would.)

'He'd better be good,' said David.

'That bloody cat,' said Sarah happily.

(The Queen of Sheba sat in his cage at the surgery and looked out at the ferrets and iguanas. He looked out at the tanks of scorpions and turtles. He settled, sphinx-like, and crossed his paws. The nurse poked her fingers through the grille as she passed Sheba's cage and Sheba, yawning, ignored them.)

The crowd at the pub seemed to part before the bridal party and they found an outdoor table, newly abandoned. Their happiness brought good luck. Sarah said, 'I should stop drinking. I might have to work.'

'You might,' said Robbie, 'and you might not.'

'This is your wedding reception,' said Clare, and she placed her arm around Sarah, coaxing.

'You need a gin and tonic,' said Robbie.

'My first gin as a married woman,' said Sarah. She sat beside David and felt the day carry them toward each other. The hours passed at the pub and they didn't go home, although this was what they looked forward to: the privacy of their bed below smudged windows, its view of small gardens, and the beat of trapped bees against glass that shook as the buses moved by. Their bed was a long way from the colleges and the river but the bells would still come over the roads and houses, and they would be alone, and married. The day moved them toward the moment in which they would face each other in their bed and see that despite their marriage there was no change, and that this was just what they wanted.

Sarah's phone rang at nine o'clock. She knew it would be work, and so did David. He creased his face at her, disbelieving, but found he wasn't disappointed. This way he would have her to himself. They would drive in the car and she would tell him her impressions of the day. He would imitate the mannerism he'd disliked in the registrar: a tendency to blink too often and too hard. He would rest his hand on her warm leg and watch the way her driving forced her to keep her usually animated hands still. This animation would pass instead into her face, where her eyebrows would knit and rise across her forehead. She would lean a long way forward to look left and right at intersections, as if she needed to see vast distances. Sarah drove as if she were landing an enormous plane full of porcelain children on a mountaintop.

'What a surprise,' said Sarah. She placed her phone on the table. 'The Queen of Sheba needs a catheter.'

Clare said, 'There must be someone else?'

'No one else,' said Sarah, standing now, slightly unsteady on her feet, but graceful. 'Sheba's all mine. He's a friend's cat.'

'And does this friend know you got married today?' asked Clare.

Sarah laughed. No one knew they'd been married today.

'Your wedding night and you have to go stick something up a cat's dick,' said Robbie.

(Sheba rolled in his cage. The pain felt familiar to him, but newly terrible, a hot pressure. He flicked his paws to shake it off. He couldn't.)

Sarah led David from the pub. He leaned against her the way he did when he was on the way to being very drunk. In fact, he was just perfectly, amiably, generously drunk, inclined to pause in order to kiss his new wife. He felt grateful when he looked at her. He felt an expansion in his brain that he enjoyed – a feeling that finally he had found his life, or was finding it, was on the verge of finding it, although he was still a graduate student and suspected he always would be. He said to himself, This is my youth, at this moment, right now, and because he was drunk, he also said it to Sarah.

The walk home wasn't far; still, they took their time doing it. Sarah felt a sense of urgency about Sheba but couldn't translate that urgency into hurry. She felt the way she did in those anxious dreams when she was due somewhere important and was unable to find the items she needed to bring with her. The light was lowering now. They spent whole minutes standing on the side of the road in order to watch a woman move around her lit basement kitchen, ironing. As they approached their flat, David said, 'You know I'm coming with you,' and she didn't argue. They changed their clothes and it felt to Sarah, briefly, as if it had been David's suit and her dress that had married each other earlier in the day. David followed her to the car. Before sitting in the driver's seat she shook her head from side to side as if she might clear it. She didn't feel drunk.

It was an old car, friendly but unreliable, that flew with dog hair when the windows were down. It required patience, particularly in the winter; even now, in June, it demonstrated a good-natured reluctance to start. Sarah turned the key; the engine kicked in and then out. David played with the radio to find a good song and when there were no good songs, he turned it low. As if encouraged by this decrescendo, the car co-operated. Cambridge was lit with orange lights. They passed through the city with exaggerated care and were in the country very suddenly, with dark fields pressing round them and airplanes far overhead. England became a long dark road, then, with bright windows visible across fields, and trees against the sky.

'What's wrong with this cat?' said David.

'Urinary tract.'

'I know that. But what's *wrong* with it?'

Sarah grew defensive on behalf of Sheba.

'He can't help it.'

'Why call a tomcat Sheba?'

'They let their kid name it,' said Sarah. 'It's the name of a brand of cat food. It uses real cuts of meat rather than by-products.'

'Crazy.'

'Don't,' said Sarah.

'It's crazy. It's like your mum naming your brother Leslie and your dad doing nothing to stop it.'

'It's a family name. It's a boy's name! And I don't want to think about my mother. Right now I'm pretending she doesn't exist. I left my phone at home,' said Sarah. 'If she calls, I don't want to tell her we're married, and I don't want not to have told her.'

'So just don't answer.'

'I'd have to answer. I couldn't not answer. And then – you know.' She spread her hands in order to indicate her predicament and returned them to the steering wheel.

'Then – disaster.'

She hit at him with her left hand.

'Watch the road!' he said, laughing. She watched the road.

'My first drive since getting married,' she said.

'First this, first that,' he said.

A car pulled out of a dark side road and turned directly in front of them. Sarah veered to the left but still met the back corner of this car; trees moved in front of the windscreen, tyres made a long noise against the road, Sarah and David jolted over the grass and stones of the verge, they hit a low wooden fence and felt the engine splutter and stall. And as this took place they were aware of something more urgent occurring behind them: the spin of the other car, its dive into a roadside tree. Sarah and David remained still for a moment, preparing for an impact that didn't come.

'Fuck,' said Sarah, looking back down the dim road. The muted lights of tiny Cambridge hung orange at the bottom of the sky behind them. The car radio continued to play.

'You're all right?' asked David, but that was obvious. He opened his door and stepped out. The other car reminded him of a cartoon dog, excessively punched, whose nose has folded into its face for a brief and hilarious moment before relaxing out again, essentially unhurt. He watched Sarah run toward the car and ran after her. The driver's door had opened in the crash and the driver sat, his legs pinioned, his right arm hanging, and his head turned away as if he were embarrassed to have been found in this position. He wasn't moving.

'He's not dead,' said Sarah, but couldn't have explained why she was so sure.

She knelt beside the car and held the man's wrist, and when she released it she wiped her fingers against her skirt. David leaned against the tree and passed his hand across his face. He felt the air press in around him and he wanted somehow to press it back. Sarah had found the man's wallet on the front passenger seat.

'His whole name is just three first names,' she said, inspecting his licence. 'Ralph Walter Ronald. He's eighty.'

Sarah looked carefully at this Mr Ronald, acknowledging his age and misfortune. She felt that his awkward name had lifted him out of a time in which she'd played no part and deposited him here, in his crushed car.

'We need to call someone,' she said.

'No phone,' said David.

8

'Where's yours?'

'In my suit, probably.'

'Shit!'

'You left yours too,' said David.

'Deliberately,' said Sarah.

'Which way to the nearest house?'

'I don't know.'

'Forward or back?'

'I don't know.'

'This is your drive to work. You drive this way almost every day.'

'It's dark. I haven't been paying attention.'

'All right, all right,' said David. He realised he was pulling at the roots of his hair. People really do that, then, he thought, in a crisis – pull their hair. 'I'll try the car. It seems like ages since we saw a house.'

'Nothing in England is ever very far apart.'

It began to rain, very lightly. The rain seemed to rise out of the ground and lift up into their faces, a cheerful mist.

'All right, try the car,' said Sarah. 'I'll sit with him. His car won't blow up, will it? Or is that just in movies?'

'It would have blown up by now. Wouldn't it?'

They stood helpless in their combined ignorance, considering Mr Ronald's car and Mr Ronald trapped within it. The passenger seat was whole and healthy, although the accordion-fold of the front of the car left no leg room. Sarah brushed glass from the seat and slid in beside Mr Ronald, tucking her legs beneath her.

David crossed to their car with mid-city caution. It wouldn't start; it would never start when he was late for a seminar or a critical train, it required tender solicitations after particularly steep hills. Of course it wouldn't start now, when his need was desperate. Perhaps it was finally beyond repair – and then there would be the panic of finding money for a new car. David tried again. It wouldn't start and wouldn't start. He ran back to Sarah.

'No good,' he said. 'Fuck it. I'll run. I'm sure I'll find someone. Another car.'

'Go forward, not back,' said Sarah. 'I think there's a petrol station. God, I have no idea of distances on foot.'

'Sweetheart,' David said, leaning farther into Mr Ronald's car, 'it wasn't your fault.'

'I know,' she said. 'It was his fucking fault. But darling, I'm a little drunk.'

She watched him comprehend this. He was drunker than she was. His eyes filled briefly. There was a scar above his right eye, half hidden in the eyebrow, left by childhood chickenpox. He often walked through their apartment on his toes, adding to his height, bending down over her as she lay on the couch. He would put his head on her stomach and look up at her face, and when he did this he reminded her of an ostrich.

'I'll be back soon,' he said. 'It's going to be all right, and I love you. Don't be scared.'

He bent down to kiss her, bent his long, beautiful bird neck, then began to run.

Sarah looked at Mr Ronald. He wore corduroy trousers and a neat shirt, a woollen vest, and bulky glasses over thick eyebrows. He lay with his head thrown back and to the side, facing Sarah, and his facial expression was bemused and acquiescing. She felt again at his wrist. His legs were caught up with the buckled car and it was impossible to tell what damage had been done. She sat on her side, looking into his face, and felt the faint breath that hung around his mouth. It smelled like a doctor's waiting room: just-extinguished cigarettes and something human rising up through disinfectant. She heard David try the car again, and she heard the car fail. Then his footsteps on the road. Then nothing. Sarah felt loneliness fall over her, and fear.

'The Queen of Sheba,' she said.

(Sheba paused in his tiger-walk, his head lifted toward the surgery door, waiting. No one came through the door, and he dropped his head again, letting out a low small sound that startled the macaws opposite into frantic cries.)

Sarah was married and no one knew but herself and David, Robbie and Clare. Her mother didn't know. She wondered now about the secrecy – how childish it seemed. They only wanted privacy. They wanted a new visa for Sarah, and they didn't want to bother about the fuss that went with weddings. The last of the gin wound itself up against the side of Sarah's head that tilted against the seat; it hung there in a vapour, then seemed to drain away. Mr Ronald's burnt breath came in little gusts against her face. Was he breathing more, or less? Sarah pulled the door behind her as far as it would go in order to feel safe, and to guard against the slight chill in the wind. This is summer, she thought. You wait for it all year, shoulders pushed up against the cold and the dark, and this is your gift: the sun and the bells, the smoke over Jesus Green, geese on the river. A midday wedding. A cat's catheter and Mr Ronald by the side of the road.

Mr Ronald's eyes opened and Sarah drew back from his face. They studied each other. His eyes were yellow at the edges. They were clever and lucid. They looked at Sarah with calm acceptance; they looked at the windscreen, shattered but half in place, and at the close proximity of the tree.

'I've had an accident,' he said.

'Yes, you have. How do you feel? Stay still,' said Sarah. She felt composed. Everything she did felt smooth and immediate.

'I'm all here,' said Mr Ronald. 'Everything's attached, at least.' He gave a small laugh. 'It happened so fast, as they say. I see I've hit the tree.' He said 'the tree' as if there were only one tree in the whole country; as if he had always known he would hit it.

'Good of you to stop,' he said.

'Of course!' cried Sarah.

'Plenty wouldn't. Decent of you. I don't suppose he even thought for a minute about stopping.'

'Who?' asked Sarah. She looked into the back of the car in panic, as if there might be someone else crushed inside.

'The lout who swiped me.'

Sarah remained quiet. Then she said, 'My husband's gone to find help.'

She had been waiting to use this phrase: 'my husband'. Her first time.

'Ah,' said Mr Ronald. 'I don't suppose you happen to be a doctor. That would be convenient.'

'Not a human doctor,' said Sarah. 'An animal doctor, though.'

'My leg, you see,' he said. 'I think it should hurt, but at this moment it doesn't.'

'You're probably in shock.'

'You're not British, are you. Antipodean.'

'Australian.'

'I thought so, but didn't venture it. From the first few sentences you might just as well be a New Zealander.'

He pronounced it 'New Zellander'.

'No, no!' Sarah protested. 'We sound completely different.' She demonstrated the difference: 'Fish and chips,' she said. 'That's us. This is a Kiwi: fush and chups.'

'Nonsense,' said Mr Ronald. 'No one speaks that way at all.'

Sarah felt chastised. She didn't resent it – there was something pleasantly authoritarian about Mr Ronald, who made her think of a school principal driving home from church, or the father of a boyfriend, to whom she must be polite at all costs.

'A veterinarian,' said Mr Ronald. 'Dogs and cats.'

'Actually I specialise,' said Sarah. 'Exotic animal medicine. But dogs and cats too, sometimes. Mostly for friends.'

'What counts as exotic these days?' asked Mr Ronald. His right hand moved slowly over his chest and toward his legs, testing for pain and damage.

'Chinchillas,' said Sarah. 'Ferrets. Hermit crabs. Monkeys.'

'Monkeys?' said Mr Ronald. 'Good god. Does anyone in England actually own a monkey?'

'You'd be surprised.'

'And is it legal?'

'I'm afraid it is.'

'And people will spend hundreds of pounds to cure a hermit crab?'

'People become very attached to their pets,' said Sarah. She had defended her clients on this subject before, at parties and college dinners, and whenever she did she saw them all in the surgery waiting room, bundled against cold and worry, holding cages and carriers and shoeboxes with holes punched in them.

'Yes, you're right,' said Mr Ronald, and he thought about this for a moment. 'Dogs I understand, and cats too, in their own way. I grew up with a bull-mastiff. He could knock me down until I was eleven, and then I could knock him. He ate the leg off a rabbit once.'

The bull-mastiff walked through Sarah's mind. Hip dysplasia, she thought. Hypothyroidism. A heavy dog. She'd need help lifting it.

'And you've treated a monkey yourself? You seem very young.'

'A capuchin once, with a broken leg.'

This mention of a broken leg seemed to remind Mr Ronald of his situation. His face altered in pain.

'Do you feel it now?' asked Sarah. The skin whitened around his mouth and he let out a sound that reminded her of a tiger, a long and drawn-out 'ooow'.

'It won't be long,' she said. 'My husband will be back soon.'

She looked out of the window. The road was dark in both directions and overshadowed with trees. There were shapes in the trees. They looked like small crouching monkeys escaped with their rotten teeth and cataracts from backyard sheds all over England. When she looked back at Mr Ronald, he seemed to have recovered a little. He laid his head against the seat and breathed quietly. A band of sweat bound his forehead. She placed her fingers on his wrist: his heartbeat was steady now, and slow. She kept her hand where it was, despite feeling revolted by the dampness of his old skin. They sat together listening for cars. Someone will come in this minute, thought Sarah; but the minute passed.

'A capuchin, you say,' said Mr Ronald. 'A kind of monk, isn't it?'

'Well, a monk, yes, I think so. But also a kind of monkey.'

'I saw an orangutan in the Berlin zoo once, painting on the wall with a dish brush. Looked just like my wife cleaning the shower. But here Douglas is, against primate testing. I can't go in for that. Douglas calls me species-ist.' Sarah decided not to ask who Douglas was. 'If they cure Parkinson's then it's worth those gorillas, I think. Not a popular stance, I'm told. I myself can't stand vegetarians.'

'I'm a vegetarian,' said Sarah.

'Well, in the abstract. It makes sense for someone like you. A veterinarian. Why heal them and then eat them? But I always say vegetarians ought to eat meat when it's served to them. Imagine being a guest in someone's home and turning down food that's offered.'

This reminded Sarah of her grandfather: perplexed and indignant, having survived a war, to find that people cared about other kinds of suffering. Food might run out – eat what you're given. Life might be lost – don't mind the monkeys. Sarah liked to argue on this topic, calmly maintaining her position, but in this case she would not.

'Oh, but I'm sure you're a charming guest,' said Mr Ronald. 'And here you are, helping an old man in distress.'

He chuckled and the pain came again – stronger, it seemed, this time. It lifted him from the seat a little, and the lifting caused more pain. He shut his eyes against it. Sarah waited for this to pass, as it had the last time, and when he was quiet she asked, 'What can I do? Anything? Is it your legs?'

He laughed again, sucking in his cigarette breath, and moved his wrist away from her hand. The rain grew heavier and the trees on the road began to move their monkey arms. The damp fields gave up their deeper smells of mice and manure. No cars passed by. Sarah worried about David in the rain. He couldn't have been gone for longer than ten minutes, she reasoned; perhaps fifteen. She wondered briefly if the woman was still ironing in her house.

She asked again, 'How are your legs?'

'Funny,' said Mr Ronald, and his breath was shorter now. It left his throat unwillingly. 'Funny, but one of them's not even a leg. Left leg, below the knee. Plastic.'

Sarah imagined him at other times rapping his fingers against the plastic of his leg, knocking it through his neat trousers while chatting on a bus. The war, she thought, he must have lost it in the war; she saw him and other men moving quickly over a French field. Poppies blew in the grass, and he was a young man, strong of limb, and the sea lay behind them all as they ran.

'Diabetes,' said Mr Ronald. 'Didn't know, did you, that it could take your leg off?'

Sarah shook her head, but she did know. She'd seen diabetic dogs, cats too. She'd cut off their legs. The French field fell into the sea, and the rain still fell against the roof of the car.

'Started as a blister, then an ulcer,' said Mr Ronald. 'Just a mishap. A blister from new shoes. No one tells the young: be careful of your feet. Feet should last a lifetime. What can be prevented? Everything, they say. No they don't. They say not everything.'

He laughed harder now, in a thin straight line, and his cheeks drew in over the laugh so that Sarah could see the shape of his skull and the crowded teeth, nicotine-stained, that swarmed in his mouth. Perhaps this wasn't laughing, but breathing. The steady rain and wind moved the car slightly, back and forth. The branches of the tree against which the car was pressed were darting shapes at the corner of Sarah's eye, like Sheba at night, stalking rats with his stomach full of jellymeat.

(Sheba lay panting in the corner of his cage, overwhelmed by the pain on which he concentrated with a careful doling out of attention. He kept himself steady but his small side rose and fell, rose and fell, higher and then deeper than it should. His eyes moved toward the door and his mouth sat open, showing pink.)

Mr Ronald's laugh was a clatter behind his teeth. Sarah huddled close to him as he moved against his seat. She placed her arm around his shoulders, touched his damp forehead, and felt her hair lift away from her skin, all along her arms and the back of her neck. The summer passed through the car, windy and wet.

'Hold on,' said Sarah. 'Just hold on.' Her mouth was close to his ear. David would come soon. You could swear at a cat that rocked this way, crowded close in pain and confusion; you could talk softly, not to the cat but to the idea of the cat, to the faces of the family to whom you must explain the cat's condition. You could sing to the cat and if you had forgotten its name you could call it kitty – you could say 'Hold on, kitty' while your hands moved and your neck craned forward and the parts of you that understood the machinery of a cat, its secret places, worked despite the cat's terror. You could set the leg of a monkey and watch it, later, as it limped back and forward across the surgery floor, scowling and shaking its funny fist at you.

Noises came from Mr Ronald's throat now, and these sounds seemed accidental, the by-product of something else. They continued past the point Sarah felt certain he had died; they rattled on in the can of his throat. After they had subsided – although this took time, and they came in unexpected spurts – she became aware of the sound of a radio playing. In her own car, or this one? Who could Douglas be? A son? A grandson?

Sarah was unsure how long she had been sitting beside Mr Ronald and how long it had been since he stopped making any sound at all. His wife cleaned the walls of their shower and he had been to see orangutans in Berlin. He was too young to have been in that war.

Without warning, David filled up the space in the passenger

door of Mr Ronald's car. She had been so certain she would hear his footsteps on the road, but here he was in the doorway as if she'd summoned him out of the field.

'I'm sorry, I'm sorry, I didn't find anyone.' He was wet and his breath came quickly. 'I ran and finally found a house but there was no one home. I thought about breaking in. Kept going for a bit but no sign of life. No cars on the road, even. So I came back to try the car again.'

He looked at the stillness of the man in the driver's seat. He saw the blood on Mr Ronald's trousers and the way that it crept toward his belt and shirt, and he searched for blood on Sarah.

Sarah concentrated on David's face, which swam in the sound of the rain and the radio. My husband. She smiled because she was happy to see him. Then she placed the wallet in Mr Ronald's lap. She moved to step out of the car and David made space for her.

'How is he? How does he seem?'

When a cat died during an operation, when a macaw was too sick, when a snake was past saving, then Sarah must tell its owners. It was difficult to tell them this true thing, and so along with it she added other, less true things: that the tumour caused no pain, that the animal hadn't been frightened to go under anaesthetic. Still, it was difficult. It made no difference to Sarah that words were inadequate to her enormous task. Of course they were. There might be a time when she would have to tell her friends, Sheba's owners, that he wouldn't survive his infection. Each loss of which she had been the herald seemed to have led to this new immensity: Mr Ronald, dead in a car. But they didn't know Mr Ronald. David had never even spoken to him. She had been married that midday, with no rain. There were only two witnesses.

'He's dead,' said Sarah.

She stood and shut the door behind her. David fought the desire to lower his head and look through the window. It seemed necessary to make sure, but more necessary to trust Sarah. He held his hands out to her and she took them.

'My god,' he said. She shook her head. He knew that when she shook her head in this way, it meant: I'm not angry with you, but I won't talk.

'What now?' he asked. 'Should we take him somewhere?'

David felt that Sarah owned the wreck, owned the tree and piece of road on which Mr Ronald had died, and that he need only wait for her instructions, having failed to find help. He thought of her sitting alone with the unconscious body of an old man, and he thought of the moment at which she must have realised that Mr Ronald was no longer unconscious, but dead. David saw with certainty that Sarah was another person, completely separate from him, although he had married her today. His wife.

'We'll try the car again,' said Sarah. 'We just have to get to the surgery.'

'We can use the phone there,' said David.

Sarah crossed the road and he followed her. She didn't look back at the wreck. Waiting on its grassy rise slightly above the road, their car had a look of faithful service, of eagerness to assist. It started on the third try with a compliant hum. Sarah had always been better at coaxing it; even before trying the ignition she'd known it would work. She was unsure if this resurrection was good or bad luck, or beyond luck – simply inevitable. Now that she could see the rain in the headlights, she realised how soft it was, how English. She missed home, suddenly: the hard, bright days and the storms at the end of them, with rain that filled your shoes.

It grew bright and then dark in Mr Ronald's car as their headlights passed over him, and it remained dark as they left that piece of road and that tree. David watched Sarah drive. They didn't speak. As the distance between their car and Mr Ronald's grew it seemed that the roads were all empty – that all of England was empty. It lay in its empty fields while the mice moved and the airplanes flew overhead to other places, nearby and far away.

They reached lit buildings and the surgery so quickly that David was embarrassed at having failed to find help. Sarah walked calmly, and she spoke calmly with the nurse about Sheba. She didn't look at the telephone. There was no blood on her clothes. David watched his wife as she made her way toward the cat, who rubbed his head against the bars of his cage. He was waiting for the pain to stop. And then he would be let out, healed, to hunt mice in the wet grass.

Art Appreciation

Henry Taylor had always known he would have money one day, and this confidence was vindicated when his mother won the lottery on a Thursday in the August of 1961. He could afford to get married. But he wasn't yet sure if he could afford to quit his job, so he went to the office the day after he heard the news. The sun came through the window blinds in long tedious slats and time passed outside, far below, with the noise of the road and the joy of boys on bicycles. Above, where Henry was, women walked among the men, delivering coffee and papers. They were all decorous, even the young ones – even those reproachable few who lingered with one hip against the corners of desks. One particular girl had caught Henry's attention. She was new to her job, but had already made a name for herself with her prettiness and good nature. She dressed modestly, with a sense of pleasures offered all the same: a heightening of her body's secrets through her polite attempts to conceal them. Her name was Eleanor, and she called herself Ellie.

Henry thought, now he had money, that he would marry her.

He didn't tell anyone that his mother had won the lottery, and a considerable amount of his delight had to do with his windfall being secret. That was the great thing: to sit at his desk, observing as he always did the movements of the office – and Ellie's movements among them – but as a profoundly different man, with a new and superior perspective. There was no longer anything to keep him from approaching Ellie, but he held off even so, not out of hesitation but in order to savour his own intentions. Henry noticed that she stole frequent looks at him. She had the quality of a bird among grasses, peering out in nervous excitement, eager for a mate but afraid to abandon safety. He was certain she was in the office not to make flimsy dates with different men but to find a husband.

As he left work that Friday afternoon, Henry made sure to say goodnight to Ellie. She was flattered and demure.

'Enjoy your weekend,' he said, and she said – she almost sang – 'You too!' She wore her hair pulled back with a navy ribbon.

Henry, as usual, took the stairs to the ground floor of the building – this was part of his fitness regime, to exercise his legs in the morning and the evening – and when he reached the lobby, the elevator doors sprang open and Ellie stepped out from between them.

'Fancy that,' Henry said. He looked at her with pleasure. Her waist was small, she had pale, plump arms, and her hair had a good-natured sheen.

Ellie stood swinging her handbag this way and that.

'Walk me to the station?' she asked, and he offered his arm, which she took.

It had begun to rain, and they walked beneath his large black umbrella. She tucked herself in beside him and her small, uneven steps limited his stride. He wanted to lift Ellie up in his arms the way you might a child at a parade.

'I'd like to take you out some time,' Henry said.

'That would be lovely,' she said, with a small frown.

'I'd like to take you out right now,' Henry said.

'Tonight's impossible,' she said. 'I have a class on Fridays. But some day next week?'

'What kind of class?'

Ellie gave a little smile, the bashful twin of her frown, and said, 'Art appreciation.'

They arrived at Wynyard station and there, between the sound of the trains passing underneath the street and the sound of traffic passing over the street, she leaned her head into his shoulder for one unexpected moment. Then she ran down the steps into the station. Henry watched her bright brown head move among the commuters and disappear in the direction of the North Shore line. He considered her his girl from that moment.

Henry was fond of Sydney on a Friday afternoon. It was late winter, so the sky lowered early, and there was that week-end feeling of relief and consequence. There was a place near the station where he liked to eat after work. The whole establishment smelled boiled – boiled meat, wet raincoats, and the undersides of shoes. He ordered a hamburger – no onions, never onions – and ate it while imagining Ellie on the way to her Friday-night class. He had a vague sense that art appreciation involved bowls of fruit and flowers. But his mind didn't stay on her for long; he began, without quite knowing it, to think about his money. He wondered how much of the ten thousand pounds his mother would give him and concluded that it would be at least half. He thought of her clutching his arm the night before, saying, 'I'll set you up, you'll get married.'

Although Henry's mother had promised to set him up, he still went to the dog track, because it was Friday. He had a weekend schedule: Friday night the dogs, Saturday the horses, Sunday lunch with his mother, and Sunday night with Kath, a girl he knew. For so long he had dreamt of a windfall, of a sudden fortune, and of what it might make possible, because every week there was a chance: the dogs ran, the horses flew, and Henry was always there to see them. There was money on every race. He won, and sometimes he didn't. This was the greatest pleasure he knew: a little profit and a little loss. He also liked the company of gamblers. They're cheerful people, he would say; they're optimists.

Henry might have taken a bus to the dog track, but he preferred to walk: down George Street and Broadway, through Glebe, and into Wentworth Park. The Friday city was so festive in the rain, full of women running from warm taxis into warm houses and men standing at street corners waiting for the lights to change, holding newspapers over their heads. The gum trees lining the streets of Glebe took up the easing rain and shook it out again in heavier drops. In every one of the terraced houses Henry passed, a woman like Ellie waited for a man she loved amid the furniture and finery he had bought her.

Because he was careful with his money and lived with his mother, Henry had a small but steadily growing savings account, which was commendable for a man of twenty-eight with a mid-level job in an insurance firm. The thought of his nest egg produced in him a simple, serious pleasure as he entered the Wentworth Park greyhound track. It pleased him to think that he would be here, with money he could afford to bet, whether or not his mother had won the lottery. And because he was a man who enjoyed weighing his odds and his options, it didn't occur to Henry to bet any more recklessly on that Friday than he normally would. Still, he had an unusually successful night. He sat in the good feeling of the crowd as it hung on those few moments that mattered, when the dogs flattened against time and won, or failed to win. Then men erupted around him in victory or regret, and there was a new surge toward the bookmakers, who stood illuminated above the throng. The bookies were the men Henry admired most of all. They spoke in a ribald and rhythmic way, singing out the odds like a sea shanty. Henry was covetous of their easy authority, which he believed came from handling large sums of money.

Henry stayed three hours, passed jokes among his track acquaintances, rolled on the balls of his feet as he waited to see which dog would emerge from the starting tangle, and collected his winnings. Then he walked to Central and took a train south. He never drank (he hated a fogged mind) and that night, as he walked home from the station – late, with the streets dark and his mother waiting for him, even in her sleep, her lamp bright in the window – he felt a new clarity to his brain, as if a frost had settled on it. It was still there the next night, at the horses, and he won again – a larger sum this time, and still without undue risk. It interested him, in an offhand way, that his weekend could look the same as always, even when his life had changed. But his wealth had already altered things: made Ellie possible, aided him at the track, kept his mind clear.

At lunch on Sunday his mother told him that she was planning to move to Victoria to live near her sister. 'I'm giving you this house,' she told him. 'I want to see you settled.'

His mother was a small woman – it was as if her thrift extended even to the size of her body – but on this day she ate heartily of lamb and potatoes. She seemed to have entered a new and generous state of perpetual surprise; she'd bought lottery tickets for so many years, without the least expectation that she would profit by them. Now wellbeing radiated from her unlikely face, with its thick nose and thin eyebrows.

'That's the second day this week you've given me good news,' Henry said.

His mother answered, 'Good things come in threes,' and Henry wondered, What will the third thing be? Ellie? A car? A big win at the dogs? And so he limited himself.

He would sell the house, of course, and buy something closer to the city, where he would be known in the neighbourhood, known by the greengrocer and by the paperboys, and he would have a straight garden path leading to his front door, flanked by a hedge that he would trim himself on Saturday mornings. Because, he thought, I'm a working man, and I won't forget it. He would buy a car and drive to the track; he would still go to the track, because it was the spectacle, not the money, which drew him there. And there would be days with Ellie by the harbour, visiting all those brief bays on the northern shore where she lived, swimming and picnicking and maybe sitting on the water in a little boat. The benevolent future spread out before him, and he felt an immense satisfaction.

After lunch with his mother, Henry went to see Kath. He lingered into the evening with Kath's compact body. Later in the night, he read the newspapers by lamplight; Kath preferred lamplight. Henry had ambitious plans, but he considered anyone who worked too hard for his success a dupe; he read in the newspapers of the rigorous transactions of wealthy men and stabbed at these pages with a contemptuous finger. Kath yawned on the bed. She had the sort of long, streamlined face you sometimes see in tall women. She was more beautiful than Ellie, but less pretty. Kath was always making distinctions of that kind. She worked in the beauty salon of a flash hotel. Henry had met her at the hamburger place at Wynyard station; how odd and blazing and fine she had looked in that cheerful din.

He shook the newspaper and told her that this would be their final Sunday.

'What's her name?' she asked.

'Ellie,' he said.

'You like your girls with cute little names, don't you,' Kath said, and he considered this petty of her.

'If you must know,' Henry said, without looking at her face, 'I've won the lottery.'

'How much?' she asked him, and when he told her, she sat up in bed and hooted like an owl.

'You're not serious,' she said, swinging her long boyish legs over to rest her feet on the floor. 'Let me pour you a drink then, you bastard.'

She began an uncharacteristic sprightly chatter, telling him of every lucky instance in which a person she knew had won something: money, meat, flowers, jewellery and large appliances. Then she handed him a drink and said, 'I thought you didn't rate the lottery? I thought you didn't even buy tickets?'

'Just this once,' he said, with a shrug of the papers, and she growled at him from the corner of her mouth and said, 'No one's that lucky.'

That Sunday night, a wind moved over the city. It rolled through in one direction, out of the sea and into the west, and it bent trees behind it. The wind brought rain at times, in orderly diagonal sheets, but there was no chaos to it, only consistency. On Monday morning, Henry stepped over fallen leaves and other storm litter on his way from Kath's flat to the office. The wind rearranged his hair, so he combed it with his hand as he climbed the stairs. While climbing, he considered the fact that he liked his job, that he liked the idea of insurance, that it suited his temperate, ready mind. It occurred to him that he might not quit, even now that his mother had promised him the house. There was no need to make big gestures; after all, she couldn't spare him such an enormous sum of money that it would do for two people, and children, for another sixty years. He sat at his desk and watched for Ellie all day, and whenever she was in sight he made sure she knew it. He mentioned the lottery win to one or two people. He told them that he knew he could rely on their discretion.

Ellie was waiting for him at the end of the day, wearing a funny little blue hat that hid most of her hair.

'I wondered if you'd walk me to the Art Gallery,' she said. 'There's a lecture tonight, and we could eat afterward.' She laid one hand against his shoulder, in the same spot where she had rested her head on Friday, and although he was reluctant about the idea of a lecture and the Art Gallery, and about her having asked him before he could ask her, he said, 'Let's go, then.' He took the elevator with her down to the lobby and Ellie leaned into his arm as if she couldn't be near him without some sort of physical contact.

The wind was still about, and it funnelled through the streets and caught at Ellie's skirt until they reached Hyde Park. Ellie stood for a moment beside the park's great circular fountain and looked up at the figure at its centre.

'Hi, Apollo,' she said, and pointed. 'I like to say hi whenever I pass. Isn't he beautiful?'

The statue was naked, with one green bronze hand pointing toward the cathedral and the other holding some kind of harp. Henry supposed that this was art appreciation. He tried for a moment to replicate the position of Apollo's knees.

'He's the god of poetry and music,' Ellie said.

'Do gods let birds do their business all over them?' Henry asked, and Ellie laughed in just the right delighted way. 'Come on,' he said. 'Or we'll be late for your lecture.' In this way, holding his hand out to her, chiding, pleased, he corrected the tone of the outing.

They were late, and Henry's shoes squeaked on the marble floors of the gallery. There were chairs set up in the high, arched lobby, and a number of the people sitting in them turned to look. Henry thought the audience appeared well fed but somehow pinched. There were a number of fashionable hats. He saw a single vacant seat and urged Ellie into it; he stood at the back of the crowd with another young man.

'Get dragged here, too, did you?' this man said, and Henry gave a mock grimace. They leaned together against a yellow wall in the easy company of their mutual conscription.

The lecturer was a man who described himself as a conceptual artist. Like Henry, he wore a light grey suit; in fact, he might have come, moments before, from an office like Henry's, except that his hair was slightly longer than Henry would have allowed himself. He was talking about his latest work, which seemed to involve a photograph of a chair, an actual chair, and a card printed with the dictionary definition of a chair.

'Bet it took him half an hour and a couple of beers to come up with that one,' Henry said, in a low voice, to the man beside him.

'You're on,' the man said. 'A fiver.' He shook the note out of his pocket like a magician producing a bird. But they only laughed, and the man put his money away.

Henry could see the back of Ellie's head from where he stood, and he watched her listen. Her blue hat sat in her lap. The hat was for the wind, he realised, and he approved of her foresight. The artist coughed into the side of his mouth and said something about the impossibility of totality. Henry stirred with discomfort, the man beside him shifted, too, and Ellie turned in her seat to look at them. She gave Henry a small sweet smile. When the artist called for questions, she slipped from her row, took Henry's arm, and hurried him out into the night.

The Domain was dark under the fig trees and Ellie walked with her head resting against Henry's arm. 'Now we can eat,' she said, as if the lecture had been a regrettable obstacle to this activity. The ground was soft underfoot with the ripe, wet leaves of the figs, and bats tittered in their intricate branches. He wasn't sure where to take her to dinner, but she steered him toward a place off William Street that she said was Italian. There were brothels on the street and Ellie looked at their red lights with sad and serious eyes. American sailors, drunk and dressed in white, ran up out of Woolloomooloo. They called to Ellie as they passed and shook Henry's hand. He was proud of her.

Over dinner he said, 'What was all that about totality?'

And she answered, 'Wasn't he marvellous?'

Apparently he was, but there was no more to say about it. Ellie ordered expensive things, and Henry paid for them. She seemed somehow to have been his girl for a very long time. For example, she spoke of her friends and family as if he already knew them.

'And Jimmy,' she said, 'is livid about Ann. But you can't blame him.' Or, 'When we see her, you have to ask Mary about her surfing accident. It's the funniest thing I ever heard.'

It was as if, with the new clarity of his mind, he had willed her into a relationship with him. She didn't ask him any questions, but listened with her chin perched on the neat palm of one hand whenever he talked about himself. He told her about the money. He had been unsure whether to mention his mother or to claim the lottery win as his own, but was pleased to find himself telling the truth; it made him seem filial, respectful, the fortunate son of a lucky mother, and no dupe – *he* would never waste his daily bread on lottery tickets. Ellie listened, and watched him with her serious face. She was calculating, he thought, and he didn't blame her. He wasn't an unattractive man: there was his height and the vivid blue of his eyes, which Kath, in a mood, had once described as 'hygienic'. But with his tall, loose frame he looked as if somebody had knitted him together, and his ears sat out too far from his head. There was nothing wrong with defects like these, as long as he knew about them. Ellie leaned across the table and took his hands in hers.

'I'm very happy for you,' she said, in a conclusive tone, as if the shape of her life had now been decided. They walked back through the park to St James station, neither of them speaking much, and he kissed her there for the first time.

The wet winter became a clear spring, and Henry bought a car and wooed Ellie among all the secret suburbs of Sydney's northern coast, their palms and coves and their small significant bays. They swam together in the hot honeymoon water and manoeuvred behind the tricky rocks to kiss. She remained faithful to her Friday-night art-appreciation classes, so Saturday became their weekend night: Henry stopped going to the horses and took Ellie out instead. On Sundays he still lunched at home, and afterward – now that his Sunday evenings were free – he helped his mother sort through her possessions in readiness for her move to Victoria. She had acquired more in her quiet life than Henry could quite account for, and she spent a great deal of time over each object, as if every Christmas ornament or book or porcelain figurine were worthy of attention. Something was slowing her progress and delaying the move – a nostalgic tenderness, Henry thought, a formless sentimentality. It worried him, until he realised that she was waiting for him to announce his engagement. She would move when she knew he was settled.

During this period Henry cultivated a brittle beard. He bought a suit of navy wool and knew he looked significant in it. Naturally, his good fortune had become news in the office. He was promoted to a new floor of the building, where he didn't see Ellie until he called to fetch her for lunch. Usually they ate sandwiches in Hyde Park, but sometimes he took her to a restaurant on Pitt Street where the waiters wore bow ties and the wood-panelled walls made Henry think of a gentlemen's club. All around them sat feverish men in suits, eating steaks with their square teeth. Business was transacted here, true business, the acts of men. Secretaries and girlfriends and wives slipped neatly in and out of the booths. Here, Henry was expansive and proud. He was a little afraid of the waiters, but they would never know it. He was gracious with them and paid the bill as if handing over a dowry. Ellie was the prettiest girl in the restaurant. Over lunch, he asked her to stop attending her Friday-night classes.

'Surely you know by now how to appreciate art.'

'It's my passion,' she said, and averted her head in a

becoming way, like all those Madonnas she'd shown him in books about Italian painters.

Maybe it was just as well; he could keep going to the greyhound track. He made a profit every week now, though his bets remained modest. He took fewer risks and studied the dogs more carefully. He was concerned about his savings, which had been depleted by the car and the courtship, and he was preoccupied by the idea of marriage: the pressed cotton, the resolute ecstasy, the begetting of children (he had hopes of a dynasty). Henry's mind vibrated with these possibilities. He sat among the men at the track and saw the singed quality of their thinning hair and the thick ridges of flesh in the back of every neck. He was less and less charmed by the singsong of the bookies, the pointless silks of the trainers, the false lights, and the sharp dogs – all that stinking fuss in the sweet evenings of spring. This dissatisfaction, he thought, was not a sign of growing maturity (he wasn't ashamed of his past love of racing), but it suggested to him a loneliness that he had been unaware of before his mother won the lottery, a loneliness that had driven him out into the city and to public congregations of men. It had also sent him, he supposed, to Kath, whom he thought of infrequently now, with something bordering on a wistful impatience, most often when Ellie stopped him short of handling some coveted part of her body. Ellie had a hasty, hot manner, girlish and at the same time proper, which in retrospect pleased him more than Kath's smooth surety. They hadn't slept together yet. He'd heard something, somewhere, about weak men redeemed by the society of good women.

He brought Ellie to meet his mother one Sunday. He was disappointed to see towels on the clothesline; otherwise, the house was orderly and he was proud of it. Perhaps, when they were married, he and Ellie needn't have the largest of houses. There was something to be said for quality on a modest scale. Not modest, exactly; humble, in the sense of an extraordinary man who conceals the extent of his own greatness. That was dignity, Henry thought: to have, but in private. Possibly they would stay in this house and have work done to it.

Ellie excused herself to use the bathroom and his mother leaned in close with a confidential, sprightly face, and whispered, 'She's a delight.' There was a newly set quality to his mother's hair, a thin blush of colour over her cheeks, and she wore an unfamiliar dress. He remembered her telling him that she had once worked in an office.

Ellie returned from the bathroom with a water stain on her pale blue blouse, and the way she held her hand over it – above her heart, above her breast – made everything she said seem particularly sincere. It was as if she were swearing allegiance to the meal, to the house, to Henry's mother, and to Henry.

After lunch, he took her out into the garden and asked her to marry him. She answered, without hesitation, 'Yes.' Unsure of what to do next, he held her hand and kissed her. It was one of those days on the very edge of summer, when the light falls blankly from a strong sky and the grass is already beginning to brown. The towels on the clothesline flipped in the light wind. The kiss was not their most successful, and raising his eyes from it, Henry saw his mother's face hovering in a window.

'I don't have a ring yet,' he said. 'I thought you might want to choose it yourself.'

Ellie was looking around the garden as if she were not so much excited as interested by the turn of events, and Henry was surprised by the feeling of admiration that rose from somewhere beneath his feet and rushed toward his heart. His mother, unable to wait any longer behind the window, came running down the brick steps and embraced them both. She held Henry's hand, and she held Ellie's, out there on the browning grass, and said that she would see them married and then she would move. So Henry had been right: she had been waiting for him, and now things would proceed more quickly.

Ellie decided on an April wedding. Cool, blue April was her favourite month. Her mother approved, and so did Henry's, who finally set a date for Victoria: the first of May. Henry's mother wanted to pay for the wedding, so Ellie arranged a meeting with her parents at a city restaurant. Her parents were a poised pair: he was a teacher, though retired with back problems; she liked to paint, and had even sold one or two watercolours of the view from their dining-room window. There had once been money somewhere in her family. Everyone was grateful for Henry's mother's generosity, and there was a minimum amount of embarrassment, which was a relief to Henry, who found himself unexpectedly anxious for his mother among the sombre hover of the waiters. Ellie's father also unsettled him, for no good reason; he was a pale, greying man, gentle with his back to the point of womanliness, but at one point he leaned across the table, took Henry's wrist in a pinching grip, and said, in a low voice, 'Isn't the groom meant to ask my permission?' Then he winked – the kind of sharp, jovial wink that bookies master and Henry never had – and carried on eating.

That summer was damp and close: white skies and pressed heat. Henry had been busier at work since his promotion. It was the season of bushfires, and a mid-sized sugar company whose policy he managed lost a mill and much of a small township among its more southerly canefields. This involved some travel for Henry, who had never ventured far from Sydney. He caught the train up the long green coast, and although the sea on his right and the hills on his left looked very much like home, he was struck again by the new horizons opening before him with money and marriage. He was now prepared to admit that he had been a lesser man before his mother's win. He resolved, in the flickering carriage of the northbound train, to stop going to Wentworth Park on Friday nights. This resolution survived his return to the city. Ellie, pleased with his decision, and unusually permissive – she had missed him, she said, while he was away – made no similar offer to give up her art classes.

They spent Christmas at Ellie's parents' house because Henry's mother had gone to her sister's. Henry was wary of the differences between this house and the one he would soon inherit: the strong grey-green light that filtered through the gum trees and was reflected in the vague watercolours hanging on the dining-room walls, the simplicity of the furniture, and the surprising number of books. There was a balding in the carpet; his mother would have covered it with a rug. After the meal, Ellie's father rose before the assembled guests – there were quite a number of cousins – and delivered his annual speech, in which he summed up the events of the past year, both private and public. Henry, who was attentive to the gestures of other men, to the small and large ways in which respect was granted and withheld, noticed – much as he had noticed the worn carpet and the books – that Ellie's father never once met his eye during the speech, not even when announcing his daughter's engagement. Her mother, in contrast, peered at her future son-in-law from behind her glasses.

At an appropriate time that evening, Henry steered Ellie out into the garden and quizzed her about her parents. At first she wouldn't say much, except, shyly, 'They have ideas.'

'What does that mean?' he asked.

Ellie made a small, anxious motion with her hands, as if someone, from a long way off, had thrown a ball in her direction.

'Do they like me?' he asked.

'I told them you wanted me to give up my art appreciation,' she said, without looking at him, and when he made a noise of irritation she began to speak very quickly about things that didn't seem to matter. She told him that her mother was, in fact, a remarkable woman, and that if her family had held on to their money she would have done so much more – she'd have trained as an artist and would be famous now. Ellie said that her father had been adored by every student he'd ever taught, but that his pride had suffered when he was forced to retire; that they wanted, more than anything else, to see her go to university, but she was tired of living beautifully on too little money, tired of her parents' belief that education was worthy of any sacrifice, and wanted to prove to them how possible it was to take a job in the world, so far into the heart of the world as an insurance firm, and still love art. Because she did love art. Then Ellie pressed herself into Henry's arms and laid one damp cheek against his shoulder. All this while the mynah birds plunged from the junipers, frightening other birds away.

He said, gently, 'Did you tell them about the lottery?'

Ellie shook her hidden head to say no.

'Why not?'

And she raised her face and said, 'They would think I was only marrying you for your money.'

Her face disappeared again, and her thin shoulders rose and fell. Now she was crying. She was so young – only twenty – and passing into his keeping. If marriage was going to be like this, with Ellie at his shoulder, exhausted by honesty and, despite her parents, sure of the way to happiness, then he could manage. He could flourish, in fact, and win; the threadbare carpet and the watercolours could no longer laugh at him. He moved his mouth amid her dark hair and said, 'My Ellie, my sweet girl.'

Henry's mother returned from Victoria on the arm of a man named Arthur. Arthur was short and fox-coloured, with freckles and a muddled smile under a neat red moustache. Like Henry, he was in the 'insurance game'; he also liked to spend his 'bit of money' on a Friday night and was disappointed to learn that

Henry no longer went to the dogs. He had a habit of jogging his shoulders up and down as he talked. Henry viewed him with suspicion and had to know everything. His mother offered it all up: how they had met (on the train to Melbourne), where he lived (in Sydney's west), what he expected of her and she of him (she couldn't say – not yet). There was no question she wouldn't answer; there were also some she answered that he hadn't asked. There had been no intercourse. She told Henry everything and then went away and told the telling of it to Arthur, so that Arthur sat Henry down one Sunday afternoon while Henry's mother produced a purposeful clatter in the kitchen and said, 'What you want to know is, am I on the make?'

Henry liked Arthur's candour; he liked straightforward talk. It showed a respect, he thought, for all parties. So the two men talked it all out in the shuttered light of the Sunday house: Arthur's wages, his savings, what he knew of Henry's mother's winnings, what he knew her to have promised Henry.

'Never an actual sum,' Henry said. 'But it's understood. She wants to see me set up in life.'

'Like any good mother,' Arthur said, lifting and dropping his shoulders, 'who has the means to do so.'

Henry approved of Arthur after this discussion, and, when Ellie expressed doubts, came to his defence. She was jumpy in Arthur's presence, and her refusal to respond to his mild flirtations made her seem prudish and ill-humoured. Henry could see that his mother was happy and that happiness suited her; that she was made for contentment, for padded hips, for the kind vulgarity of a man like Arthur (that was how Henry saw him – clearly, he thought, through Ellie's eyes as well as his own). When Ellie kept away from the house and from Henry's mother, Henry accused her of being a snob, which made her wrinkle her nose. He knew she was afraid of snobbery (afraid of having caught it from her parents). Arthur made jokes about Ellie's art appreciation and Henry laughed at them without feeling disloyal. As the summer faded, he felt an increased impatience with the sanctity of Ellie's Friday nights.

One Thursday evening in mid-March, Ellie and Henry walked together in Hyde Park. Whenever Ellie made movements toward St James station he held her by the hand and wouldn't let her go. The fig trees swung with bats and somewhere in the park a possum cried out. The water in the fountain threw light over the green legs of Apollo, who was otherwise lost in darkness. Here Henry pleaded with Ellie in a low, shameful voice to give him her Friday nights, to give him everything, to love him and only him, and he told her other things which before tonight he could never have predicted he might feel, let alone say, about his need and his loneliness and all the ways in which she had changed him. She was angry and wouldn't promise; she said to him, hurt and soft, 'I can't believe you would even ask,' and when he began to defend himself she raised her voice to say, 'I didn't know you doubted me.'

And then, without thinking much about it, Henry thrust one arm into the water that poured from the fountain until it had soaked far beyond the elbow of his navy suit, and he held it there, or rather the water seemed to hold it, although it was cold and Ellie begged him to stop. He saw her confusion, but from a distance. He felt her kiss his face and submerge her own arm in order to take his hand and draw it out of the water; only then did he seem to be free of the fountain. They held each other and cried, both of them – in public, in Hyde Park, with other lovers and lustful young men skirting them, whistling and smiling and making comments. Henry considered his behaviour remarkable; he felt Ellie's warm tears and the compassionate pressure of her shaking body, but was unable to believe that he was physically present for any of it.

Their wet arms chilled them both. She led him through the park and down William Street, and this time, instead of going to a restaurant, they went to a hotel she knew of – how did she know? – and there she let him see all of her, all at once. There was no doubting her beauty and her devotion, and the most extraordinary thing about her giving herself up to him was that he felt, equally or perhaps with even more certainty, that he was giving himself to her. The room had a sour smell like turning fruit, not unpleasant. Afterward, they lay together, damp and listless, until he felt himself return to his body, and then he forced them both into action: dressed her and himself, took her out to the street to find a taxi, and gave her the money to pay for it. He walked to Central station in a state of luminous calm. It was two weeks until the wedding.

The next day, after work, Kath was waiting for him at the hamburger place.

'I don't know what you think you're doing,' he said in a low voice, with a polite smile, as if someone might be watching them.

'I stopped by for a bite,' Kath said. 'It's a free country, last I heard.' She was pert and proud. There was a new copper to her hair.

'Suit yourself,' he said. He ordered his hamburger at the counter, distracted, and Kath called out, 'No onions!' People turned to look at her, as they always did. He took a deep breath. 'No onions,' he said. Nothing wrong, he thought, with sharing a quick meal with a good-looking woman, a friend of the family. He kept his eye on the station for any sign of Ellie, although he had already walked her to the train and ushered her with tender regret (on both sides) to her Friday class.

'You look . . . greenish,' Kath said. 'A bit green about the gills. You all right, Henry? Not eaten up by remorse, are you? Now that you've thrown away the best thing you ever had?' Kath laughed, delighted at herself.

'What's all this about?' His hamburger arrived, steaming. But the solitary pleasure of it was entirely lost.

'I just wanted to know if you were off to the dogs tonight,' Kath said. 'I fancied it, is all. Fancied a night out with a friend.'

He had lifted his hamburger and now there was no putting it down. This placed him at a disadvantage. The thick slice of beetroot threatened to slide onto his plate – it purpled his bread and his tongue – and juice of some kind, silky with fat, ran over his fingers.

'I'm getting married in two weeks,' he said between bites.

'Where's the bride, then? Shouldn't you be painting the

town? It's Friday night.'

There was something submerged about Kath's face – something private and sly. Henry disliked it. It reminded him of how well suited they used to be; of how they'd both liked to cultivate a secret life to which they could make coy allusions.

'She's got a class,' he said.

'And you're not invited?'

He snorted. The final bites of a hamburger were impossible in company; he abandoned them.

'Take me to the track, then,' Kath said. 'We'll go on a date.'

'You never wanted to go on dates before,' Henry said.

'You never won the lottery before,' Kath said, laughing, and two men at the counter looked over at her. They laughed, too, and she seemed to absorb their approval and turn it back on them, brighter. The men watched as she put her hand on Henry's arm. 'You're not a married man yet.'

Well, that was true, certainly. Kath smiled from her long immaculate face.

'I guess I've missed you,' she said.

They stood together and went out into the street.

The city was scrubbed and pale after the summer, and the buildings rose from the street with a mineral sheen. There was a leisurely rush on the pavements. Henry was aware, as he hadn't been in some time, of the anxious thrill of Friday evening. He bought a copy of the *Daily Mail*.

'I usually walk to Wenty,' he said.

'All that way?' Kath showed him her heeled foot.

Henry liked the authority of hailing a taxi with a girl on

his arm, and of getting into the back of it with her. Kath was wearing a short blue coat which drew attention to the bareness of her immoderate legs; Henry admired them, but with disapproval, as she stepped out of the taxi. Ellie was pretty in such a sensible way, but Kath required adjustments. She stood out on his arm. He and Ellie, he thought, stood out together. Ellie would be at her class by now. And here he was, at the dogs with Kath. Passing through the gates with this long girl at his side, Henry felt as if something had fallen over him: a soft cloak, maybe, made of silky stuff, invisible, that made him hot with knowledge and pride.

'This feels like the Easter Show,' Kath said, pressing him forward, lifting her face to the lights and the noise. 'How do we make a bet?'

'Over there,' Henry said, and he pointed to the bookmakers, who stood under their umbrellas above the crowd, shouting, with their heavy bags strung around their necks. 'You leave that to me.'

'No,' Kath said. 'I want to know everything.'

Henry found it gratifying to teach her. She frowned at the racing form in the *Mail*, tracing one polished finger over the names of the dogs, creasing her forehead and saying things like 'I like Young Lightning. He's got a good feel to him.' She paid no attention to all the other information on the form, so he ignored it too. Kath took a small gold pen from her handbag and as she bent to mark the dogs she liked the names of, Henry saw the darkening roots of her copper hair.

She held his hand and let him lead her to the bookies, and

once there she scolded him for wanting to bet so little on each race. 'For a man who talks big, you have no ambition,' she said.

Henry was enjoying himself. He felt as if he'd been drinking; he felt the warmth of the crowd, of Kath's body against his, of having money to spend. If Kath liked Young Lightning, he would put five pounds on Young Lightning to win. Henry knew he would lose. And Ellie, right now, was in a room on the northern side of the harbour, among all those pink Madonnas, those green Apollos. She would never like it here with the noisy dogs. She would ask the wrong questions, and she was sentimental: she would worry about the treatment of the greyhounds. Kath sat beside him on the benches, tense in her blue coat, and watched every race. Young Lightning fell in the sixth race, but Kath only laughed; Henry couldn't care about his five pounds. This time last night, he and Ellie had been on William Street, at the hotel.

Kath turned to him and smiled. 'These dogs love to run,' she said. It was the right thing to say, and he kissed her mouth. The kiss was friendly and without conviction. She squeezed his knee with her left hand.

'I'll just pop to the loo,' she said, and she went quickly, taking her handbag with her. Then it was as if she'd never been there, as if she were only a good feeling Henry had every now and then. He wondered how many of the men sitting on the benches around him were married. They leaned easy on their comfortable knees; they wore open coats and drank from brown bottles. He loved them, and everyone.

Henry turned around to look for Kath's return and there was

Arthur, freckled and ruddy under the lights, sitting higher in the stand with a paper folded over his knee. He was watching the dogs parade before the seventh race, and making notes; he wore the kind of flat green cap that Henry associated with butchers or publicans or plucky men down on their luck. Arthur gave no indication that he had seen Henry, but it was difficult to tell with a man like him, a man of winks and nods and innuendo, a man of showy discretion. Henry turned back to the track, where the dogs were filing into the starting traps, and Kath passed in front of him, one hand on his shoulder, to resume her seat. She wore fresh lipstick.

'Who've we got in this one?' she asked, inspecting the form. 'Is this Rowdy Jack?'

Henry's chest shook. He saw the future and Arthur in it, steering his mother by her happy elbow, smirking above the Victorian table, giving Henry quiet, confidential looks, tapping his nose, hating Ellie and wishing on the two of them a dull revenge. And in this future Henry saw himself in his mother's house, always and only the lucky son of a lucky mother. An inheritor, before she was even dead. There was something indecent about it. He would be living in debt to his mother and to Arthur and to Ellie, and they would all make demands on him, and on this free and shouting life he'd given up: the bookies under their umbrellas and Kath beside him with her copper hair and lips. Generous Kath, who was his friend even now, was so quick and alert, and had never asked him for anything. And another life occurred to him, a life in which his wife came with him to the track and the rest of the week was happy Sunday lamplight, with a bed and newspapers.

Henry stood. 'Let's go,' he said, and she followed him out, her hand on his back, and he let it stay there. He didn't look at Arthur.

'What's the rush?' Kath asked, and he pulled her by the hand into the darkness of a stand of trees. This whole part of Sydney had once been a swamp, and then an abattoir. There was rot and filth under all of it. Kath's lipstick tasted chalky and sweet, and he felt with hectic hands under her coat; but she pushed him away.

'Henry,' she said, and he stopped. Her face was as pale as the bark of the gum behind her. 'I could use some money,' she said. 'Just a loan.'

He waited for the shouting of the crowd inside the racetrack to subside, and then he asked, 'How much?'

'I could use a hundred,' she said. He didn't answer. 'That's nothing to you. That's a hundredth of what you won.'

Henry reached out for her coat again, and this time she unbuttoned it for him. She was as thin as she had always been underneath it, and she shook like an arrow. She didn't raise her face or body into his, and kept her arms behind her, wrapped against the trunk, so that he felt, kissing her, as if he were only pressed to a tree that had once had a girl inside it. But her mouth moved. She was willing. It was her being willing that made him stop.

He stepped away from the girl and the tree. He took all the notes he had in his wallet and passed them to Kath, who accepted them without looking.

'Thank you,' she said. She began to button her coat.

Henry walked out to the part of the street that was most illuminated by the floodlights of the racetrack. The invisible cloak still lay across his shoulders; it was heavier in the light. He shook it off and walked home to his mother.

His lucky mother, who was waiting now for Arthur with a lamp in her bedroom window.

Mycenae

What a terrible thing at a time like this: to own a house, and the trees around it. Janet sat rigid in her narrow seat. The plane lifted from the city and her house fell away, consumed by the other houses. Janet worried about her own particular garden and her emptied refrigerator and her lamps that had been timed to come on automatically at six.

'Is six too early? Too obviously a timer, do you think?' asked Murray. Janet was disturbed by this marital clairvoyance, and this was a new feeling, very recent. It had to do, she thought, with seeing the Andersons again. She took Murray's hand and together the Dwyers leaned toward the small window and watched as the horizon lost authority. When the attendants came with trolleys they would know they were safe, but until then they held hands as they tilted into the sky.

During the flight Janet allowed herself to remember her fear of the Andersons. She had forgotten this fear – or placed it aside – during the flurry of preparation. There had been an efficient period of To Do lists and of telling people, coyly, that they were 'meeting old friends in Greece'. Now, necessarily idle on the plane, Janet recalled the Andersons' sophistication; the decisiveness of their actions, which had always been without tremor or negotiation; the fact of their being American, which placed them at the centre of the world. Suspended above the revolving deserts of the Middle East, she feared the Andersons, who were from 'good families', however that might be understood – this was clear because they used to mention expensive New England schools and exotic family holidays. Or Amy Anderson mentioned these things on behalf of herself and Eric with an air of begrudging tenderness, as if obliged to give up a shameful but pleasant secret, and this fascinated Janet, who'd grown up in an asbestos house owned by the Australian government.

Murray would never say he feared the Andersons, though in his anxious way that's what he meant by 'Is six too early?' And Janet worried about him coming into daily contact with a man like Eric Anderson – what that might do to her husband's self-esteem, given that Eric, since they'd met him, had gone on to an illustrious academic career and Murray's contribution had been so small, though very solid. And to be seeing them again in Greece of all countries, in an old place that mattered, among the ancient terrors of history. The best thing was to be afraid along with Murray, to retain that sense of unity; later they could rally, once they'd been reassured by the goodness of Greek food and the number of people who spoke English. So Janet nurtured her fear over peanuts and warm washcloths, and pressed her leg against Murray's, and together they watched the same in-flight movies and walked up and down the night-time aisles of the plane in their compression socks, treading softly over the slipped blankets of other passengers.

In this way they flew to Greece, as if that were an easy thing to do: to board a plane in Sydney, spend a few hours in Hong Kong and then in London, and finally to arrive in Athens. They stepped out of the airport terminal and were surrounded by offers of help and information; they'd expected this and made their way to the official taxi rank with resolute faces. Murray held a piece of paper with the address of their apartment on it in Greek letters; he handed this over to the taxi driver like a man entrusted with the delivery of a sacred object. The driver understood. The apartment was, it seemed, a real place in a real city.

The apartment had been Amy's idea. Both couples would find one and spend the week as if they really lived in Athens. They would be neighbours, they would cook experimentally with market vegetables, they would carry keys and not hotel swipe cards. Here were some vacation rental websites Amy had looked at. Here was the apartment the Andersons were booking, a large white space with a roof terrace. Amy was sure Janet could find something similar nearby. Janet was less sure. She preferred the idea of a hotel. The apartments on Amy's websites were too expensive, or unavailable. Her son Damian offered to help. This wonderful trip to Greece, said Damian. He'd talked her into it. Damian was an experienced traveller – he'd been to places like Lebanon and Cuba – and he would help them. Now he worked for a law firm in London, and they would visit him after Athens. They would visit Damian in London and take him to the town Murray and Janet had lived in all those years ago, when Murray was a graduate student and they were newly married. They had met the Andersons in those days, in that town.

Damian found something not very close, but not so very far away from the Andersons' apartment: a student sublet with too many stairs, crowded with plastic furniture. It was cheaper than it needed to be, but it was something and it was somewhere; it was their apartment in Greece. And Damian had spent time finding it. And the relief Janet felt, despite the furniture and the view of TV aerials, countered, briefly, almost all of her disquiet. Murray sent a deposit. Then came an email of apology from Amy: their apartment had fallen through, last-minute, a shame, hotel after all, so disappointing. Here was the hotel address – the website – the tasteful lobby – the Acropolis view. The computer screen gave Athens to Janet and Murray, and they peered at it from the safety of their house in Sydney. They saw the white buildings, cement towers among the hills, the brown smudge low in the sky, the many roads, the temple high above. A sensation of having made a terrible mistake, of having sunk into something disastrous. But they would survive this city. In their apartment.

'We'll save on breakfast with our own kitchen,' said Murray. 'Make tea of a night.'

And Janet was reassured; they both were. When they entered the apartment – finally, having crossed the world to find themselves in it – they both looked for a kettle among the furniture. There it sat by the stove. It restored their confidence. They carried their suitcases into the small bedroom and lay on the student bed. Their limbs pressed into the sheets as if they were made of metal. Janet wanted to phone Damian at once but they fell irresistibly asleep, and when they woke later that afternoon it was time to meet the Andersons at their hotel.

Janet was worried she wouldn't recognise Amy. But of course she recognised Amy, who cried out, 'It can't be!' and advanced across the lobby with a look of delighted surprise on her face, as if their meeting were accidental. Amy wore slim white pants and a navy shirt with its jaunty collar turned up. She gathered Janet against her ribs. Eric's great height still gave him an air of magnificent remoteness; the grey of his hair only amplified the effect. When he bent low to kiss Janet she felt there was something exaggerated about the slow hinging of his body to reach the level of her cheek. She refused, at first, to stand on her toes to meet his approaching face, but capitulated in the end.

'Welcome to Greece,' said Eric. He said it with great seriousness, with a kind of weighty pride, as if he personally had prepared Greece, with effort but with no complaint, and with no particular thought for their pleasure; but he would share it with them anyway. Janet realised she was being uncharitable. She smiled apologetically at him. The Andersons had been in the country about five hours longer than they had.

'Welcome!' echoed Amy. 'How was the flight? Such a long way!'

'It's just good to be here,' said Janet. Amy was still holding her hand.

'Isn't it amazing to think: forty years, and here we are!'

Forty years ago, Murray had been completing his chemistry PhD and had, in a state of constant anxiety, crashed their small car three times. He and Janet were exhausted by England, by its complicated rules and the constant worry about where they would live next and how they would pay for it. Reflecting on that time, Janet saw herself eating toast and carrying shopping bags through rain almost continually, as if there had never been a summer (but there had been – three and a half of them, each glorious). They lived in a little college flat, and next door: Eric and Amy, not yet married, Eric a year ahead in his PhD and a philosopher, Amy on a Fulbright; they had painted their walls red without asking the college's permission. Amy invited them in one afternoon, fed them tiny pickles and gin, and after this had befriended Janet in a confiding, collegiate way, lending her books, giving advice. They had little in common and were very intimate, and their men were forced to befriend each other.

Eric was famous for refusing to engage in small talk. At parties he used to sit in the most comfortable chair, holding a glass that was always refilled for him, quietly, unasked, as if he were actually asleep, when in fact he was reading; finally, later in the night, he would materialise in the centre of a group and begin to talk with an irresistible urgency about Kant or sex or Nixon or Freud. This used to fill Janet with fury. She complained to Murray that *no one* liked small talk, but only Eric Anderson felt he was above it. It's *sociopathic*, she said, it's *intolerable*. But Eric's behaviour was not only tolerated, it was admired. Among their college acquaintances, Eric was always referred to, reverently, as a genius. No further explanation was offered or required. Alongside lively Amy, who danced and smoked, Eric seemed taintless and incorruptible; strange, then, that he should choose Amy, and apparently love her.

The Athenian Amy was a trim, ingenious woman, a walker in the early mornings, a subtle rearranger of hair, a gatherer of people and a maker of plans. Observant. The first to admit her ignorance – 'I know nothing whatso*ever* about Greece!' – and the first to master it. Within hours of her arrival she could direct taxi drivers, expertly manage her currency, and give a number of personally observed examples of the civility of the Greeks, their candour and charm. She had been, in England, a large girl, well made, with blonde limbs and hair. There was a ripe blaze upon her. Now she was thin in what Janet thought of as an American way: hard-won. Janet admired it. She admired the smooth shellac of Amy's adult hair. During the week in Athens it made her, for some reason, ashamed of her persistent desire to browse among the cheap ceramics of the tourist shops in Plaka, to shop for plates and bracelets rather than take a dusty tour of the Agora. In Amy's presence she became a shy glancer in mirrors – glances accompanied by brave smiles and the rubbing together of lips. She and Murray walked behind Amy and Eric through the Greek streets, and they smiled a great deal. They walked hand in hand until they noticed the Andersons didn't. They never voiced strong opinions on where to eat or what to see, except that Janet wanted to go to Mycenae.

When Amy had contacted her with this Greek idea, Janet recalled a *National Geographic* article she'd once read about Mycenae, ancient home of kings. It had stayed with her for years: the death masks made of gold, the old name 'Agamemnon', the gate carved with two lions. When she looked up the magazine – Murray kept them all in yellow rows – it was just as she remembered it. There were the death masks with their precise eyebrows, there was the grey-green valley, and the ruins on the hill. She showed Murray, knowing it would interest him: he liked the layers of things, the way they fitted together. 'Look,' she said, 'it was already a tourist destination in Roman times.' She liked to think of the warriors buried in the old grave circles, sleeping for centuries with their gold faces, and of Agamemnon setting out for Troy. Janet checked the distances involved and found it was possible to make the trip from Athens in a day; she suggested this day trip to the Andersons.

'I *did* hear it was just a hill with rocks on it,' said Amy. Clearly she hadn't factored Mycenae into her itinerary; she must be polite to Janet, but it would occupy a whole precious day. 'I guess we could hire a car and driver. The hotel could organise it. I don't like that phrase, "day trip", do you? It sounds so artificially lively. A minivan might be better. Then we'll have room to stretch our legs.' She looked pointedly at long-legged Eric, as if to emphasise the efforts she was making to preserve his dignity.

'It was just an idea,' said Janet, who knew she was being shrill and deferential. 'We're happy to go along with anything.'

But Murray cleared his throat and said, 'You've wanted to see it, haven't you, for some time?'

So Mycenae was decided upon as a special favour to Janet. Amy arranged it, just as she made the other plans. All week she led them through the streets of Athens with the enthusiastic gait of a tour operator; she was a sort of Hellenic shepherd. Eric co-operated with her silently until he noticed something that interested him. Then they stood and watched him be interested in it. He seemed oblivious to their waiting. When he was finished he stirred himself a little, a bear in spring, and they all moved forward again, the Dwyers wearing their accommodating smiles. Alone, Murray and Janet would have fussed about where to eat and when to withdraw money. They had done this in towns across Australia and England. Here in Greece they withdrew sums in the early mornings so as not to inconvenience the Andersons, and they allowed Amy to lead them into any café she liked the look of. There was one in Plaka she particularly favoured, a small place with tables on the street; she enjoyed watching the crowds of people as they took the sloping road up to the Acropolis, and observing their faces as they returned. The tourists made respectful space for these tables, looking at them longingly as they made their way up the hot hill, and they collapsed onto the café chairs in relieved exhaustion, crying out for cool drinks, as they descended. Amy never ordered cool drinks. She ordered coffee for herself and for Eric, but the Dwyers sipped at Cokes.

The Dwyers were both too large for the chairs at the café in Plaka – they teetered, with the chairs, on the cobblestones – but Janet was relieved to be sitting down, however precariously. She was made uneasy by the marble pavements of Athens, over which she slipped in the soft soles of her comfortable shoes. The Parthenon was humourless above them; it meant too much. It was almost offensive. Janet felt that it was wasteful not to look at it while she had the opportunity; at the same time, it exhausted her. She could find nothing human about it – nothing like Mycenae's shining masks.

'Let me see your passport photos,' said Amy, who was plainly proud of hers.

'Oh, no!' cried Janet, reaching into her handbag.

Her passport was so new next to Amy's. She saw Eric compare them. He turned to Murray, uncharacteristically expansive, and said, 'Nothing prepares you for the Greek light.'

The Dwyers nodded and smiled. Australia had prepared them for the Greek light. But it was still something different, if familiar: the great, burdened light, the Attic light. They sat among the flowers of the café as if prepared for sacrifice. In her embarrassment, Janet wanted to speak of Damian. It was a struggle not to talk about him too frequently. Into the silence of the table she wanted to say, 'Damian has a lovely Chinese girlfriend.' Or, 'Damian was promoted last year.' Instead she shifted her glass with her fingertips and noticed with surprise the dirtiness of her nails. She would have liked the café to smell of fish and rosemary, but instead there was the sun on dust, and sunscreen.

'I had quite an adventure this morning,' announced Amy, whose meaningful days began hours before anyone else's. She told of setting out from the hotel at sunrise, of her walk among the early-morning streets and markets, her coffee at a café crowded with workers, her encounter with a man named Christos who wanted to take her to Marathon. She spoke with solemnity of her lone walk, of the café and workers, but her tone altered for the story of Christos: she became amused and worldly.

'Why Marathon?' asked Janet.

'That's where he lives,' said Amy, crumbling a floury biscuit between her droll fingers. 'The man from Marathon.'

Eric stirred his coffee and looked toward the immemorial street.

'And what did you say to him?' asked Janet. She felt a small throb of envy. Before the trip, as she brushed up on the Greek dramatists, she worried that she couldn't possibly do Athens justice, and here she was, tired and hot, with dirt under her nails. But here was Amy, not reading about Greece, but actually *living* it, and all this from a hotel, not an apartment. And still beautiful enough for a man in a café to ask her to go home with him.

'I told him I was happily married,' said Amy, with a brief look at Eric, a brief hand on his mammoth arm, and Eric inclined his head toward her, stirring, stirring his coffee. 'I said I didn't trust his intentions. In no uncertain terms.'

'And what did he say?' asked Janet. Murray pressed her foot

under the table with the firm undersole of his sensible shoe, because they had decided last night, under the sweltering ceiling of their apartment, that they would stop encouraging Amy by asking questions.

Amy pursed her lips and leaned back in her chair in preparation for laughter. 'He said, "I'm hungry, but I'm not that hungry."'

And Eric let out a great, unsuspected laugh, a bark of laughter which Murray later described as a guffaw. It drew attention to their table, it silenced Janet, it left Amy adrift in the end of her story about Christos of Marathon. They sat startled among the plants and crockery. Eric tasted his coffee and pushed it away.

Janet all at once regretted every moment of the trip. Murray hated to travel. Damian had talked her into it; she'd talked Murray into it. She was furious with everyone. Travel was ridiculous. The dead plants, the fled cats, the concern at mounting mail. What could someone like her possibly be doing in Greece? The Greek light sped over the streets, the marble pavements tilted. So much marble. Restaurants in car parks, the blue dusk, doves among the stones. Greece was life, Amy said. But the Greeks must water plants and feed cats and answer mail. There were people here who taught high school, just as she had. Where were those people? They were speaking all around her, she supposed, but she couldn't understand them, and never would.

The light ticked on and the real sun fell. The couples arranged to meet at the hotel for cocktail hour. Janet and

Murray, arriving early, drank wine, intimidated by ouzo and carefully aware they were not paying guests. They drank too quickly as they waited for Eric and Amy to appear, and the sight of the Andersons made them drink faster still.

'I'll get drinks. A Scotch?' Murray asked Eric. They were the patient husbands of friendly wives. Their conversation had been reduced to a funny little parody of manliness: liquor and modes of transport and the distances between places. Among the sharp, pointed objects of the male world they sat quietly and Murray asked again, 'Scotch, Eric?'

'Oh no,' said Amy. 'No, he's just brushed his teeth. So have I. We'll wait. Wouldn't go, would it – toothpaste and whiskey?'

'If for no other reason,' said Eric. Sombre. Janet looked, and he winked. Don't wink, thought Janet. You're not a boy. She was susceptible to winks. They prevented her from feeling over-looked, and notice of this kind caused her heart to flower with gratitude. Made nervous – more nervous – she reached for her empty wine glass, then drew back. A funnel of lamplight fell over Eric and Amy. Janet told Murray she would join him at the bar.

'What was all that about?' said Murray. 'The not drinking?'

'Yes, what?'

It was about too much, or too little.

'Do you think he's . . .?'

'Couldn't be.'

'What's he drunk other nights?'

'Not much. Never what you'd call too much.'

'The truth, then? Toothpaste?'

'Don't they want us paying? Is that it?'

They could only conclude: don't worry, not our business. People arrived at the bar later than they had and were served first. The Dwyers tested out their Greek on each other, then ordered haltingly in English. Behind them the music rose in volume and couples began unexpectedly to dance – unexpected to Janet, although she had imagined hotels of this kind and people dancing in them. The lights were lowered on the tables and the dance floor was illuminated. The Andersons were dancing. So the Dwyers hesitated in the semi-darkness. Diminished, utterly, by their fear of the Andersons, who had found Greece – Amy had found Greece – and now moved as if through grape vines and olive groves, over the hard ground toward the mountains. The sea would rise up to meet them; the original sea. The Dwyers waited beyond the lights with extravagant drinks in their hands. They stood foolishly, and they stood without speaking to one another. They were afraid, and they waited.

You might say Janet had brought the Andersons together, although this wasn't quite true. They were engaged when the Dwyers first met them, but toward the end of Eric's PhD Amy considered breaking it off. She'd fallen in love, she confessed to Janet, with someone else, someone whose *greatness of character*, whose *kindness* and *deep commitment to love* were qualities, lacking in Eric, she couldn't afford to be without. Janet approved of these vague qualities – she recognised them so acutely in Murray that she worried, briefly, that Amy might have fallen in love with her own husband – and disapproving of Eric's magnificence, she experimentally encouraged her friend to pursue this new man.

'First I have to leave Eric,' said Amy. 'There needs to be a definitive break.'

It was decided they would go away together, Amy and Janet; Amy had finished her Fulbright year and Janet could be spared from work – her teaching credentials weren't acceptable in England, so she filed records in a doctor's surgery. Then it became clear that Murray would have to come too, because without Janet he floundered in their dim flat, which felt at this time of year exactly like a sad hotel. Janet had always wanted to go to Cornwall. When they began the drive, with Amy in the back seat, it felt to them all a little like a kidnapping.

This was a bad time to be in Cornwall: early December, the cold days after a flood. Water remained in the low streets of the town in which they rented a small house. The town had gathered itself on the cliffs as if in preparation for a springtime suicide. The houses were narrow and grey, the hills were green, and continual sleet fell over the sea. Amy and Janet ran from their house to the post office, where furniture subsided gently on the spongy floor, so Amy could send a postcard to Eric telling him it was over. They ran home in the wind. They remained inside during a storm that lasted, it seemed, for two days, playing cards and reading novels. Then someone came shaking the door and demanding to be let in.

Janet, afraid of reports to the landlord, opened the door and Eric arrived among them in a gloomy suit. Massive among them, and silent, with an air of inevitability.

'How did you find me?' asked Amy, quite calmly, from the couch.

'The postcard. Then I asked someone at the train station,' said Eric. 'You're the only tourists in town.'

He sat beside Amy on the sofa and rested his head against the wall behind him. It was as if he had run all the way from London, dressed for a funeral. Janet and Murray announced they would go for a walk. It was far too cold to walk. They dressed importantly in boots and hats. Janet imagined herself blown from the cliffs of Cornwall, but Murray held her arm and they struggled to a tearoom. They stayed three hours among the brown wallpaper and granular tablecloths and when they returned it was as if to Amy's marital home: Eric, shoeless, spread across the floor, coffee made, and Amy pleased with herself among newspapers.

Eric lay on the floor the way a marble statue sits indifferently on grass. His suit jacket steamed over the radiator. Janet felt herself redden with worry. Was everything settled? Would he stay the night? Should she ask? She didn't ask. He stayed the night in the tiny house, in Amy's bed, which struck loudly against the wall between them and the Dwyers. Janet and Murray giggled into their pillows, they clutched each other with the silly primness of the newly married. Amy and Eric's bed rocked, their own bed shook; all the beds in the riotous house. Murray's mouth fell against his wife's and she pulled away, smiling.

'They'll hear,' she said.

They buried themselves in the pillows again. Then crept to the floor. There was a rug that smelled of shoes.

'Bring down the quilt,' said Murray.

The quilt over the rug; the Dwyers over the quilt. The Andersons next door, rocking. Only not yet the Andersons – they were married two months later.

'Aren't we happy?' said Janet, rolling on the rug, and they were.

Late in the night she walked through the dark house checking the security of windows and doors, the safety of stoves and electrical cords, afraid that her great happiness might be taken away from her by divine accident. Amy, also walking the house, moving silently on felted feet, met Janet filling a glass of water at the sink. The water poured slowly and quietly, and Janet held one finger in the glass so she could tell when it neared the top.

'Sorry,' said Amy.

'For what?' asked Janet. She had felt all afternoon that Amy had something to apologise for, although she couldn't have defined it. But at this moment, her finger bent into the glass, she was certain that none of them need apologise to each other ever again.

'For creeping up on you in the dark.'

'I'm just getting a drink,' said Janet, and the water touched her fingertip. She let it fill the glass and moved her hand so it flooded over her wrist. She felt as if her intimacy with Murray, the privacy of her love and happiness, had expanded so that it now encompassed Amy and Eric. Her happiness pushed against her chest. If she could preserve this, somehow: the town pressing round her, the floodwater soaking into the post office carpets, the bedrooms of the house hanging over her head, with men in them. She felt the security of a house. The water ran into the sink and she turned off the tap.

Amy stood by the kitchen table.

'Janet,' she said, 'you won't tell Eric about the other one, will you? The man I mentioned?'

'Of course not. Is everything all right?' Janet shook her wet fingers.

'Everything is perfect,' Amy answered. It seemed that it was. The windows and doors were locked. The men slept on in the house.

Athens gave Janet unexpected allergies and she fumbled continually with sodden tissues – too thin, they clung to her fingers. She laughed, embarrassed, and brought attention to herself. Amy walked into the hot, quiet hour of the day and returned with a box of smooth handkerchiefs, scalloped in blue.

'How clever,' said Janet. 'I'd never have thought.'

'You're the suffering kind,' said Amy – not true, surely? – 'who won't put others out.' Possibly true, and Janet had never felt so guilty. She was shy behind her quaint handkerchiefs. Money was offered and refused. They were all up on the roof terrace of Amy's hotel. Husbands lay on lounges behind them, Eric with the newspaper, Murray asleep, hands clasped over his ribs, a midday saint.

'Hasn't it been forever?' said Amy, as if they'd just encountered each other in a supermarket. Forever might have been eight months. 'Hard to imagine. So many years since Cornwall. Remember Cornwall?'

'Oh yes,' said Janet.

'Cornwall was wonderful. Lately it's all I think about. Remember that adorable little house? And drinking sherry from those tiny glasses?'

'The sherry,' said Janet. She didn't remember the sherry.

'Remember how cold it was? And the coin-operated heating? How worried we were that we'd run out of coins?' Amy sat with her chin in her hands, and her head was older, thinner, than it had been in Cornwall. 'You have to wonder what would have happened without Cornwall. Marriage is like that, isn't it,' she said. 'It reaches a point.'

Janet was unsure what point Amy's marriage might have reached.

'Why don't we take a walk, just the two of us?' said Amy.

Janet was tired. 'What a good idea,' she said.

'We're going for a walk,' Amy told Eric. He nodded behind his newspaper. Murray looked so defenceless, asleep on his lounge, that Janet hated to leave him. She and Amy walked out into the exhausted afternoon.

'You know where I'll take you,' said Amy, 'I'll take you to that café I was in yesterday morning. Now, if I can just remember how to find it.'

She remembered how to find it; it was only around the corner. It was a very ordinary café, and there were racks of post-cards among the outdoor tables, where tourists sat drinking

Cokes. Janet had pictured something else. She looked at it from across the street, disappointed.

'Is this where you met Christos of Marathon?'

Amy was unexpectedly anxious. 'Oh god, I don't know what you're going to say,' she said. 'I'm just going to be up front with you. I need a favour.'

'Of course,' said Janet, imagining a small loan, imagining confidences about Eric.

'I need to borrow your apartment for a few hours this afternoon.'

'Oh,' said Janet. They were walking toward the café, and a man, a little younger than they were, stood up from a table when he saw them. Everything was so predetermined; it was embarrassing. Amy introduced them. They all stood there, embarrassed, and perhaps Christos was the most discomfited of all. He was the kind of man Amy used to see in England and say to Janet, 'Look at the quality of his shirt!' Janet never noticed the quality of any man's shirt. She thought Christos had a pleasant face, a face you enjoyed looking at; it seemed so sensibly arranged. She went to pass her key to Amy, who turned away, suddenly fastidious, checking for something in her handbag, so Janet handed the key to Christos instead. Then he stepped away toward the road, discreetly.

'Do you know where it is?' Janet asked Amy.

'I have the address. Christos knows how to get there. You must think I'm really something.'

'No, no,' said Janet.

'I shouldn't have brought you out. You should be locked up

in an air-conditioned room, taking care of your nose.'

'I'm fine,' said Janet.

Amy's face creased into a shape of exaggerated concern. Janet waved her blue-scalloped handkerchief, a little flag.

'I'm fine,' she repeated.

'See you here at four,' said Amy, and then she was gone and Christos was gone, and there was Athens. Janet couldn't go home, or to the hotel. There were no men to meet in a café. She walked to Plaka, carefully, over the marble. Her nose ran. The streets were full of stores selling blue and white and yellow ceramics. She bought three heavy platters, then worried about how to get them home.

The minivan drew up to the hotel with the look of a bashful turtle. It was a generous vehicle, with room for many passengers, and Janet felt conspicuous as they drove away in it, as if the four of them had been abandoned by a crowd of friends and left to the Fates and to Mycenae. She felt a particular anxiety because today was her doing. Why had she suggested Mycenae? The night before, she'd pulled the *National Geographic* article from her suitcase. She was hesitant to sit on any surface; every object in the apartment was suspicious to her, although there were no clues to betray the afternoon's activities. The photographs of Mycenae showed blank and barren hills and a spread of vaguely room-shaped rubble.

'Let's call it off,' said Janet. And tried not to picture Amy and Christos in the bed.

'No,' said Murray, rubbing his weary feet. 'She can't have everything her way. This is the one thing you wanted to do, and we're doing it.' He was bold and aggrieved when they were alone; they also held hands in the apartment, as if to make up for their separation during the day. Janet was grateful, but she didn't tell him about Christos. How else to protect him?

So here they were in a bus, air-conditioned, on their way to Mycenae. They left Athens very early because of the weather – it was going to be the hottest day. Murray, anticipating the heat, had frozen bottles of water overnight.

'Couldn't do this in a hotel,' he said, with some satisfaction.

Now the bottles were sweating cold liquid, staining their laps but still too frozen to drink, while Amy and Eric sipped at the bottles provided by the driver.

'You know, I'm excited about this,' said Amy, inclining her attentive head toward the window. Eric sat in the front with the driver, and didn't turn to look at her. No one else spoke, but Janet cooed a little, like a pigeon.

The heat was worse at Mycenae. Janet saw with dismay that it was a hill with rocks on it. She said to herself, *Agamemnon. Agamemnon.* They abandoned the cool of the minivan and began to ascend. They could stay in the shade of the walls until they passed under the Lion Gate, but after that there would only be the sun.

Eric walked kingly among the stones. The heat was similarly dignified. It lay impersonally over them all. It filled Janet's lungs and pressed against her face whenever she stirred her head. And Eric walked unmoved among the stones. Janet watched him, and she watched as Murray picked his faltering way among the shaded rocks. He struck her as elderly, without being exactly old, and she felt an additional fondness for his vulnerable head. His bottle of ice rattled against his hip as he walked. Dizzy, she sat on a low wall and looked to see if Murray, ascending the slope – soon he would be completely exposed to the light – might turn to find her. He didn't. He passed with determination, with his trim calves and ankle socks, beyond the reach of the shade and out into the heat's flat plain.

'Come on, you!' cried Amy.

But Janet couldn't bear to look at Amy.

She waved and smiled and watched them all disappear under the Lion Gate. There was dust at her feet and strange birds flew overhead, and the rocks she sat on had been shaped and set in this place so long ago they may as well have occurred naturally. Then Mycenae seemed to her a growth, rather than a construction. It had nothing at all to do with human life. All of Greece seemed that way: as if some other species – the gods – had lived here carelessly then abandoned it. And she could only crawl about on it, take some photographs, go home.

A man in uniform called out and she understood that it was forbidden to sit on the stones. That seemed right to her, so she stood. She wanted to apologise to someone, but the only person she saw when she passed under the Lion Gate was Eric. He was standing on the edge of the slope with his right hand shading his eyes, his right hand pressed against his great American head, and in this stance his Viking ancestors were so visible, sailing the North Sea in their longboats, that the whole country of Greece became the frigid ocean and there was nothing to do but hurry into the boat with Eric, who would captain it so surely.

Janet stood beside him and read aloud from a small sign: 'Grave Circle A.' Grave Circle A was a ring of stones laid out beneath them. Archaeologists had pulled the men and gold from it many years ago. Eric didn't even look at it; he stared across the valley. Janet realised that she had never really been alone with him before. She might say to him, Your wife slept with another man in my apartment yesterday afternoon. With Christos of Marathon, who was hungry after all. She might say, Your wife fell in love with another man in England.

Eric said, 'Nothing prepares you for the light.'

It was impossible to pity a man like this. He was a god, really – remote and ineffectual. He belonged in this kind of place, in the ruins of something he'd fought for and won. But she noticed his hands were shaking.

'I've finished my water,' he said.

Then he fell. He dropped the way a jacket does, slipping off a coathanger: an elegant, draping subsidence. Soundless, and although he collapsed on himself at first, he then rolled out across Janet's feet, so that by the time people came she'd fallen too and couldn't quite understand how to get up. Murray ran toward her, curiously nimble. Eric lay heavily across her legs but Murray moved him without difficulty, lifting her out and away and to her feet. She was dazed by the sun and the dust, by Eric's mournful face and upturned hands; painted clouds above, rocks below, and doves among the stones. The view over blank hills that were green without being green, the constant haze at the horizon. Janet thought of this later as the failure of a man, the great, impossible end of Eric, although Eric didn't actually end but woke drearily, halfway to Athens, in the back of the van with spit dried at the corners of his mouth. It was only sunstroke. He was thirsty, his head ached, and he cried a little – Murray and Janet heard him cry in the seat behind them. His head lay in Amy's lap and she stroked and soothed him.

'Shhh,' she said. 'Shhh.'

Janet sat beside Murray. They held hands. Greece took place outside the windows of the van. She rested her head on Murray's shoulder and said, 'It's far too hot. We never should have come.' But she was glad they had.

In Sydney, it was six o'clock. The lamps came on in the Dwyers' house, all at once, in the empty windows.

Man and Bird

In the hour of his humiliation, Reverend Adams still wore his hat: a black bowler that sat upright on his narrow head, like a fortified town on a hilltop. His clerical shirt was also black, and his single-breasted jacket (all three buttons firmly fastened), and his trousers and shoes, but all in slightly different shades, which gave him a regrettably scruffy look, simultaneously prismatic and funereal. The parish had great hopes for him at first. He'd had excellent theological training, came with good references and was moreover unmarried, which stirred the ashes of many a virgin breast; and so, in the beginning, when he entered his new congregation, it was as a bridegroom into a rose garden.

His appearance was promising. The slope of his nose, echoed in the angle of his chin, gave an impression of profound endurance. There was a suggestion of sculpture in the marble-like whiteness of his skin. Yes, he was prim and pallid, in excellent health, with well-made ears, and in his battered blacks he presented a respectable, even slightly romantic figure. Also, he was kindly. He walked with an incongruous maritime swell that might, in another man, have passed for a swagger, and was careful in the maintenance of a small yellow car that he rarely drove faster than seventy kilometres an hour. He spoke in long, dignified sentences, rich in clauses, reminiscent of a veteran's parade on a memorial holiday, and as he delivered his sermons he had a tendency to rise to the tip of his toes, so that finally he appeared to be levitating behind the pulpit. This was disconcerting, but forgivable. He also caused a minor stir early on when he removed two ancient trees from the churchyard because, he said, they interfered with the grass.

What worried people most of all was his parrot.

It was fitting that a man of Reverend Adams's calling should have acquired few objects on his way through the world, but why should one of them be a parrot? An entirely white parrot, too, as if it had once been red and yellow and green and blue but was now in some kind of Chinese mourning, except for the sulphur crest on the back of its head. Every member of the congregation can still recall, with perfect clarity, the appearance of that prodigious bird: the stiff crinoline of its feathers, the Pentecostal lick of yellow flame on its head, the tiny eyes and wormy claws, that grey, awful beak. When it fixed you with its enigmatic eye, it suggested nothing so much as the sorrowful ghost of a parrot, but you were aware, nevertheless, that it was not above a kind of solemn cheekiness. And when the parishioners saw man and bird together, they were reminded of certain ordinary dining rooms on whose walls fantastic wallpaper repeated bamboo and nightingales. It unnerved them to think of Reverend Adams and the parrot, alone together, eating their bachelor meals.

As Reverend Adams settled into his position, the congregation developed the opinion that he talked too much about death, and with the wrong emphasis. The way he described it, it was as if the arrival in Heaven, the longed-for meeting with God, would be about as melancholy as you might imagine the reunion of a father and son in a railway station, under artificial light. Eternity seemed less glorious, then; it seemed a cheerless thickening of time, rather than a new expanse. And so Reverend Adams was given to understand, by certain older and well-respected members of his congregation, that his flock had begun to pray for him, that he might receive insight into the mysteries of Heaven and the inheritance awaiting him there.

Reverend Adams withdrew to his rectory, troubled by this rebuke; trouble drawn into the furrows of his brackish brow, which he mopped with a handkerchief he kept stuffed in the pocket of his black trousers. But that night, as he slept, he dreamt of Heaven. It was a sleep so close to sleeplessness that when he woke he was able to recall every detail of his dream of paradise: the river that flowed with dull silver, the endless walls of the City of God, the streets paved with gold, and the holy clamour of the passionate elect, who worshipped God day and night without ceasing. He was led through this vision by a strange figure, half bird, half human – an archangel, he assumed – with white feathers and a tongue of fire on the back of its head. There was a quality to the light which was, it seemed to him, something like an old photograph, taken at night, in which white becomes silver and every other colour a shade of blue. This dream left him both elated and bereft – he felt he'd been born into entirely the wrong tradition to take advantage of it, and so, in his sermons, he skirted its great thicket and made instead for the sparser grove in which he'd been trained.

Nevertheless, the slight oddness of his person increased, imperceptibly at first, but more obviously toward the end of that year. He began to pause mid-sermon as if made curious by what he'd just said. Yes, it was as if his beliefs were surprising to him; he appeared to be baffled by their mysterious survival. He resembled his parrot most uncannily at these moments because he was so like a bird suddenly given the power to understand its own speech.

Of course, even this might have been tolerated if his behaviour hadn't become stranger still. He took to carrying his parrot everywhere with him, perched on the back of his right hand. The bird sidled on his hand. It stepped to the left and stepped to the right. There was no distracting it from its great love: Reverend Adams. It had eyes only for him. And the Reverend, in turn, would gaze at the bird in respectful consultation, as if waiting for some message. This was not a particularly talented parrot, the kind that can repeat whole sentences, the kind suggestive of a soul; it only made strange stops and clicks with its plump bird tongue, bobbing up and down as if kneeling to pray or to take communion, its head cocked to one side. Stop, and click; warble, click; and stop. Even the stoutest of the Reverend's suitors withdrew at the sight of him waiting for his parrot, and turned their hopes elsewhere.

Of course, even *this* might have been tolerated, if it weren't for the sermon he delivered on Christmas morning – a joyous morning when an old truce is declared, so that the sinners of a parish, the neglectful and the ambivalent, the absent-minded and the repentant of spirit, can flock with the faithful to church and expect to be met with cheerful news of the life everlasting. But on this day of days, overwhelmed, no doubt, by the goodness of his news, Reverend Adams chose to stand at the pulpit, on his toes, and inform his congregation that their prayers had been answered: that on the previous night, and every night for months now, he had been visited by visions of Heaven so magnificent, so vivid, that the world around him seemed almost to no longer exist, and he had come to rely on his bird, that messenger of God, to guide him through it, so that he could keep his inner eye fixed on the paradise in store for God's people. Then Reverend Adams began to weep, and as he did so his bird lifted from his arm and flew, in perfect calm, into the vast expanse under the roof of the church, which had been designed long ago to encourage men to raise their eyes Heavenward. It seemed now to have been designed for the flight of the white parrot, which continued for some time until finally the bird came to rest on the great cross in the chancel. By then the Reverend had been led away from the pulpit and, as his congregation sang carols and murmured the benediction, could be heard sobbing in the vestry. He pulled himself together, however, to stand outside the church door in order to perform his regular duty of greeting each parishioner after the service, and it was here that certain older and well-respected members of his congregation suggested to him that he might consider taking a long and possibly permanent break from his ministerial responsibilities, which appeared to be taxing him beyond endurance.

This was the hour of his humiliation. He left the church at once. He drove with his yellow car pointed toward the sea, because this was the pattern of his annual holiday and he was unsure where else to go. A long flat plain and a range of mountains separated the Reverend from the sea. His bird rode above the steering wheel, on his right hand, as they crossed the plain and climbed the mountains, and as they descended the clouds broke open and admitted a column of sun. Reverend Adams was moved to lower the window of his car and thrust his bird-heavy arm into the void, so that his parrot was obliged to take flight. He withdrew his arm and sealed himself in. And the white bird flew in the shaft of light above the car, above the revolving earth, until finally, man and bird together reached the sea.

Unnecessary Gifts

James is being a sea lily.

'Look, Dad,' he says, 'I'm being a sea lily.'

Unhurried, and with a submarine expression, he waves his small arms backward and forward and drifts around the room.

'What would you call this kind of movement?' he asks, waving and drifting.

'I don't know,' I say. 'How about "undulating"?'

He takes this on board. 'I'm a sea lily undulating above the ocean floor. I look like a plant, but actually I'm an animal.'

'You look like an animal to me,' I say.

'And when I die, I'll turn into limestone.'

He's on the couch now, on tiptoes, and the way his arms wave into the room it's truly as if they're long green stalks. Somehow I have produced a child who is capable of pulsing with a creepy aquatic languor.

'I didn't know small boys turned into limestone.'

'I may look like a plant, but actually I'm an ANIMAL. I swim around the ocean with my ROOTS.'

James launches himself from the couch. He spends a fraction of an airborne second transfixed by the compact floating disguised life of the sea lily before landing among the carpet fluff – one arm over his face, one foot through the plywood of the china cabinet door. For this he is sent out to find his older brother. He knows he will be able to find Greg at the Wolfsons', the Barters', or possibly at the Carrs', although Blake Carr has fallen from neighbourhood grace owing to the recent demise of his trampoline.

'God,' says Glenda, coming in damp from the kitchen as usual (the kitchen always unaccountably damp, and Glenda always arriving thirty seconds after an accident). 'Your mother will love this. She hates that cabinet.'

Glenda's bringing me a gin and tonic. Alcohol plays no part in this story; it's just that taking the glass from her requires me to lean forward in my chair, and this means I see James out on the street on his one true possession, a bicycle with silver pedals, heading in the direction of the Wolfsons'. This is the last moment I can account for him with any authority for some time, and what I want to do now is re-create those hours after

James left the house, a sea lily disguised as a small boy. I want to know what those hours were like for him. It's not easy. There's the police report, the security tapes, and Tony's brother's statement. These things help. But the difficulty lies in the task of remembering childhood, that busy time of waiting.

Glenda's back is to the window. She doesn't see him.

Glenda gave birth to Greg and then James with the flustered enthusiasm with which she approaches most activities. For some time afterward it was very easy to keep track of their movements. My parents supplied us with state-of-the-art devices intended to attach children to other things: strapped across our chests, immobile in the back seat of the car, bouncing in small buggies that fastened to Glenda's bicycle. Initially, we functioned as tour guides to their lives, arranging for them to be moved from place to place. It didn't last. First Greg, then James, acquired additional life. Their tiny bodies seemed designed for the express purpose of running quickly and cannily through department stores. Glenda showed the strain, so my mother took her to a day spa to be smothered in cool creams that smelled of supermarkets.

'Philip,' my mother said when they returned from the spa, 'I'm worried about Glenda. I hope you're looking after her. She seems subdued.'

Glenda, uncharacteristically immobile with aromatherapy, lay across the couch waiting for my mother to leave as the boys stacked brightly coloured plastic blocks around her feet.

It's not that Glenda doesn't get on with my parents. It would be difficult not to get on with them. They're tanned, wear crease-free clothing, and play sociable tennis. They love Glenda and the boys with the kind of generosity that means they'll come by for an impromptu visit and, if we're out, wait in their car until we get home. Glenda will sigh as we pull into the driveway – a small sigh that I can hear but the boys can't.

'We were just passing,' my mother will call, extracting herself from the hot car with the plucky expression of a dehydrated dog. My father's arms will be full of bread rolls and newspaper cuttings and a book Glenda mentioned she liked the sound of a week ago. Our house feels smaller when they're in it, more untidy.

My mother has expressed her concern at our practice of allowing the boys out to play unsupervised in the neighbourhood. She once discussed it with me in the garden, where only the magpies and I could hear her.

'It was fine when you were young,' she said, with her thin, tanned voice. 'But things aren't the same these days.'

'They never go more than three blocks away,' I told her. 'And we have Neighbourhood Watch.'

'You know I don't often comment on your parenting,' she said, looking around the garden, from fence to fence, window to window, as if scouting for disguised dangers about which I know nothing.

The boys' social life may be confined to two or three streets but it's still complex, fluid, and frequently involves Glenda and me in unexpected situations. James, then, on this hot afternoon, experiencing the injustice of being barred from home, the humid repetitive earthbound feeling of not occupying the ocean floor: James goes in search of his brother on his silver-pedalled bicycle. As soon as he received this bicycle from his grandparents – for no reason, I might add, it just arrived one day – James customised it with stickers of half-men, half-monsters. Glenda's reaction to the stickers was: 'Your grandfather gave you that bike and he isn't going to like these.' I couldn't tell you the exact moment Glenda began living as if my parents were watching her every move through secret cameras embedded in unnecessary gifts.

'This one is especially gruesome,' I said, inspecting a particular sticker. It featured something green which appeared muscular despite its delicate tentacles.

'I know,' said James, conspiratorial. 'He doesn't eat. He photosynthesises.'

This is the bike James rides away on, basically homeless. That's how his head seems – small and homeless. I look at the china cabinet, then at Glenda.

'You can take the boys to the hardware store tomorrow,' she says. 'They love it there.'

That's true. Even Greg never fails to be impressed by the number of small shiny things in the world.

This is what I think happened. James found his brother one street away at the Wolfsons', and Greg was unhappy to see him. The accumulating sorrow – evicted from home and now unwelcomed by a brother. I know the Wolfsons' yard well because I've negotiated it when tipsy. It's all paving, swimming pool, and plants in pots. Bev Wolfson holds parties lit by candles and the moist glow of this obstacle-course greenery. Glenda and I wonder if their plants are fake because we're jealous of their swimming pool, despite the temporary feel of its above-ground installation.

'Imagine having a swimming pool like that,' says Glenda. 'I'd spend all day in it, naked.'

My answer to this is that I would reapply her suncream.

This is the world of patio foliage and older boys that James has entered, the flimsy pool full of children, water coming over the side like surf. Greg damp but dressed and ready to leave, the brief argument, James sullen and imploring, Bev Wolfson shimmying around with towels and Diet Coke and painted toenails. Greg is unimpressed at James's arrival because he has plans to meet his friend Tony whose older brother is a shopping-centre security guard. When were these plans made? Some interior minute we couldn't monitor. Greg makes phone calls when we least expect it, curling his entire body around the phone, giving and taking quick instructions and behaving afterward as if nothing has happened. He sends emails from my computer. Every now and then I surprise him at my desk, looking like a small efficient workday version of me. At any given moment he could be making arrangements to meet up with a security guard one Friday when we are tired and lax and stunned by the end of the week.

A street away, safely at the Wolfsons', Greg is shrugging his shoulders and agreeing to let James come along to an empty shopping centre. There are times when he shrugs that way at me, too, slouchy and resigned. It's like I'm literally on his back. Then he shrugs and I'm off.

The bicycle stays at the Wolfsons' because Tony's security-guard brother has a car. Bev Wolfson will find the bike later, after the rainstorm, stickers wet and peeling, collapsed among the pot plants in a blur of mosquitoes. The police report doesn't give the colour of Tony's brother's car; let's say it's blue. My first car was blue – almost navy. It shook on the highways and leaked in every kind of weather. My parents wanted to buy me a new one, but I insisted on paying for my own. Glenda filled it with apple cores and covered the door of the glove compartment with the fruit's stickers. Tony's brother's car is only minimally insured because the sound system is worth more than the car itself. This is the kind of information you can pick up about a person. Glenda's sister works in an insurance call centre and we had her check him out. She typed his name into the system with those long pearly artificial nails that make her do everything with the last-minute flicks of a flamenco dancer. Tony's brother drives his car to work, although he could walk; the shopping centre is only three blocks from his house, through the roundabout at Hughes Road, and across the car park. It's true these places aren't designed for pedestrians. Who knows what might happen to security guards, leaving shopping centres alone on foot at dawn.

Tony sits up front and our boys climb into the back. They fasten their seatbelts without being asked, just as they always do. Tony's brother looks over his shoulder from the driver's seat. He's good-looking, sports promising jowls, grooms a bit of stubble, and wears a zip-up jacket.

He asks, 'How old is this kid anyway?'

'Eight,' says Greg.

At the same time as James says, 'I'm eight.'

The boys have been to this shopping centre hundreds of times, but not when it's empty and not behind the scenes. They'll enjoy this, James because he likes knowing how things work, Greg because he likes knowing things other people don't. Tony's brother takes the boys into a room and says, 'This is my office.' James and Greg both know it isn't exactly an office. They've visited me at work. But there are more interesting things to touch here: switches, telephones, television screens. James finds a map of the shopping centre and walks his fingers around it. He's particularly good with maps. He brings them home from school and sits at the kitchen table to colour them in. This, I think, is what our table was made for. James enjoys school in the same way that Greg enjoys ball sports. This week he has learnt about unusual underwater animals. Dense, dark-water fish with built-in light globes. Poisonous rockpool octopi. Sea lilies.

What if we'd had two girls? Bev Wolfson has two girls, twins just a little older than Greg. Last time I saw them, they were in the kitchen sharing headphones, each with a pod in one ear, jumping up and down in sync. Glenda would like a girl – it's something she'd like, but doesn't feel she needs.

'You know what,' she's said more than once, 'one day your mother will walk in here and give me one, gift-wrapped.'

'All right, boys,' says Tony's brother. 'Let's take a walk.'

Now that they're in the shopping centre it doesn't matter what time of day it is. The lights are dimmed and for hours it will be evening. The place looks as if it's just been evacuated after a disaster warning. James is thinking about the time. I know he thinks about it because it's often a topic of conversation for him.

'In a minute,' he'll say while I'm combing my hair or brushing my teeth, 'Mum's going to come in here and tell you we're late.'

And she does.

Greg is walking up front with Tony's brother. Tony's on the loose, stopping and starting, running ahead, falling behind. It's like he's playing tennis with himself. He's one of those kids. He gets nosebleeds, but on him they look macho: blood on his lip, making fists. He's chunky and quick, checking things out. He'll exchange a few words with James.

'Hey,' he says. 'That huge Christmas tree is hollow.'

They're in the central court of the mall now, and it's set up for Christmas. There's a plush red and gold Santa's throne looking vaguely degenerate on a stage. There's tinsel and holly, fake snow, and a bright green, three-storey Christmas tree – fifteen metres of plastic pine. I wonder how they assemble those enormous trees, how many pieces there are to them, and where they live for the months they aren't required. James is wondering this, too, as he inspects the tree, the globes of red and gold floating in it, the fact of its hidden cavity. His gaze follows it up and up among the shopping-centre levels that are strung together with escalators and boughs of synthetic holly and the cameras whose video screens Tony's brother is supposed to keep an eye on. And being James he is struck by the tree's undersea immensity in the half-light. The end of the sun comes through the skylight above them, and it's like looking up from the other side of water.

Greg is on Santa's throne. Here comes his voice – girlish and convincing. He's saying something like 'I am the lord of all I survey, of half-price CDs and ladies' underwear and small white fences designed for keeping kids in line while they wait to see Santa.' Greg is a keen observer of concrete objects and we have high hopes for his sense of irony.

'James,' he says. 'Get up here.'

'Hey,' says Tony. 'Why are all the escalators blocked off? They're stopped anyway.'

This is when Glenda looks out the window and says, 'Where are those boys?'

What's Tony's brother doing now? What do security guards do in empty shopping centres? Here are some possibilities: they stroll around with torches, wearing caps and pretending to be burglars. They window-shop. They pluck tiny spiders out of fake foliage. I've heard that celebrities sometimes come to malls after hours and things are kept open for them. Princess Diana did, some time in the eighties, on one of her visits. She strolled and chatted and did some shopping. I've also heard that in the eighties, shop mannequins were modelled on her features. It must have been quite a life, shopping amongst yourself in an empty store at night.

Could be Tony's brother is noticing a lot of things at once. The rain that's started up – brief, sweaty summer rain, with the sky yellow and no clouds that you'd noticed. Tony fooling with the escalator barriers, trying to swing them back or push them aside. James heading toward his brother on the throne. Something about James is that he's always neat – no laces undone, nothing creased, never sloppy, like a miniature version of my father. Glenda always says 'His hair falls in a natural part' with a kind of subdued wonder, because hers doesn't. Could be that Tony's brother is sitting on the raised red stage smoking a cigarette and knowing no one will stop him. He must bring girls here.

'So James,' says Greg, kicking affectionately at his brother, 'what do you want for Christmas?'

'A new china cabinet.'

Greg laughs. He has a spooky laugh, man-sized, though he's not a man. James's face gets the look it does when he's made Greg laugh: happy and speculative. There's always the risk that Greg will stop.

'Get up here,' Greg says. 'I'm Santa.'

James sits on Greg's knee.

'Hey,' calls Tony, halfway up the escalator, 'this tree's so big you could sit in it.'

Glenda makes a call to Bev Wolfson. The rain stops while she dials. Bev says, 'Glenda! Come for a drink. The boys are probably in the yard. They'll be among the hordes. Why don't you come over? Bring Phil.'

Bev's talking so loud I can hear her. I shake my head at Glenda and Glenda shakes her head into the phone.

'Do you mind checking, just quickly?' Glenda asks.

Where's Tony's brother at this moment? Checking out a noise in a loading bay? He may have a walkie-talkie somewhere in his zip-up jacket. The smoke from his cigarette is going up up up.

'What about you?' says James. 'What do you want for Christmas?'

'I've got a list,' Greg answers. 'I've sent it already.'

This concerns James. He knows, in a solemn and informed way, that Santa Claus isn't real. He assumes Greg knows this too, but now he isn't sure. He looks up to the second-floor mezzanine, where a diminished Tony is circling the tree like a compact angel, inspecting it from all directions.

'Who'd you send your list to?' James asks.

'To Grandma and Pop. Who else? They give the best stuff.'

James knows this – we all know this. Even Glenda has buckled under the pressure.

'Mum and Dad give good stuff,' says James.

Greg says, 'Mmm.' Then he says, 'It's all educational.'

Maybe Tony's brother is right there, thinking about Christmas, the nuts and candles and bad wine, the old people who knew you when they were young. He leans against the stage, removes his jacket, places his walkie-talkie beside him. Tony has finally found himself the perfect position: a bench, the balcony rail, a small step into the tree. He yells down to them, his voice echoing and enormous.

'I could get into it from here,' he says. 'Think it's stable?'

Bev hurries in from the yard – imagine her agile steps among the plants.

'The boys aren't here,' she says, and she reports James's bike. There's a small moment when you begin to wonder, and in the middle of it, you remain calm.

Glenda finds more phone numbers – the Barters', the Carrs'. I say I'll take a drive.

'It's not *all* educational,' says James. But he's scanning through a mental list of every gift we've ever given him, and it's true that there's always an agenda: Keep quiet! Learn to read! Hand-eye coordination! Ancient cultures!

By now Tony is in the tree. Who but a kid like Tony would think to climb into that tree? He just stepped right into the middle of it – I've seen him on the CCTV tape, quiet and at a distance. Tony slightly fuzzy in black and white, stepping into the tree like a chunky Chaplin, slapstick and crazy. He's got nineteen seconds and he lets out what I'd call a whoop. Some kind of sound that has to do with height and secrecy and finding things out, with disobedience, with being in space – the new view, the absurdity of it. He pockets a bauble, like a thief or a bird, and he's both, making a place in the tree, rearranging it, shifting things round up there. Tony's got it – he's riding that tree, he's found his footing. What a feeling to be in the middle of all that, a kid like Tony looking around, looking down.

The tree shakes a little, unhappy, like something in a fairytale waking up.

I'm driving slowly with my window down, watching pedestrians and making people uncomfortable. Everyone's out after the rain, walking on the wet grass, following dogs, peering into flowerbeds. The birds are crazy with the late sun. The houses are transparent and available, curtains open for early Christmas trees, back doors visible through front doors, and pieces of smoke-filled garden. In each house, someone is on the phone. You can hear their phone voices in the street, and it's as if Glenda has called every one of them, all at the same time. There are small boys kicking soccer balls across yellow front lawns. There are boys climbing trees to retrieve lost objects, and boys at windows pressing their open mouths against cool glass. I wonder when this place got to be so wholesomely full of childhood. None of the boys look like James or Greg, not even for a hopeful moment.

I go through the Hughes Road roundabout twice. The shopping centre rises out of exit ramps and bright banners and the kind of low bushes that can withstand drought and exhaust fumes. There are barriers over all the entrances. In my head, I compose a list of the things I need to buy there tomorrow: a new belt, bulk laundry liquid, stamps. I'll take the boys for a milkshake before we go to the hardware store. I keep floating the car through our avenues and drives and boulevards and crescents until the streetlights turn on. They say: Nothing to worry about, nothing to worry about.

So does Tony. 'Nothing to worry about.'

Then the tree comes down.

It takes forty seconds, at least, for the tree to fall, and for Tony to fall with it, and for the shaking of the knotted branches to subside. The tree settles against the stage and the tiled floor and the columns wrapped with holly leaves – once this settling has taken place, the tree has fallen. It has fallen in two pieces but the star that sat on top of it is hanging in midair, held by an invisible cord, three floors up and circling like a disco ball. There are gold-coloured globes rolling across the floor, speeding down the slope that accelerates shopping trolleys toward the car park. The tinsel and the fake pine needles rustle in a peculiar way, windblown and floor-stunned. The tree is so fake it smells like Christmas, like plastic ribbon and shopping bags and wrapping foil. If you look closely at the branches you can see the way the short brown fronds have been woven into long green ones to replicate the look of a real pine tree just past its perfectly green prime. You can see the way plastic pine cones grow out of the branches like natural accidents.

The tree covers the children. Viewed from above, with the security camera's eyes, they're completely hidden.

Here's Tony's brother. He's been hired for a reason: he's unafraid, highly trained, possibly armed. He knows first aid, and I mean really knows it. He's assisted more than one old-aged pensioner overwhelmed by the size of the shopping centre. Apparently, this is how he spends his day shifts: crouching next to old men as they lie with their heads on his folded zip-up jacket, waiting for their children to arrive. This is the kind of information you can pick up about a person.

Here's Tony's brother finding Tony in the branches. Tony isn't moving.

Where are Tony's parents at this moment? Their names are Aldo and Lara. We know them in the abbreviated way that comes of having children in the same year at school. Tony and Greg haven't been friends for long, so we haven't yet memorised the angle at which you must back out of their driveway or the smells that emanate from their house just before dinner. Maybe they're at the supermarket buying steak or oranges. Maybe they're taking advantage of Tony's absence and having sex; maybe they're too tired for sex. Maybe Lara is showering while Aldo walks the dog. Whatever they're doing, they're intact.

But Tony, at this moment, isn't moving. He's managed, somehow, to keep his grip on the tree's thick trunk, but his hands are held there by twisted wires and his back against another branch is bent too far. His brother knows not to move him. He's trained for this, or a version of this. But Tony is his brother.

Tony is not my son.

Tony's brother calls out to our boys, still sitting on Santa's throne. The tree has fallen just shy of them, on their right side. Its wide branches form a glade over their heads, and in this forested darkness the boys sit quietly, unsure of how to answer. Tony's brother has forgotten their names – he calls, 'Kids! Kids!' and eventually they call back, 'Yes?'

James, eight. Greg, eleven.

In a testament to his luck and ball skills, Greg has managed to catch a flying red bauble the size of his brother's head. James has a lapful of PVC pine needles, and these make scratch marks on his knees. The throne, bolted to the stage, has held back other branches. Thinking of this, the boys in their felled forest, I wonder, Really? Can this be all?

Our boys can see Tony through a tunnel of green, and they see Tony's brother climbing over him, in the tree.

'You boys all right?' says Tony's brother. He's dialling emergency.

Greg says, 'Yeah.' The boys are pushing now through the branches, which bend away with ease and then spring back. Greg jumps down from the stage and turns to help James do the same. It looks like they're emerging from the carcass of a monster.

'You know the way back to my office?' asks Tony's brother.

Greg doesn't.

'I know your office,' says James. Then he runs. I can see him running, arms moving backward and forward, good at reading maps, knowing how to find an office.

And Greg follows him, wondering how he knows.

I know what happens next; there's no need to speculate. I'm down at the train station when Greg calls. I've parked the car and am standing on the bridge across the tracks, looking at the platform and checking the illuminated tops of heads. A train comes as we speak, and it doesn't stop or even slow, but races through.

'I'm coming,' I say. And I go – I drive to the shopping centre, to the loading bay, and there among the lights of the emergency vehicles I see our boys. I haven't called Glenda yet. I will, when I've seen them. I don't want her to have to wait for bits of news, but to hear it all at once. And I don't want to go home to her without them. This is how I explain it, later. But the truth is that I don't think of her, not really, until I see them sitting there on a pile of flattened cardboard. Their poses are identical: hands in fists and placed on knees, and they look up and out beyond themselves, as if waiting for a photo to be taken. They are fine, they are whole, and I wonder for the first time, Really? Can this be all?

It's dark when we turn into our street. My parents' car is in the drive, and my father helps my mother out of it. I see the way he holds her elbow as she bends and straightens. Glenda must have called and asked them to come; I know this because they have no gifts, and because she's waiting there on the lit front steps. They go to her and my mother holds her, my father puts one hand up on her head. There is a day in the future when one of them will fall and find it difficult to recover, when one of them will receive a diagnosis or become forgetful or weak. I wonder which of them will be the first.

Those Americans
Falling from the Sky

When I tell our husbands the story of the bad-luck Americans I begin with Edith because when the Americans came, moving into the airstrip out of town, expanding it with new buildings and sheds and hangars, bringing with them a brass band that practised in the streets of a Saturday, I thought of the planes that hummed over our newly crowded sky as tiny Ediths with their parrot faces pointed toward the sun. Edith was a short woman, short enough maybe to count as a dwarf, and from the back she looked like our kid brothers. From the front she was about sixty, and looked like a parrot. Her lips were pale and hard and fused. Her eyes were small and dark. They rotated backward, first one way, then the other, whenever the kitchen in which she was talking was invaded by a man.

Edith called us Eleanora and Jean Louise when Nora and Jeanie did at home and everywhere else. She was one of those people who act out every story they tell, waving her arms, reproducing facial expressions, running around our kitchen like an unfamiliar cat. She acted out the air raids on London – a miniature plane tilting at our table, dropping erratic bombs that rattled the teacups. These gymnastics tired our mother. When the Baptists came every few Sundays, leasing our pond to wash their sins away, Edith was always among them, hopping side to side with her parrot step. Our mother would pull the shutters to shut out the hymns and say, 'Don't let them come in, not today, and not that Edith. If she comes up inside I'll die of tiredness. I know I'll die. She just tires me and tires me *out*.'

When we saw her in town she was brisk and chatty. It was Edith, for example, who explained to us, one Saturday morning on Merrigool's main street, about the internment camp.

'They're bringing in Chinamen, by the truckload,' she said.

'They're not from China,' said our mother. 'They're from Japan.'

'Well,' said Edith. 'They're all Orientals, aren't they.'

I thought of a missionary talk she had taken us to about the work of God in China, the blessed and dangerous work of God among the delicate foods and feet of China, with a woman in Chinese dress telling us not to be confused between the Taiwanese and the Chinese, and especially not the Japanese, and certainly not the Malays.

'God bless the Americans,' cried Edith, raising her bird hands to heaven right there on the street, 'and our boys.'

Despite this blessing, the Americans brought nothing but bad luck – for us, but mostly for themselves. They blustered through town and held dances and attended church, or so we heard, dressed in uniforms so stiff they could hardly expand their lungs to sing. They were shiny and good-looking. After the war plenty of girls packed their suitcases and, clutching letters and photographs, departed for promised love in exotic places like Texas and Montana. With their easy walk and their well-combed hair the Americans seemed brave and fortunate. But as it turned out, they had a strange aptitude for dying on the outside of the war.

Our father, on the other hand, Nora's and mine, died on the very inside of the war. He always succumbed to things quickly. When we were younger, before the war, he panicked at the thought of financial difficulty. Word of crashing markets and worthless bank accounts reached Merrigool by train and newspaper, and our father leased out our fields amid speculation about the future of beef and milk. A little later he sold the farm off, piece by piece, until we were left with the house, the yard, the pond, the gully and the creek. Also, the drive reaching out to the Merrigool road, and the yardy, pondy, bushy strip leading from the house back to the hills. Then he left on a truck for Sydney, looking for work, and never came back. At some point he and our mother were no longer married. Frank arrived and became our stepfather, and then there were more children, and the war. Our father sent us a letter to say he had enlisted, and in the envelope, a photograph of him at a wedding, standing by a woman in white we'd never heard of.

He died in Egypt, in a yellow-walled hospital, in the midst of befriending the nurses, taking sips of smuggled whiskey from strangers, cradling a crushed arm. He sent us letters, childlike and left-handed, or dictated to someone who added comments in French that we couldn't understand. One day we received a letter from a woman named Hélène, also from Egypt, accompanied by a rainbow school of foil fish, all neatly cut from sweet wrappers by our father's careful, concentrating left hand. There were over two hundred of them. We played with them for a week before abandoning them in a silver-backed pile. For many years afterward we found stray fish around the house, blue and gold minnows beneath loose tiles, brilliant green sardines swimming in the dust behind chests of drawers. Hélène sent the fish and her sympathy and her admiration for our father. His love for his daughters provided solace to the end. In the valley of death he had heard the Word of God, and was comforted.

This letter reached us before the one from our grandmother in distant Melbourne telling Nora and me that he was dead. Our mother wasn't included in either letter and we felt adult and private as we showed them to her. Nora was sadder than I was, so I learned from her how to be sad. She refused to believe the letters and persisted in a private conviction that someone else had been mistaken for our father, who had lost his memory, been rescued by the Americans, and now lived in New York City. He would find his way back to us, someday. I was three when he left. Back then, he would pick me up and pretend to throw me off the veranda, over and over, and I would laugh with terror, again and again.

For a while after that the war passed over us. The year between the letter from Hélène and the arrival of the Americans moved quickly. Things always moved quickly in our house. Spiders ran up the walls and weevils hurried through the flour and settled into their crunchy camouflage before you could be sure you'd seen them. The final baby was born, white as a turnip. The Americans came, and the Japanese, crammed into the hills around our town, a small piece of the war delivered directly to us, and to Frank.

Before he married our mother, Frank was one of Edith's favourite subjects, because a city policeman moved to a country town like Merrigool was news. She didn't know he wasn't really city, but from the part of the city that's scratchy and open, half town and half bush, on the flat baking plain under the mountains where no one really from the city would ever think to go. Frank was large and ugly. There was something so definite about him. He had country arms, though he wasn't country, and hair the clingy colour of cicada shells. He had the use of a car that wasn't his, though we never found out to whom it actually belonged.

'This car isn't mine,' he'd say, stern and formal, whenever we climbed into it, 'so watch yourselves.'

For a year after his arrival in Merrigool he fought bushfires, came limping and roaring off the football field, calmed the drunken flurries of old men in the streets, and swam the flooding river to rescue a dog that bit his big arm. Then he met our mother. She had the best legs in – and out of – town and carried with her the self-sufficient weather of a widow. Their courtship was private: late nights, swimming, driving in the car that wasn't his, walking through long grass. Edith, who had always flapped to us with athletic stories of misdeeds and miracles, who always followed the scent of misfortune, of divorced women and almost-orphaned children, found one day the grassy, stubbly smell of Frank, massive on her chair in our kitchen, with his arms laid across the table. That afternoon, she addressed all her talk to Nora and me. Every time she visited us after that, she peered hesitantly into the kitchen before entering, unsure of what she might find. When Frank married our mother, she stopped coming. She didn't visit their unbaptised babies – one, two, three, eventually four – and rarely acknowledged Nora and me in the scripture classes she taught at our school. Edith continued to sidle reverently on the pond shore, singing with the Baptists, and I watched her from the house and surprised myself by missing her in our kitchen.

Of course Frank wasn't ugly, I now realise. But he had a mammoth face that loomed over us, and when he brought it to our level – shaded with new hair, blue at the roots – it looked as if parts of it had caved in. Nora tells me now that he was very attractive to women. 'Jeanie,' she says, when I talk about him, when I tell our husbands how ugly he was, sculpting his lion's face with my hands, 'Jeanie, you know, he was very attractive to women.'

One day he came home from work at dusk in that car he

had the use of and found Nora cycling back and forth on the road by our drive, toward town and away from town, while I sat on the gatepost kicking my dirty feet. He stopped the car and unfolded himself from it. He watched Nora pedal away from him and began to jog after her, a jog that was long and slow and nevertheless covered the ground between them with unexpected speed. When Nora found him keeping pace with her, his knees lifting, his arms moving the air, she thought it was a game and threw her head back to laugh. But he reached out suddenly, took her under the arms, and lifted her from the bicycle, which wheeled along riderless, skidding and shaking. I watched Frank put Nora down and speak to her as he went for the bike. They walked back toward me, Nora nursing her arm. Often we rode the bike double, her feet moving in a swift blur, mine suspended over the dust-coloured road. Now we sat in that car with Frank, cruising slowly down the drive to the house, and Nora wouldn't turn from the front seat to look at me. He spoke to us quietly, his left hand lightly on the wheel, about the things girls could and could not do. He explained to us that when he came home from work he expected to see us waiting for him, clean and ready for dinner.

That was not long after they married. The bike came out later for his eldest boy, clattered over the veranda, and was pronounced too rusty to ride.

Our father had sold the farm but the pond was still ours, half hidden among trees in the low folds of the beginnings of the hills. A waterhole, really, shaded by dry bush, sticky with duck mess, floating in the spring with the froth of the frogs that sang through the summer. The water was soft and brown and took the heat away, momentarily, until we resurfaced and it cupped over us again like a wet hand. The younger children, Frank's, were tied to the big dead gum tree to stop them from rolling down the yard in the way they tended to, irresistibly drawn to the pond, into which they blundered and bobbed like pumpkins. Tied up, they circled the tree, getting tangled and tired in the shade, while Nora and I waded, bug-bitten, waterlogged, and out of sight of our mother. We stepped with long feet over the sunny banks, warm with worms and mud. We lay on the grass and the earth felt dry and clean between our fingers, and the sun was big and good, the flies busy on our foreheads and above our lips, the places where the sweat gathered. We knew we would burn to a purply-brown, and when we did we would lie awake heating the air in our bedroom for hours and make midnight trips to the bathroom to dip towels in cold water. We'd lie under our towels in a humid cloud. And in the subsequent days we'd itch and itch until the skin came off in raspy, silky skeins.

That's how we all became so brown. Brown all year, brown feet, brown ears, brown in the parts of our hair. And stiff white hair, all of us, that later in our teens turned yellow and then unexpectedly dark. But when our hair was white, our mother cut it on the veranda every few weeks in the late afternoon. It grew quickly. Nora's especially, which left uncut shimmered down her back in a wet white coil that distracted farmhands and diverted the loyalties of dogs. The haircutting took place on the veranda so we could watch for signs of Frank returning. The land in front of the house was flat as far as the road, and in the dark of winter the lights of the car carried a long way across it. In winter, we knew for five minutes beforehand that Frank was about to arrive and could make ourselves quiet and good.

Summer was different. The sun stayed until eight, the light until nine. The birds stayed too, scratching in the grasses, screaming in the trees. By the time we heard the sound of him we only had a minute to prepare. We all liked to be busy, or hiding. Or we sat in a row on the veranda, knees pressed together, a towel on every knee shining with a lapful of stiff white hair, our mother poised above us with her scissors.

Frank always took time leaving the car. It wasn't large, but he was. The engine would stop its noise and he would sit in the car for a minute or more, collecting himself, I suppose. Nora and I – and probably our mother – had given up our attempts to predict what kind of mood he was in by watching his dark figure behind the windscreen. We all waited cautiously for his arrival in our evening lives, except for the baby, fat as a cabbage, who cooed from a cot and knew no fear. Sometimes the younger children would run down the steps to meet him as he rose from the car. They shuffled around him offering their services for the carrying of hats and documents, and some days he accepted their offers, other days he swatted them away. On the best days, he swung one of them high into the air and onto his shoulders. The best days were usually ones on which he'd had some run-in with the Americans and come home ready to complain about them. Then he seemed to leap from the car, and the children laughed and flew, and when he stepped up onto the veranda even Nora looked happy to see him.

At first we only saw the Americans in town. They played darts in the pub. They crossed the street in their meticulous uniforms to talk to pretty girls. They held dances in their hangars, and if the wind blew in the right direction the music reached our bedroom on Friday nights. They played their brass instruments in the main street of town. An American flag appeared at our school, next to the Australian one, and always caught the wind first, the real wind that came from the distant sea.

I performed better at school after the handsome Americans came to teach us about their handsome country. We learned of river chasms miles across, and thick trees, and coyote dogs that prowled the uproarious night. Our own rocks and reefs and strange marsupials paled beside these natural wonders. Our men in the Papuan jungle and North African sand had left us in capable hands, and Merrigool felt a kind of blessing in this stylish American presence, a safety it loved and claimed to have prayed for, as though the Japanese soldiers were at that moment advancing across the wheat plains with maps of our muddy river.

But Frank didn't like the Americans. He said so in the evenings. They were bored, I suppose, and glossy and hilarious. Frank was never those things. They also didn't think much of the local police.

'They think,' said Frank, 'they're a law unto themselves.'

Their behaviour on the weekend streets of lean Merrigool did leave a little to be desired. Even Edith's faith must have wavered the Saturday night some descended on the town dressed as girls and painted black. I wish I'd seen them walking past the lit windows, revolving their droll hips. At first there were only these pranks, and flirtations, and lectures at the school. At first there was no bad luck. Then they began jumping from the sky.

They fell on our farm when the wind blew east. From a distance it looked soft – the billowing descent, the padded green, all the silk folding onto the warm yellow grass, like our mother pouring thick cake batter into a tin. Sometimes we were closer, watching the fields from the bush, and saw the Americans' light-limbed run across the paddocks, the wind catching in their parachutes while the cows looked on, sleepy. We watched the morning jumps from our cloudy kitchen windows until our eyes tired from the light and we dragged through our chores. Our mother was never interested. Men fell in the yard and tangled in our washing. They scared her hens. One skimmed our roof and floated away down the gusty drive, his slim legs dancing. Our mother never cared one way or the other.

'Tell me when it's raining,' she said. 'Tell me when the Baptists are at the door to pay for the pond. Tell me when there's cows in the yard and the barn's on fire. That's worth telling. Not those Americans.'

The Americans drifted back and forth, even in the night. They carried lights and radios. They carried ration packs they didn't need. If we located them in the long grass, dizzy with gravity and knotted ropes, we helped them find the right way up and they gave us dried apples and chewing gum and smoked beef. They let us flap the green silk into the sky and run underneath it. We loved the terror of feeling trapped, the increased sound of our own breath. We stumbled and rolled and found each other, clutching at arms and shoulders, nostrils flaring, scrambling for a way out. We helped fold the chute, surprised at the size of it spread out like water and the size of it folded to nothing. The men who had fallen from the sky, in the way the men routinely did, shouldered their packs with their great green nets inside them. They left in the truck that came for them, always, riding with radios out of the hills.

With the sky full of Americans, I didn't fear war. I didn't fear the Germans or the Japanese. I didn't fear the return of Jesus, though the Baptists prayed for it, wading in the pond, and I didn't fear my father's ghost staggering in the hallways with his ruined arm and scratched face, followed by tinfoil fish. I was also less afraid of Frank. I was silent around him, and watchful. For long stretches at a time, I was able to pretend he wasn't with us at all.

Then, one Monday afternoon in the hot late March of that year, a plane crashed in the hills and all eight airmen died. An ordinary training flight, readying for tropical bombing over the green Pacific. They had been in our sky, looking down over our yellow town with its yellow river and fields and hills beyond it. All they had seen, before they fell, was the expansive sea and palmy islands and the paths of bombs across them.

We didn't see the plane go down, though we all claimed we

had, somehow skidding across our schoolroom windows and over the rooftops of the town. We did see the smoke: a plume of black that split the sky in two and resisted the half-hearted rain of the late afternoon. Nora and I hurried home that day. As soon as we arrived, we threw our school cases onto our beds and ran across the yard, down into and out of the gully and through the patchy bush that separated us from the hills. We wanted to run into the hills and find the plane. We wanted to follow the smoke for days if necessary, to see the collapsed airmen, none of them dead but piously calling for our help.

By the time we cleared the trees, however, it had begun to grow dark. The hills rose above us. We knew Frank would be driving the car that wasn't his down the Merrigool road. Nora and I looked up at the hills and the smoke that was blurring into scrappy clouds and twilight. We turned around and made our way home.

There was no sign of the rain in the roots of the bush. The creek hadn't risen, hadn't budged from its course. In the dark, among the trees, we thought we could hear the Americans calling for help that wouldn't come. Back in our yard, we paused to look up at the lit house. Dinner was over. Behind us the plane and the airmen smoked.

'God help us,' said our mother. 'Here you are. Here they are. Where have you been? Wait, don't tell me, I'm not interested. You disappear like rabbits, not a word, you don't come home for tea. For all I know you've been bitten by a snake, both of you, lying in the bush bitten by snakes. That's the last thing we need. Nora, what do you say? You're fifteen years old, for god's sake, Nora.'

Nora said nothing. Our mother pushed us through the kitchen and into the front room that we used only for winters and punishments, both unexpected. She straightened our clothes and neatened our damp hair and brushed leaves from our legs, as if preparing us to enter a church.

'Here,' said our mother, 'is your father. Who has been worried sick and is very disappointed in you.'

I imagined our father slumped in the corner, his fishy feet worn out from pacing to and fro with worry. Then she left and we heard her moving about the kitchen, calm now, with no responsibility. She clucked at the baby in the way she liked to. There would have been a time when she clucked at us.

Frank did not look disappointed in us. He sat in the best red chair, which smelt of dogs and used towels, and eyed us thoughtfully, his bare policeman's feet planted square on the yellow rug. In that undersized chair, his vast and neutral face was almost at our level. His knees rose higher than his belly. He wore a vest and his trousers and, keeping up his trousers, a belt. When I touched it much later, after Frank was dead, the belt was old and supple with use. That belt felt soft as a calf the day it's born.

'My children,' said Frank, 'never miss dinner.'

He ordered us to turn around, and he stood up. I remember his shadow on the wall. It was strangely diminished by the low-hanging light fitting, which swallowed his legs; I saw his arm, though, as it rose and fell, and the belt flying at the end of it. I remember being grateful that he did me first, and I wondered if the Americans might even then be flying overhead, dangling on their strings, and knew they weren't, because of the smoke in the hills. I think I cried, but Nora didn't.

That night, the American flag at school stirred at half-mast in the meagre wind. The interned Japanese – doctors and painters and wives and plumbers – wrote letters of panic to the mayor and the police, to the Americans, to the Baptist minister and the Anglican, declaring their innocence in the matter of the crash. I wanted, more than anything, to throw myself into the pond, to touch the surface lightly once, twice, three times, like a skimming stone, and stay there underwater until the sun rose again and Frank was gone.

Because they hadn't been buried, the souls of the eight dead airmen began to cause trouble in the area. They played with ladies' stockings, tearing tiny holes in them that ran and ran. They bit apples on the trees and left them swaying and rotting, with teeth-marks. They sent bugs scurrying through oats, and they spooked cows so no bulls could rut. We saw their shadows at times, swimming in the pond among the knees of the Baptists, delaying the return of Jesus because their bodies hadn't yet been put back together. That, we discovered, was Frank's job, with the help of the airbase surgeon.

We imagined the airmen gruesomely neat, each a jigsaw of distinct pieces: arms, legs, torso. We rarely thought of the heads. We learned the names of the Americans: James Milner. Curtis McAvoy. Kevin Roberts. Roy Brand. We repeated them over and over, skipping them into our games, clapping out the rhythm. Leroy Bump, of North Carolina. Poor Bump had a nasty bump, we joked. Clarence Sullivan. Eugene Jackson. David Young, who died once and always young. We talked of Frank's methods, the eight tables accumulating parts and the fitting together of a Sullivan arm with a Sullivan shoulder. We thought of mothers fixing dolls, and of the detachable tails of bloodless lizards.

As Frank's task wore on and those stubborn pieces would not fit back into eight bodies, we were impressed by his silence, the way he simply sat at dinner with us, chewing and drinking. At night, in bed, I discussed with Nora his nerve and his courage, his secretive profession, and his strict rules about a subject's suitability for children. No war, no details of other people's marriages, no religion, no airmen in a scrambled heap. He was unfazed by his difficult and gory work, even when the town, plagued by the dead Americans, became impatient with the time he was taking.

We noticed one difference in him: he became more tender with his children, if not with Nora and me, and seemed to understand the cries of the baby in a way that not even our mother could, walking it on his huge hip and feeding it raisins he had chewed and softened in his own mouth. He read to his children until he became frustrated with them for wanting the same stories over and over again. He taught his boys to play football. Nora and I watched from the veranda as they stumbled and fell on their fat legs, bewildered and violent, knocking each other to the ground.

After nearly two weeks of concern among the Merrigool citizens, uneasy in the presence of the Americans, alive and dead, and the interned Japanese, with Frank politely accused of incompetence in every kitchen, word came that Curtis McAvoy of Iowa City had never been on the plane at all. He had abandoned the plane and the base on the morning of the crash and found a truck on its way to Sydney – just as our father once had – where he lived it up in the bars and in the soft tanned arms of the Woolloomooloo whores and watched for Japanese submarines sneaking into the harbour. The eight airmen, it turned out, were seven, which explained Frank's difficulty with their jigsaw bodies.

Our mother cut our hair that day. We sat on the veranda, watchful, quiet, while the lorikeets picked at the afternoon grass. Because the cut was unscheduled and it was a wash day, all the towels were wet, so our collars filled up with white hair that clung to our necks and worried us all evening, itchy but elusive. Eventually our mother took Nora inside to help prepare the meal. The rest of us stayed on the veranda listening for any sound through the dusk. The dogs barked at nothing. They barked at birds and each other. Finally they barked because he came.

It took him some time to get out of the car. We all stood when he did, and our mother came to the door. Nora watched from the window through the batter of moths. We realised then how dark it was. He climbed the steps purposefully, looking everything in the eye, and then put his hand on top of my head.

'We're all hungry, aren't we,' he said, moving his fingers in my hair. 'We're a family of good eaters, and we like to sit around a table for our tea.'

We filed in, our bare feet soft on the floor, treading our hair into and around the house. Frank's belly growled all through dinner, loud and complaining, and he turned this into a joke, holding it in both hands and soothing it like his baby. We laughed at it and fed the dogs with furtive scraps of meat.

With the seven Americans reassembled at last, Frank took a week off work, and this free week coincided with our school holidays. His presence made the days tricky and unpredictable. He worked all morning beneath sinks, along the fences, hidden in the roof. He chopped down a huge dead tree so that it lay across the yard like a giant squid, pale and horizontal, its enormous sideways branches cut back to stumps. But in the afternoons he lurked in chairs and on steps and by the pond, lazy and hazardous, and we played around him, alert, never nearing the bush or water.

He remained in a good mood, against our expectations, and one day set up an obstacle course of tin cans on boulders and fences. Then he got Nora and me and the boys into the car and told us we'd take turns leaning from the front passenger window to grab as many cans as we could.

'Someone will get hurt,' observed our mother, but she did nothing to stop it. She sat with the baby on a rug in the yard, shelling peas, her long fingers working quickly in the shade. It was hot, and hotter in the car. Hotter even when there was a breeze, because the breeze came from the desert and blackened our necks and snot. The car bucked over the uneven ground and we barrelled from side to side in it, collecting tin cans, missing tin cans, awaiting our turn to lean out over the burning metal and squint into the moving, rolling sun. Nora at first refused to try, sitting behind the driver's seat with the window down, leaving the wind to mess her hair, keeping her eyes on the horizon. Eventually Frank persuaded her and of course she was the best of us, hanging from the car with one brown outstretched arm and her bum filling the window. Then the youngest boy vomited over the backseat. Frank stopped the car and we all ran and lay on the grass beside the pond, panting and burning. Except Nora, who walked back in the direction of the house. She moved as if she were underwater, lifting each leg higher than necessary, letting her arms trail behind her and turning her head slowly from side to side. Then she stopped and pointed at the sky.

'Look,' she said, and we looked. Beside the sinking sun, men were falling. They rocked in the dusty wind, their parachutes opening and catching, and the birds flew away from them and into the trees. We knew where they came down – out on the fields, past the bush by the creek, where the cows had chewed the last of the grass and the ground was powdery ash. Each of us imagined feeling the earth shake, almost imperceptibly, as one by one the men landed, gathering their nets around them and feeling again the weight of the sky. We hadn't seen them jumping since the plane crashed.

Frank was watching transfixed. He'd never been home when they jumped, and it seemed he'd never watched them from the windows of the station, or his car, or the houses he drove to daily, where thefts and suspicious fires occurred.

'How high up are they?' he said, and we looked at each other and then back at where he stood, one hand shading his narrowed eyes. With relief, we realised he didn't expect us to answer.

'Maggie!' he called to our mother. 'Have you seen this? Would you look at this?'

And our mother didn't say, Tell me when the soup boils over, tell me when the pond dries up, tell me when the minister arrives naked, but don't tell me those Americans are falling from the sky again, again, again. She smiled and looked up toward the airborne Americans and said, 'Just as long as they don't land in my henhouse.'

'They're half a mile up,' said Frank. I knew that to be the distance of our house from the Merrigool road, so I tilted that length into the sky and mentally ran along it, tiring quickly, as the Americans followed it down. 'Half a mile up or more.'

Our mother sat the baby on her knee and let him throw his hands in and out of the peas. The frogs were beginning to sing, their bellies full of hard, cross music that sounded at the bottoms of our ears. That's how we knew the day was ending. Now we would start to wait for Frank to come home. But here he was.

'And how do they get home again? Do they walk?' asked Frank.

We knew the answer to this. The youngest boy, smelling of pond weed and still a little of vomit, said, 'The truck comes.'

'The truck, eh?' said Frank, and he turned to me.

'Yeah, Dad,' I said, surprised that he had looked at me, and proud. 'They send a truck to pick them up and take them all back to base.'

The sky was empty now, and the truck was crossing over the hills, over the fields, filling up with Americans who laughed about holding their breath as they jumped.

'All right,' said our mother. 'Who'll help cook peas? Who'll help cook the sweetcorn?' It was a special dinner, and there was a job for everyone – everyone except Frank. We followed our mother into the house and moved among the different foods while Frank stayed outside, scanning the sky for a tiny plane half a mile up or more.

It was a special dinner because Frank was returning to work the next day. Our mother had killed two chickens and baked five different kinds of vegetable. The meal took a long time to cook and very little time to eat. There was fruit salad for dessert – oranges and apples. Frank told us stories about fruit picking in Queensland.

'The queen of fruit,' said Frank, 'is the mango.'

He told us the mango tasted like sugar and cream and peach and banana all at once. He told us the sap could burn your skin like a hot stove. He told us about German men wrapped in shirts – one for the body, one for each arm and leg – who could pick a hundred mangoes in ten minutes. The possibilities of Frank's previous lives occurred to me suddenly, and they tasted of oranges and apples.

Frank leaned back in his chair, looking at the ceiling as if he might see the Americans dangling there. 'Tomorrow,' he said, 'I'll cook us sausages for tea, burned on the skins the way we like 'em. Eh?'

'You're working tomorrow,' said our mother.

'Saturday then,' said Frank, still inspecting the ceiling. Only he said it Satd'y, the way fathers do, the way their sons do: Tuesd'y, Thursd'y, Satd'y, familiar and friendly with the long days of the never-ending weeks.

That night I dreamed of rain. It started with clouds so low I could touch them if I stood on a chair. They were dense and solid; I could break pieces off and even taste them. They tasted of burnt sugar. I held one out to Nora and said, 'Try some mango.' When the clouds burst into rain, the noise on our iron roof was terrible. Nora was trying to sing, but no one could hear her. There was nobody else in sight – no American airmen, no Baptists, no brothers or mothers or Frank. Just me, and Nora, and rain and more rain, which looked like white hair. I stirred at some point, very early, and heard unfamiliar voices in the hallway, then swam back into my noisy dream of rain.

Later, Nora woke me to say that an American was missing and they were searching for him on our farm. My heart slowed. I thought of my fear, a secret until now, even to myself, that Frank had taken Curtis McAvoy, limb by extraneous limb, and buried him by the creek. But this was another American, Nora said, who'd jumped from the plane yesterday and never come back. We had watched him fall, shading our eyes and wondering if he was watching us: children lying on the grass by a pond, a mother on a rug with a baby, a father's face lifted to the sky, looking like a family.

'But the truck?' I said, remembering what I'd told Frank,

with such confidence, calling him 'Dad', and I thought of being wrong. I wondered if I would be punished.

Nora took me outside. Planes flew low overhead. We saw men we recognised and men we didn't climb out of the creek gullies to be served cold drinks by our mother. Frank led the search. We spent the day watching him, proud of his authority, proud that he was stern and unforgiving, and pleased to see lesser men try to satisfy him. We stayed far from him, and kept quiet, and managed through a combination of helpfulness and invisibility not to be sent away somewhere less exciting.

We heard the sound of dogs at the creek and drew our feet in beneath us, squatting on the veranda. Other women came and we listened as they speculated that the American had copied Curtis McAvoy: shaken off his parachute, walked up the weary roads, found a travelling truck, and disappeared. We heard these things could be contagious. An old man stood with his foot on the veranda rail and said, 'What we need is a tracker.' Everyone laughed and then nodded, as if to say, Yes, we need a tracker. But there was no prison in Merrigool anymore, no mission, and only a small police station. Frank didn't have a tracker working for him the way he might have years before. There were no black men in Merrigool.

In the late afternoon we helped our mother peel potatoes. We knew by the density of the air around the house that the American had not yet been found.

'Where is he?' I asked Nora, my hands brown with sticky dirt.

'Maybe in Heaven,' she said.

I thought of all the things I had done since watching the parachutes fall the night before. I had boiled peas and eaten my part of two chickens. I had learned about mangoes, and German men in shirts, and dreamed of rain. I had helped my mother bake scones and carried them to the gathered men and waiting women, fully conscious of the importance of my task. I had served drinks and peeled potatoes. The American had been lost this whole time.

I realised suddenly that any of the men we had helped untangle, who had fed us army-issue chocolate and showed us photographs of their sweethearts, could have been on the plane that crashed in the hills, could be this American who might never come back, and even if he was found, or that plane had never fallen, they would all be sent, anyway, to the war that had killed my father. I felt the way I did when I ran under the chute silk into a green world without sky or air.

And there in that world was Edith. She had arrived at our house with the sixth sense of lonely and loving and meddling people who fancy a crowd and an emergency.

'Jean Louise,' she said, in the old way, the way she used to before I was just another girl in one of her scripture classes. 'Follow me. And you too, Eleanora. Follow me. And we'll pray together for the return of the American.'

She spoke with kindness and authority, as if she had never stepped out of our kitchen and left us alone with Frank. We followed her, and no one saw us go.

The pond was gold in the late light, the colour of good wheat. Edith took us there, I suppose, because she was used to praying at the pond, a place of wet and joyous rebirth. Her footing over the sloping banks was uneasy but she maintained her constant bird chatter to God on the subjects of rescue and redemption. She held her tiny arms out like airplane wings to steady herself over the mossy rocks. And in her effort, praying and balancing, she didn't notice what we did.

The American floated above the pond, his feet partially submerged, greenish with weed and his parachute. I don't know how he got there, or how they had missed him. The trees had caught him and hung him by his strings on the edge of the bush and the war. He had a scratched face and only one arm, whiskey breath, and the fish that swam at his booted feet were silver as tinfoil. Seeing his face was the very worst of our luck, Nora's and mine. But as I tell our husbands, it didn't last. We grew up, didn't we. We left Merrigool, Nora first, me later, and found our husbands. We instructed our half-siblings on methods of escape and eventually they did, to lives that rarely involved us. We made telephone calls to our mother, and when Frank answered he never spoke to us for long.

Our mother died, and then Frank, and we returned to the house to clear it out. We walked to the pond, dry in the drought and empty of ducks. Once again, we heard Edith praying with her face to the late sky. We heard Frank calling our names, his voice soft as leather, only this time we didn't go to him. And the American still floated above the water, turning in the wind, and the wind smelled of dinner.

Rose Bay

Susan telephoned Rose at work to say she'd decided, finally, to accept her in-laws' offer to visit California, and would be in Sydney for three days before the ship sailed – it sailed on the Monday, but there was shopping to do, the children had never been to the city, and there was no need for Rose to put them up, oh, but if she could, if it was no trouble, well, that would be lovely, and no, of course, a little flat would be more than big enough for the three of them, they would take up no space, almost none at all. Rose agreed to everything. The thought of her sister being in Sydney filled her with curiosity. Here was an opportunity to be kind to Susan, who was after all a widow. Rose said she would meet them off the train at Central, but Susan wanted to double-check her address and, as usual, laughed when she heard it.

'Isn't that just like you,' she said. 'To live in a place called Rose Bay.'

Rose laughed too. She made an effort, always, to be pleasant. Her boss referred to her as 'particularly pleasant'; she had heard him. Her instinct to please people, without being over-eager, came from a dislike of disagreement. She knew Susan considered it immodest of her to live in a place that shared her name; it was the sort of thing Rose did in order to draw attention to herself.

'It's lovely there by the water, that's all,' Rose said, as she had before. 'The name is just a coincidence.'

The name was not entirely a coincidence. Robert, the man who paid the rent on her flat, liked the idea of her living there. But walking home from the tram that night, Rose suspected her bay. It was too lovely. It was fragrant streets and bright water, schoolgirls in grey uniforms, nodding nuns, a golf course above the harbour. Flying boats landing on the bay and rising again, heading out for Lord Howe and Singapore. From her flat Rose looked over low rooftops and lower gardens onto the water, and the world was lamplit, lavender, particularly pleasant, and she belonged here, and was neither sad nor lonely. But her sister coming made her wonder, and she saw the lights on the other side of the harbour and understood that she was not entirely content, and not always quiet. Still, not sad. Not lonely.

A few days before Susan's arrival, Rose went to the theatre with Robert to see an American dance company on tour in
Australia. This company was very fashionable, according to the
girls in the office, and very modern, full of Americans with illustrious pedigrees and Jewish refugees who'd danced their way out
of the war. Tickets had sold out almost immediately; the girls
wanted to know how Rose had come by one, but she couldn't
tell them because Robert was a partner in the firm, and married. Rose had her hair set and wore a new grey dress. She was
interested in the Americanness of the dancers because Susan's
husband, Jonathan, had been American. Rose used to enjoy listening to his unanticipated voice, never knowing where it would
rise or fall, but the rest of her family – even Susan – imitated
him in his absence. Rose assumed they'd stopped after he died.
She hadn't been to see them in over a year, not since the funeral.
They lived hours inland, in the kind of town this dance company would never visit.

The star of the troupe was a dancer called Adelaide Turner:
diminutive, sprightly, with long expressive arms and a broad
doll-face. She was famous even in Sydney, so many thousands of miles from the city she was born in, the name of
which – Chicago – might as well have been the name of a fruit
Rose had never tried, or an animal she'd never seen. Adelaide
would dance that week in Sydney, the end of the company's
Australian tour, then sail home on the *Coral Sea*. The same ship
was to carry Susan and the children to California to meet the
other half of their family, which seemed to be full of healthy,
sunlit cousins, expectant grandparents, and many uncles and

aunts. It may have been for this reason – the shared ship – that Rose felt connected to Adelaide Turner; her face, too, reminded Rose a little of Susan's. Jonathan had laughed at Rose once for seeing in famous people she admired a resemblance to someone she knew. But when Adelaide first came on stage, dressed as a girlish clown in a black smock covered with stars and red circles on her cheeks, Rose felt a funny tug at her own limbs. As Adelaide moved, left and right, above the lights and below them, her arms flying, her feet, Rose moved imperceptibly along with her – left, right, above, below. Her arms, her feet.

Afterward, walking through the night-time city, Rose noticed how many gulls hung in the light above office buildings and street lamps. Bats crossed overhead, quieter. Robert talked about the music and staging, but Adelaide Turner had made an impression on Rose that was too tender for discussion. She was filled with a longing she knew would occupy her for days, then disappear suddenly, as if cured. Rose was conscious of her body in the warm air. She enjoyed the movement of her arms by her side, and the muscles of her legs felt new and within her power. She listened to Robert and thought, I'm much younger than you are. Later that night, lying beside him, she felt her body lift from the bed and hang, for just a moment, in the half-lit room. Not long after, Robert got out of bed to wash and dress and leave for home; Rose lay still and pretended to be sleeping. The next morning, in her empty flat, she cut Adelaide's picture from the programme and propped it on the mantelpiece.

Rose met Susan and the children off the train on Thursday evening and was relieved to be happy to see them. Lizzie and Alex were mute with the movement, the lights, and the station's domed ceilings. They were nervous of their aunt and stumbled among the cases and bags. There was a great deal of luggage. It accumulated around their feet as they embraced and enquired and smiled. Then the effort of gathering it and directing Susan and the children and stepping into Rose's city, into Rose's life, as if this were natural and easy.

It was dark by the time they reached Rose Bay. Susan was a tourist peering into the small, lit rooms of Rose's flat.

'Well, this is very comfortable,' she said. 'What do you think, little ones? Isn't Aunt Rose's house nice? Isn't it, Lizzie?'

The children's tired, formal faces looked up at Rose.

'It's smaller than our house,' said Lizzie. 'It's prettier, but we don't have to climb steps.'

Susan made the children eggs and toast for supper while Rose moved bags into bedrooms under the surveillance of her niece and nephew. They were more distinct here than they had been at the funeral. Lizzie, the eldest, seemed clear-headed and observant. Alex was more uncertain. His upper lip was puffy and folded to a sweet point in the middle, which gave him the look of a stiff cupid. Rose thought they were delightful and perhaps a little dull. She searched for their father's likeness in their faces and failed to find it. Perhaps later, as they grew, they'd acquire Jonathan's looks, the furrow between thick eyebrows she'd mistaken for good judgement. Upon being shown where he would be sleeping, Alex became raucous and insisted on displaying his navel to Rose.

'This is my button,' he announced, over and over, although his sister told him to stop. He lay on the bed, flexing his plump stomach, watching his navel and checking, every so often, that Rose was too.

'My button!' he cried.

'Stop it,' said Lizzie.

'I don't mind,' said Rose.

Lizzie ignored her. 'Alex,' she said, 'can't you see Julia would like to make the bed?'

Alex froze on the bedcovers. Rose wasn't sure how to remind her niece that her name wasn't Julia.

'Julia doesn't need to make the bed,' said Alex. 'Aunty Rose made the bed already.'

Lizzie sighed with a laboured patience. She said, in a gentle, teacherly tone, 'Julia brought a silk robe and a patchwork quilt from home to put on our bed so we'd be comfortable here and sleep quietly and you won't get up in the middle of the night and cry.' She tilted her fastidious head to look at Alex in a way Rose recognised as Susan's.

'No, she didn't,' said Alex, but he rolled off the bed.

'Julia is Lizzie's good friend,' said Susan from the doorway. She emphasised *good friend*; she was benevolent and motherly, wise when it came to imaginary friendships, indulgent with her children who had lost their father. She expressed this to Rose with a significant smile. 'Supper's ready, darlings,' she said, and Alex charged from the room so that his mother was forced to follow.

Lizzie took Rose's hand as they walked to the dining table. 'Julia *is* my friend,' she said. 'My very best friend. She's coming to America.'

'Really?'

'*Really*. I know you can't see her, but she's not a ghost. She's not dead. She looks a bit like that lady over there.'

Lizzie pointed to the picture of Adelaide Turner on the mantelpiece. Adelaide was in costume for her clown dance: red cheeks and starry outfit, hair plastered in two curls at her temples.

'Then she's very pretty,' said Rose.

Lizzie smiled as if she liked the thought of this but didn't believe it to be true.

Susan's three days in Sydney had been carefully planned. There would be, on Sunday, a trip to the zoo. On Saturday the children would go to the pictures and Susan would have her hair done; they would all shop for gifts and new clothes. On the Friday, when Rose had to work, they would come with her on the tram into the city and walk to Macquarie Street and down the hill where the white sails of the water would rise up to meet them. They would stroll in the botanical gardens and count the steps of the library and sit under palm trees eating ice-cream and reading from comics and magazines. Then they would meet Rose after work. They would all travel back to Rose Bay together, into a quiet Friday night of sleeping children and the hum of the harbour. The thought of them waiting for her at the end of the day made Rose nervous; she recognised in herself an unusual conviction that she owned something that ought to be protected.

Rose left work with the other girls, typists and stenographers and telephonists, all trim and efficient with busy plans and singsong weekend voices. Susan and the children seemed diminished by comparison. They stood on the pavement, waiting, and Susan turned her head from left to right as if Rose might appear from anywhere except the direction she was walking from.

The office girls enveloped the children. 'Do you live on a farm? Do you ride ponies? How old are you? Nine! Five! Is this your first visit to Sydney?' The children, bewildered and loving, stared up at these bright faces and forgot how to talk.

On the tram, when asked about her day, Lizzie said, 'Alex needed to use the toilet but we couldn't find one and then Julia knew where they were. I saw flowers in a glasshouse that grew in the Bible.'

'They were ferns,' said Susan.

'Is that old?' asked Alex.

Lizzie looked at him with concern. 'Of course it is,' she said.

The children were restless at bedtime. Julia wanted a light left on. Rose waited with them for tiredness to come, and was delighted by the sure and sudden way it did. Once asleep, they breathed like birds. Their bodies lifted, briefly, then fell back. As Rose returned to the living room, Susan said, 'There's so much dust in the air. How do you keep your skin cool? And so much noise in the street. I hope they'll sleep.'

But the children slept long and evenly, their soft arms rigid over the sheets.

Rose and Susan sat by a window with one lamp on and the curtains open. They looked almost identical in this pliable light. Ships sounded out on the harbour and a buoy in the bay fell and fell in the tide. Susan composed lists in the lamplight: errands, letters to write, shopping to be done. One finger was bright with her wedding ring. Rose disliked the publicity of wedding rings. Or perhaps she was only irritated that Robert was out with his wife tonight, at a fancy-dress party to which Rose had also been invited. She would have gone as a dancer, with red circles on her cheeks and her hair curled around her face. At some point during the party Robert would have placed his hand on the small of her back, but he would have left with his wife. Usually, Rose was happy to go home alone to her bay, but there were times when her envy of Robert's wife felt like a stone resting at the base of her spine, a reminder that she was wanted, but not singly, and not enough. She remembered feeling that way about Susan, once. Maybe even now. Rose seemed to have made a career of this doubleness, as if she always came in pairs. Jonathan had listed for her all the animals that do not mate for life. Chinchillas, he said. Bison. Deer, bears, sea lions. Elephants with their old memories. Waterfowl of various kinds. He said these names lying in bed beside her in that flat and pollinated town, in those new days after Lizzie was born, and Rose, who had already decided to leave for Sydney, loved this menagerie and was made impatient by it.

'Many whales,' he said, 'don't even mate for a season. Swans,

beloved by the sentimental – that's you, Rosie – don't even necessarily mate for a season.'

Susan looked up from her list. 'I hope you don't disapprove
of the way I indulge Lizzie. I mean with Julia,' she said. 'It's all
been so hard on her. But I thought the passage over, our time on
the ship, would be a good chance to wean her off.'

Rose said, 'Yes, I suppose it would.' I know nothing, she
thought, about the hearts of children.

Susan sat quietly for a moment. She was very pretty, still,
and at thirty-five a widow. Then she said, looking out across the
harbour, 'Oh – America.'

The zoo rose out of the water on the north side of the harbour,
a hillside of animals with Sydney's best views. It pleased Rose to
think that as she looked across the bay from her window there
were giraffes looking back. A city with a harbour-side zoo was
a happy city, in Rose's estimation. It was a city playing a sweet
joke upon itself.

To reach the zoo on Sunday they caught a ferry from
Circular Quay, that busy square of water. The wharves hovered
out upon the harbour, covered over, like Japanese pavilions. The
day was warm and windless. The *Coral Sea* was already docked
in the quay. The ship was a vast wall in the water, with small
windows, and it seemed ridiculous that something of this size
could remain afloat over the profound Pacific.

'One of those windows will be yours,' said Rose, kneeling
beside Lizzie. 'Isn't that exciting?'

'Which one?' said Lizzie, turning her face up to her mother. 'Which is our window?'

'We'll find out tomorrow,' said Susan.

'And that will be Julia's window too,' said Lizzie.

Susan kissed the top of Lizzie's head. Then she said, 'No, Julia will have her own window.'

'Next to ours?'

'Near ours,' said Susan, 'but not next to it.'

Alex pressed against his sister's side. He said, 'Will the boat go fast or slow?'

'Very fast,' said Lizzie.

'Soon we'll all be flying in planes to places like California,' said Rose, and this seemed to disgust Lizzie; she turned away from the *Coral Sea*.

The zoo ferry, in comparison, was toy-small and overly bright. Alex ran toward it and had to be held back; he was thrilled and loud, as he had been about his navel. But Lizzie seemed sceptical. As they were walking across the narrow plank onto the boat she gave a sudden cry, full of grief and fear, and people around them turned to look.

'Are you frightened, Lizzie?' said Rose. 'Hold my hand. Don't look down.'

Lizzie held her hand and took small steps across the plank, all the while looking down at the water, but once she had settled into a seat on the deck she no longer seemed afraid. As the ferry moved away from the quay, Alex complained of a 'tummy feeling', over which Susan fussed. Rose sat quietly beside quiet Lizzie, irritated as she always was by sick people, even children.

Rose herself was never sick. But she helped Susan hold Alex against the railing as he threw up into the harbour, and she loved and pitied him, this small pale boy over all that water. They returned to their seats, where Lizzie waited tense and white. Rose and Susan bent their heads over the children as the ferry rocked.

The Sunday zoo was full of people, but Rose identified the dancers right away. There was a man she recognised with conspicuously red hair. She heard their accents and noted the surety and discipline with which they walked. Last night had been their final show and tomorrow they sailed on the *Coral Sea*; for now they were seeing the sights. They eddied about in same-sex groups, interacting with loud jokes and theatrical gestures. Passing aviaries on the zoo's sloping streets, Rose saw half a dozen of them sitting among the tropical birds, coaxing them onto arms and shoulders with a trick of the posture that was, Rose knew, beyond her own shoulders, her own arms.

Rose couldn't see Adelaide Turner with the dancers, but she hoped she might, later on. Perhaps they would meet beside the polar bear and talk together on the subject of his greenish fur and his obvious disgruntlement in the unlooked-for heat. Then, tomorrow after work, while the *Coral Sea* unloosed from the city and took Susan and Adelaide to America, Rose could tell Robert about it. Or she could not tell him, just as she pleased.

Rose followed Susan and the children to the aquarium, with its rocky grottoes and litter of Pacific shells. Afterward, they saw the Malayan bears and spider monkeys. A band played in the rotunda and children sat by a pond while a Sunday-school teacher read instructions from a piece of paper. There was a black rhinoceros calf, but Lizzie and Alex seemed annoyed by baby animals of any kind. Alex's eyes remained on the ponderous mother and Lizzie drooped against the fence.

'Is this the first time Julia's seen a rhino?' asked Rose.

Now Lizzie looked hard at the baby. 'I don't know,' she said.

Both children had begun the excursion with enthusiasm but were now almost shy. They stood on either side of the floral clock, following its fragrant moving hands; they remained silent on the little zoo train as it slid alongside emus and mountain goats. The very fact of mechanical movement seemed to have stunned them into noiselessness. It was as if their excitement for their trip to Sydney, and beyond to California, had all been worn out in the preparation for it; the actual journey was so large they couldn't account for it. Susan appeared not to mind. Rose assumed her sister knew, from experience, that careful days of planned good cheer often turn out this way.

The children were too afraid to enter the reptile house, which was dark and green and cool. Alex lingered by the doorway, terrified but unwilling to leave. Lizzie couldn't even bring herself to look at the picture of the snake on the sign. Their mother, for the first time, was visibly frustrated with them both. As Susan called Alex away, a flock of dancers ran screaming from the reptile house, women at first, then men leaping and laughing. They'd obviously given the women a scare – a snake-hiss, a careful brush against someone's ankle, a low-voiced story that ended in shouts. Now the women clapped and scolded.

Rose knew Adelaide Turner even without her costumes and wigs and drawn-on eyebrows; her round face and the agile manner of her walk were unmistakable. She looked very young. Adelaide called to one man – 'Roger, what did I tell you? No cake for weeks!' – and when Roger hung his head and arms in mock dejection, she mimicked his pose perfectly, teasing. Her blunt accent wasn't as beautiful as her dancing. Rose could have taken one step and been in her path; she could have said, 'Excuse me, Miss Turner?' But what if Adelaide were to smile as if Rose had just called her name in order to say, Your table's ready, your car is here. There was no way to tell Adelaide about the nocturnal gulls after the theatre, the sensation of her body rising from the bed. Rose watched the dancers walk down the hill toward the seal pools, the women quiet now, holding hands and resting their heads on their friends' shoulders. It seemed ridiculous, then – juvenile – to have cut out Adelaide's picture and put it on the mantelpiece.

Susan sat on the low wall beside the reptile house.

'I want the snakes,' said Alex. He had run into the building, quickly in and out, made brave by the presence of the dancers.

'Well, Lizzie?' said Susan.

Like Rose, Lizzie was watching the procession walk toward the seals. She waited until the dancers were out of sight before turning to her mother.

Susan said, 'What do you think of taking your brother in to see the snakes? While your old mum has a rest out here.'

'I'll take him,' said Rose.

'I want to,' said Lizzie. She gave a small, triumphant laugh.

'*I* was never frightened of the snakes.'

Alex seemed uneasy. He ran back into the semi-dark and his sister followed him.

'They're tired, aren't they?' said Rose.

Susan didn't answer at once. Then she said, 'We're all tired, I think.'

'You must be. So much to organise.'

'I'll tell you something. It's absurd,' said Susan. 'It's that I'm sure I'm going to see Jonathan again. I have that feeling. As if he's waiting for me in California. You know, they say the climate there is basically Australian, and there's the coast and gum trees.' She laughed the way Lizzie had before saying, '*I* was never frightened of the snakes.'

Rose held her sister's hand, which may never have happened before; Susan was years older and rarely tender. Rose didn't love her, but then she thought of love as a hasty secret that drew out, eventually, into something slow and denied and sought and carefully planned. Loving Jonathan had been small for her at first, and then grew smaller, but it was in this smallness that she had found pleasure and safety, as if the secrecy had necessarily pushed it into a tiny space of compacted intensity. Anything larger would have frightened her; would have led to change, or confession. Rose was made impatient by confession. The possibility of it had sent her to Sydney. And it was better, wasn't it, that she could sit like this with Susan, holding hands.

The afternoon was beginning to lengthen. Currawongs cried out of bubbling throats. There were also stranger sounds that travelled through the air from an indeterminate source, as if sprung from the mouths of some outlandish animal and his equally extraordinary mate. These noises hummed at the back of the ear along with other incidental roars and calls and trumpets that filled this unfamiliar world, briefly jungle, briefly savannah and mountain range. Rose understood before Susan did that the noises were coming from the children. She ran toward the reptile house.

It took a moment for her eyes to adjust. The light was low and green and the glass cases seemed to swim out of it, full of leafy foliage, full of fake creeks and desert rocks and their jewelled inhabitants, mostly sleeping.

'Lizzie!' called Rose.

'You killed her,' Lizzie was yelling, over and over. 'You killed her! You pushed! You killed her.'

There was another sound, thinner: Alex crying out, high-pitched. Somewhere in the dark he was struggling and crying. The snakes didn't move, except one python that continued to bury itself in the sand of its tank.

'You killed her!' Lizzie yelled again, and Alex cried and Rose ran through the corridors into the green darkness, afraid of what might be at her feet. Then Susan was there too; she also ran, breathing loudly, calling, and Rose saw her every now and then flashing against a lit case.

Rose found them first. They were deep in the reptile house, on the floor below the tank of a large, pouchy lizard. Alex lay on his back and Lizzie sat astride his chest, pinning his shoulders with her knees. She hit at his head again and again with her palms, her face teary and furious. Alex was half hidden beneath her; his legs rose slightly with each blow, his hands opened and closed, and his shoulders strained as Lizzie pressed tighter with her knees. She hit at him until Rose dragged her away, and even then she kicked at him with her bony shoes, and scratched and bit at Rose.

Lizzie quieted when Susan reached Alex. They were all quiet until they came out into the light, then Lizzie pulled herself from Rose's arms and began to scream. She opened her throat and a large noise came from it, much larger than she was. The effort of it shook her whole body, and closed her eyes, and turned her red. Children walking past the reptile house stopped to look; their parents hurried them on. 'Someone's tired!' called one jovial man. Rose smiled at him. She realised he thought she was Lizzie's mother.

'Elizabeth Rose,' said Susan. Alex had slithered to the ground and pressed his face against his mother's legs. Now Susan shouted, '*Elizabeth!*'

Lizzie stopped screaming. She sat on the ground, limp, worn out by the exertion of being so angry.

'Explain yourself,' said Susan. 'We are going home immediately, you have ruined our day, but first you will tell me why you behaved so badly, so terribly, I've never been so ashamed of you. And no nonsense, Lizzie, no silliness about anybody killing anybody else.'

'But he did,' said Lizzie, collected now, and sullen.

Susan smacked her lightly on the arm. Lizzie opened her mouth as if to scream again, but she looked across at Rose and didn't.

'I'm not lying,' she said. 'Alex killed Julia.' And now she began to cry in messy, unfeigned gulps, staring at her mother.

'What are you talking about?' said Susan.

'Alex pushed her off the ferry. While we were getting on the ferry he pushed her off the bridge we walked on and she fell in the sea and drowned and she's dead forever.' This through sobs full of air and water.

'She did not drown,' Alex called out. He turned to Rose and she noticed blood in his hair. 'She didn't.'

'You hurt your brother,' said Susan. 'You *attacked* your brother. Where does this come from, Lizzie? Why do you make these things up?'

'All right!' Lizzie cried. Then her voice became very quiet. '*I* pushed her. Not Alex. I pushed her because there's no room for her on the big boat. No, I didn't push her. She fell in the water while we walked across the bridge because there were too many people. I didn't help her. I didn't help her because she can't come in our window on the boat. And now she's dead forever.'

Lizzie lay back on the dirt of the path that led to the reptile house.

Rose waited for a long time on a bench outside the zoo's first-aid clinic. Below her the lions slept in the afternoon light. She wondered if the flying boats passed over the lions as they lifted out of Rose Bay. She wondered what Robert was doing now, with his wife and children; they might walk past her here at the zoo, gathered together, weary, cross, loving, bound for home; it seemed as likely as having seen Adelaide Turner on the hillside with the giraffes and Harbour Bridge behind her. The clinic door opened and Susan stepped out. She was red with worry; her eyes were swollen and red.

'The children won't co-operate with me in there,' she said. 'They won't let go of my arms. It's best I leave them. I think it's best.'

'I'm sure it is,' said Rose. She stood beside her sister; she was the taller by at least an inch.

'They'll only be a minute,' said Susan. 'Just being checked over. Getting cleaned up.'

'Shall we go right home?'

Susan nodded. Rose wished, at that moment, to be quick with comfort and easy with words. But it was Susan who spoke. She said, 'Is there anyone for you, right now?'

Rose watched the lions and their sunned flanks. They breathed deeply, rib-movingly, as if the light were a weight upon them.

'Yes,' she said.

'Will we meet him? Or is that . . . difficult?'

Rose shook her head, very slightly, perhaps to say no, perhaps to shake off her sister's question. 'You don't know him,' she said.

'I don't expect to know him. I don't know anyone in this city of yours. Just looking at it I think might be too much for me. All this water, those boats, the houses. And I don't know a soul in them.'

Rose looked out over her city.

'There are some schoolfriends,' said Susan. 'I should have looked them up, shouldn't I? A few girls. Married.'

'Married' sounded to Rose like a white, tall, marble word. It sounded like a word she might stand on – not to crush it, but in order to see farther. The city rose up out of the harbour, not far away, but it seemed to float on the opposite shore of an unplumbed sea. If Rose hadn't left for Sydney, Jonathan might have told Susan; they might have left together. There would be no Alex. But Jonathan would still have got sick. What I most want, thought Rose, is to be quiet, and private, and not to upset anybody. She knew, at the same time, that this could not be what she most wanted.

The children emerged from the clinic. Lizzie held Alex's hand, and he didn't mind. They looked happy and tired. Their father was dead.

Rose left work at lunchtime on Monday even though Robert had made plans with her for the early evening. She told people she was sick, and because she was never sick – because she was 'particularly pleasant' – they believed her. Robert could be, this once, unmet. She sat by her window all afternoon, waiting for the *Coral Sea* to sail between Rose Bay and the zoo with both Susan and Adelaide Turner on it. When it did Rose tried to count its windows, none of which belonged to Julia. She watched the small shapes on deck in the hope of finding somebody she recognised. Jonathan would have had binoculars. The harbour and the afternoon sun took turns with the light. Rose Bay rocked on the edge of the *Coral Sea*'s wake, a small sea with tides in it. Rose wasn't sad. She wasn't lonely. She sat at her window and watched the ship disappear, little by little, toward America.

Violet, Violet

Mr Kidd's bird looked like an ordinary budgerigar: blue, with a yellow face, black dots at the neck, and zebra-striped wings. It spoke three words: 'hello', 'knock' and 'Violet', which late in the night sounded like 'violent' and worried Christopher, at first, as he heard it through the thin walls of his room at the St George Hotel. His room was small and oppressively tidy; the television attached to a bracket on the ceiling above the writing desk made Christopher think of a hospital; his clothes filled no more than one-third of the wardrobe; and the words 'violent, violent' issued through the left-hand wall from a voice not quite human.

Christopher had lived at the St George for three weeks before he met Mr Kidd. If he hadn't been so wary of his surroundings, they might have met earlier: waiting for the lift, in the lobby, or in the communal bathrooms that dripped with a listless mildew. But Christopher took the stairs rather than the lift, and joined a gym in order to shower there. He walked quickly through the hotel lobby because he was afraid of being caught in conversation with a man like Mr Kidd: a man in a raincoat, a formless man, perpetually sodden, with a hopeful and lonely look, carrying an unredeemable briefcase. Being in the lobby generated a feeling of queasy anticipation, as if some terrible thing might happen at any moment. Christopher passed through at eight every morning on his way to the city library, and he returned just after six. He climbed the stairs and flung the door of his room open wide in case someone was concealing himself behind it. He urinated in his basin so that he might avoid the bathrooms for anything but more substantial needs. The pigeons in the eaves of the St George Hotel filled Christopher's room with their amorous clatter and he peered up at them through his scuffed window, most of which had been sacrificed to an air-conditioning unit. He looked at the pigeons with the boredom that comes of a temporary life in an unknown city. Who was this man he'd briefly become? He had no hobbies or preferences or appetites.

This was why Christopher crossed the lobby looking only at his feet. It was why he was so cold to Mr Kidd – in his own politely imperceptible way – at their first meeting.

This meeting took place on a Monday that Christopher

had forgotten was a public holiday. It was easy to lose track of these things while living in hotels and libraries; time took on a different, interminable aspect. He set out from the St George at his accustomed hour and discovered, upon arrival, that the library was closed. Something like panic flared in his chest. He was frightened by the thought of the librarians – those helpful, faceless beings who moved quickly through his slow days – relaxing with friends and family in unknown houses all around him. He was unmoored by the locked doors of the library, by the untried city, by his own confusion. At this moment, he longed for the surety of his room at the St George, with its cosy lamp bolted to the bedside table and his pile of scholarly photocopies. But when he returned to the hotel just after nine, his room was full of cleaning materials and the door was half open, although there was no maid to be seen. Christopher placed his backpack on the bed and sat beside it, unsure of what to do. When would the maid return? Would she leave when she saw him? Could he remove her equipment, close the door, and refuse to let her back in? None of these possibilities seemed feasible to him. Instead, he took a pen from his bedside table and the top article from the photocopy pile, stepped over the vacuum cleaner curled dragon-like around a mound of buckets and cloths, and made his way downstairs to the lounge.

The lounge of the St George Hotel was attached to the lobby by a despondent archway wreathed in floral detail. Nevertheless it was a separate room, cut off from the lobby and the lobby's promise of the street by an atmosphere of lonely sociability. Christopher had only ever been half aware of the movement of unknowable people in its indistinct corners. Now he entered it with purpose, photocopies tucked into his armpit. He noticed a table offering free tea and coffee. This discovery buoyed him; he made himself tea. The room wasn't empty. Men read papers, they tied their shoelaces on low chairs, they hummed into telephones. All men. The St George had been extending its hospitality to male travellers for eighty years, and its look of faithful resignation suggested that a war was taking place and shortages could be expected. Everything – the discoloured carpet, the honeycomb woodwork – shyly implied the hotel's former dignity, and the lounge, as a result, retained a gossipy climate in which affable, friendless men flourished. Christopher found a seat and settled there, balancing pen and tea and article. He began to read. He began to relax. The tea was barely warm. Almost immediately Mr Kidd approached him.

'About time we saw you down here,' said Mr Kidd. He offered his hand. 'Bob Kidd. I'm in the room next to yours.'

'Hello,' said Christopher, looking up. And then, on seeing the hand and feeling flustered and polite, 'I'm Christopher.' He took the hand. The shake was firm, so firm he felt himself rising, just a little, from his chair. Mr Kidd lifted the air behind his trousers as if he were wearing a morning suit and settled into the seat beside Christopher's. He seemed trim and energetic, youthfully old, with a beard-bordered redness to his face suggestive of whiskey and Sunday walks.

'Not a bad old place, this,' said Mr Kidd. 'Been a regular for twenty years. This your first time?'

Christopher looked at his article as if the answer might be found there.

'Yes,' he said.

'What are you reading up on, then?'

'It's research,' said Christopher. 'For my thesis.'

'A thesis, eh? What's the subject?'

'History of science.'

'History!' declared Mr Kidd. 'What's it about, then? In a nutshell.'

'Oh,' said Christopher, 'I don't want to bore you. It's very boring. Not to me, of course, but to anyone who isn't me. Sometimes to me.' The thought that other people might want to talk with him about his thesis always filled him, against his will, with a grateful excitement.

'What else am I here for? Go on, bore me.'

'All right, then. Actually it's about eighteenth-century medical models. The anatomical models they'd make – of pregnant women, for example, obstetrical models – to teach students and train surgeons. In the eighteenth century.'

'Oh ho,' said Mr Kidd, a look of delight on his face. 'Oh ho,' he said. 'I don't know much about obstetrics, though I've seen two children into the world, but I know a little something about models.' He fixed Christopher with an intimate eye. 'If you've got a minute I could show you quite a model.'

Was this what Christopher had feared, hurrying through the lobby of the St George Hotel, his chin tucked into his nervous collar? An invitation from a man like Mr Kidd, both blatant

and disguised, more sad than it was awful? His experiences of
seduction had been avid and unvarying; in contrast to this, they
took on a new cast of yellow-lit tenderness, as if they had happened long before and were unrepeatable.

'I'm very busy,' he said. 'I'm sorry. So much to read. But
thank you.'

Mr Kidd maintained a smile around which the eagerness
of his face shrank. He was obviously offended. His invitation
had been friendly and too quickly refused. There was a genuine
model of some kind – a train, or plane, or a luxury car, a coveted
Bugatti convertible that could only ever be owned in miniature.

'Not to worry. Give me a knock if you ever fancy a chat.
Door's always open.'

Mr Kidd stood abruptly, confused at this failure; there was
a collapsing of something, a crowding in of age or exhaustion. His disappointment revealed his years: over eighty. He
smoothed down the tails of his invisible suit and persisted with
his smile. A keen crowd of old men watched the termination
of the exchange from all corners. Christopher worried that he
might have humiliated this man in front of his lounge cronies
and would now be responsible for a disastrous slip in the social
ranks. There was that volatile feeling common to gatherings of
this kind on public holidays, suggestive of a public execution.

'Thank you,' Christopher bleated to Mr Kidd's departing
figure, which waved a hand about and moved toward the lobby.

Christopher spent a minute or two confused himself, and
unable to concentrate, before calming down enough to remind
himself that he owed nothing to Mr Kidd, whom he now

connected with the cough in the next-door room, and that his aim in this city was to lead a simple life of research, seven days a week, until he could return home with new material and nothing else to report. Settled by these thoughts, he returned to reading.

But the article on Christopher's lap spoke with intelligent fury of the violence toward women represented by the obstetrical models that were, as he described them, his 'intellectual bread and butter'; he grew ashamed and embarrassed in the lounge of the St George. From a distance – the distance of a few chairs away, by the tea and coffee table, where men continued to sweeten their cups with irregularly shaped lumps of sugar – he was sure the images accompanying his article must look obscene. He had become a man reading pornography in a hotel lounge. How long did it take to clean a room? Should he finish his tea, cold by now, before leaving the lounge, and where would he put his cup? Should he take it with him? His anxiety was something like the rolling pressure required to remove the shell of a hard-boiled egg. He sat in his chair with his cold tea and his dirty article, more and more of his composure flaking away; eventually he reached the same point of false bravado that had first led him to the lounge. He stood with purpose, gathered his things, and carried his cup with him into the lobby, nervously sipping the air. The doors of the lift stood open and he stepped through them with a sideways motion, pressing the 'Close Doors' button before selecting his floor. Fifth floor. He rose toward his room with a sensation of heavenly ascent. Stepping from the lift he could see his door still open, half the vacuum tube sticking out into the windowless hallway. He imagined a maid in crisis, called from her duty by a family emergency, and in his agitation permitted himself to pour his cold tea into a plant pot; at the same time he heard a voice calling, 'Knock! Knock! Knock!' The voice came from behind Mr Kidd's door. 'Knock! Knock! Knock!'

Christopher knocked.

Mr Kidd opened the door and took Christopher's empty cup from him with one fluid movement. It was as if he'd been privy to Christopher's concerns; as if he'd known that Christopher was worried, was ascending, was standing outside the door with a cup in his hands. Mr Kidd threw the cup into the air, where it described a graceful arc over the bed before landing in his wastepaper basket. A pair of shoes already occupied this receptacle.

'Christopher,' said Mr Kidd, with outstretched arms, and he ushered his guest into the room. It was the reverse of Christopher's not only in the arrangement of the furniture but also in its clutter, the disorder of which suggested long tenancy: piles of boxes, magazines thick-edged on these boxes, sloped stacks of books, a dish rack above the basin, a hat stand on which shirts and jackets perched on wire hangers, with the wardrobe itself taped shut, and a birdcage in the corner by the air-conditioning unit. The bird in the cage cried, 'Knock!' It shook its blue and black and white feathers against the bars and swung, one-legged, on its swing.

'I'm glad you've come,' said Mr Kidd.

'Sorry to bother you,' said Christopher. 'I wanted to

know – has the maid been to you yet?'

'You mean Lori? She has, she has. Sit down.' And he straightened out a stack of magazines on a low chair, so that Christopher understood he was to sit on them. He placed his papers on top of the pile and sat. The chair rocked a little against the floor, the bird's beak darted among its seeds, Mr Kidd sat genially on the end of his bed. At Christopher's feet, folded handkerchiefs filled a shoebox.

'It's just that she's left all her cleaning things in my room, for some time now, and there's no sign of her. Oh, I'm sorry.' Sorry because, in attempting to cross his legs, he had upended the box of handkerchiefs, which spread gracefully on the floor.

Mr Kidd hurried to right them.

'Not to worry, not to worry! I do it all the time,' he said, and stroked each handkerchief as he returned it to the box. They were all admirably smooth. 'Aren't they beautiful? I send them out, you see, to be laundered.' He took evident pleasure in this; not only in the act of sending and laundering, but the words themselves.

The bird worked intimately with its seeds, as if mending them. Christopher watched it lift its bright head and say, 'Violet!'

'Pretty little thing, isn't it?' said Mr Kidd. 'Belongs to my wife.'

Although Mr Kidd had mentioned, in the lounge, the birth of two children, Christopher had imagined the old man as a lifelong bachelor of regular habits. Now he must accommodate a wife. Actually there was a neatness to Mr Kidd's dress that suggested wifely attentions.

'Or belonged to my wife, I should say.'

So now Christopher must think 'widower', a word that always flapped at him out of Dickens, with a faint scent of camphor and a long, black, slightly feminine coat.

'I'm sorry to hear that,' he said.

'So was I, Chris, let me tell you. So was I. She brought this bird with her when we got married. I mean it – brought it with her to the wedding. It was like a, whaddya call it, a dowry. Like a ring on my finger, this bird.'

And he gestured toward a photograph propped against a box, a sepia arrangement of bride, groom and, yes, bird, although 'bird' was suggested more by the courtly lift of the woman's arm than the avian blur perched upon it.

'Nineteen forty-eight,' said Mr Kidd.

'This is the same bird?'

'It is,' said Mr Kidd.

'This bird is over sixty years old?' said Christopher, too polite to be distinctly incredulous, but he itched to take up his phone and research the lifespan of parrots.

'It's older than that,' said Mr Kidd. 'I'll tell you all about it some time. It's quite a story. You'll be interested, Chris. This is right in your line.'

He sat cheerfully on the bed, his head cocked, his arms rigid and his fists on his knees. Christopher beheld his loneliness and said, 'I'm all ears.' This colloquialism struck him as false, as something Mr Kidd would say. But it was Christopher's habit to fall into the speech patterns of those around him, and in this way he succumbed at last to the shabby sociability of the St George Hotel.

'Well, well,' said Mr Kidd, and he sprang from the bed toward the bird. It didn't cease cracking its seed until he opened the cage door; then it stood quite still and said, 'Hello! Hello!'

'Hello, darling,' said Mr Kidd. 'You won't come out?'

He offered his hand, but the bird remained motionless.

'Suit yourself,' he said, but just as he went to close the door, the bird flew in a bright flurry into the room, settling at first on top of the wardrobe, then on the basin, and finally on Christopher's leg. Christopher sat rigid with anxiety – he realised he had never actually touched a bird – but it was placid enough, and he found he enjoyed the light weight of its claws on his knee.

'I met my wife young,' said Mr Kidd. 'My parents were actors. Whole family, actually. I'm an insurance man myself – was. On the road as much as my parents were, just a different kettle of acting fish, really, if you think about it. I say actors but I don't mean Shakespeare, I'm talking music hall stuff.

'Well, Violet – my wife – was from another theatre family. Her mother was Gladys Nie – you won't know her, but she was big news back in the day, she tap-danced in gold tights and sang like a bugle, but they called her the Blue Canary because she performed with a blue parrot on one shoulder. And she had this daughter we all loved, and that was Violet. I was playing piano for our act back then – we were the Kidds & Kids, my brothers on fiddle and horn, Dad sang, Mum sang, we all danced. And I just met this girl, Violet, and fell for her. There was one song she did with her mother, she came out in a white dress like this was *The Nutcracker*, and she and Gladys sang about a man they were both in love with – mother and daughter both in love with the same fellow! – who turned out to be a woman dressed as a man, and she ran off with the father.'

Mr Kidd, laughing, unleashed a bubble of watery snot; he attended to it without embarrassment, using one of his laundered handkerchiefs.

'Now, Violet was only seventeen, so we had to wait, and we were touring all the time, not always to the same places – she'd be in Grafton and I'd be in Bendigo, say – and along comes the war and I'm called up, but they turned me down for service on account of my asthma and I end up running errands for the War Damage Commission, which is how I got into insurance.'

The bird shifted on Christopher's knee, as if to remind Mr Kidd to get on with it.

'So finally the war's over, Vi's twenty-one, and on our wedding day she shows up with her mother's blue parrot on her arm. It's a wedding present. She carries it down the aisle, it sits on her shoulder all through the wedding breakfast, and finally we're alone in this little hotel in Brisbane and here's this bird. And I say, "Look, Vi, I can't do it with a bird in the room" – there was no cage, see, to cover over. So she put it in her suitcase, and I said, "Won't it die? No air?" and she just shakes her head at me and that's that, my mind wasn't on the bird, let me tell you. What a night.

'In the morning, Vi opens her suitcase and out comes the bird, right as rain. And I say, "Shouldn't we feed it?" and she laughs at me and says, "No need." Then she tells me the strangest thing. "This bird," she says, "has been in my family since 1851.'"

Mr Kidd paused. The bird picked discreetly at its chest feathers. 'Knock,' it said, matter-of-factly. Christopher listened for sounds that the maid might have returned to his room.

'She says, "Bob, we're married now and I'll tell you everything. A Chinaman made this bird for my great-grandmother, and it isn't real."'

'Not real?' said Christopher, looking at the bird, which hopped on his knee.

Mr Kidd rubbed his hands together. 'I told you I had a model for you, didn't I?' he said, and his pleasure in saying it seemed to make his eyes water a little; he touched them with his handkerchief.

'Well, I was a newly married man, I was ready to agree to anything, but I couldn't wrap my head around it – the thing looked so real, you can see for yourself, and here she was saying it was clockwork. An automaton, is the word, but you'll know that with your thesis.'

'Yes,' said Christopher. 'There was a duck that ate and defecated, the Vaucanson duck, right in my time period.'

Mr Kidd nodded. 'So I asked her to show me its insides, and she said no, taking it apart would break it forever and there was nothing else like it in the world. And my Violet said to me, "Bob, by god, if you ever doubt this bird I'll walk out the door and never come back." She's saying this, mind, without a stitch on, and she looked so serious – what could I do? I made a vow more solemn, I reckon, than our marriage. Tell me you would've done any different, Chris, faced with a beautiful naked woman.'

'No, of course not,' said Christopher, although he thought instead of a beautiful man with a bird on his bare shoulder; and, as if startled, the bird flew to the top of the wardrobe, where its tail tipped up and down like a little lever. But only *like* a lever, thought Christopher; really, just like a bird.

'She kept it up all through the honeymoon – we only drove down the coast – all through setting up the house, and when I said, "Let me buy it a cage, shouldn't it have seeds to eat, shouldn't it drink?" she said, "I told you, Bob, it isn't real and it can't eat – ask me another question like that and I'll be out the door." For the longest time, you know, I thought she fed it on the sly. There was no mess. And of course I was gone all day at work, then for days at a time, weeks eventually, out on the road. The boys came along pretty early, two boys, but the third baby was stillborn, and after that it was a string of miscarriages, very hard, and one day she says to me, "I don't mind, we have our boys, except I wanted a girl to take the bird, it's supposed to be a girl."'

'Does it have a name?' asked Christopher, because only now did it occur to him that Mr Kidd hadn't mentioned one.

'She wouldn't name it,' said Mr Kidd, 'on account of it not being real. Anyway, by this time I'd forgotten about it being an automaton and all that, it was just The Bird, and she didn't make a big song and dance about it, except she told the boys to take care when they were playing. But when she said the bit about wanting a girl for the bird, I thought, Hang on, that thing must be getting a bit long in the tooth, how many years does a budgie live for anyway? I asked at a pet shop and they said seven or eight, maximum ten. Well, we'd been married for seven, and I figured old Gladys had been replacing the bird on and off and she probably got a fresh one to give Vi, so our time with this bird was nearly up and then we'd see.'

'Ah,' said Christopher. Mr Kidd's nose had begun to well, but he didn't seem to have noticed. He rubbed his thighs with his fists. A strange high hum entered the room; it took Christopher a moment to realise it came from next door and was a vacuum cleaner. The bird, as if insulted by the noise, ducked its head and said, 'Violet! Violet!'

'But a year passed, and a few more, and the bird was still with us, the bloody thing. I'd inspect it whenever I got home from a trip and wonder if it was the same bird or if she'd gone out and got herself a new one. But they all looked the same to me. One day she sees me peering at it and asks what I'm up to. I thought fast, Chris, and I said, "I'm trying to figure out where you wind it up." She gave me a kiss for that.

'So the boys grew up, and when the first one got married I asked Vi if she was going to give him the bird, and she said no, and I asked if it was because he wasn't a girl. And she said it was because he didn't believe it was mechanical. I was glad to hear it, but I said to her, "You told me you'd be out the door if I didn't believe you," and she said, "I'm his mother, not his wife." And the second boy got married and he didn't get the bird either, but I knew better than to ask. All this time, it's still going into the bath with her, sitting on her shoulder all day. It'd perch on the telly at night while we watched. It wasn't till after both boys left home that it started to talk – Hello! Knock! All of that, and her name too. So I figured she'd finally bought a smart one.'

'Violet! Violet!' said the bird.

'It used to come on holiday with us, camping and road trips, but then we planned a trip to England – Vi always wanted to go to England – and I found her putting it in her suitcase. So I said, "You can't do that," and she said, "I have to, they won't let it on the plane with us," and then it all came out, Chris – that I'd never believed her, that I thought it was a game, that she fed it in secret and bought a new one every ten years. She was spitting mad, and I said to her, "Well, take it apart, show me its insides, *prove it*," and she refused to go on the trip, shut herself in the bedroom and wouldn't come out. It was all I could do to make her eat. The boys came over and talked her out of it, but it was never the same after that, she never really forgave me.'

'But she didn't walk out the door?'

'That's what she couldn't forgive, she said it one day – "Bob, I've left it too late, I could walk out the door but there's nowhere to go," and I tell you, I could've killed that bird, but she wouldn't leave it alone with me. She died later that year, unexpected, never saw England, and I still remember coming home after the funeral and there's the bird sitting on the back of a kitchen chair. I hold out my hand for it to come over, I was ready to snap its neck. But I got to thinking about something she'd said when we had the fight. "Have you ever heard it sing?" she said, and I thought, Nope, not a note. Budgies don't sing, do they? But it gave me pause, and next day I went off to a pet shop and listened to all the budgies squawking and chattering and chirping away, and it was true, I'd never heard the bird make a single sound like that. So what I did was, I bought a cage and some seed from the shop, I took it all home and set it up, and waited to see what happened.'

'What happened?' asked Christopher, because Mr Kidd was very still on the bed and seemed to expect it. The vacuum sounds had stopped. Christopher noticed the rising of a sour smell from somewhere in the room, which might have been drain or birdcage or something worse.

'It hopped right in and played with the seeds all right, but it didn't eat them. It washed itself in the water dish, but it didn't drink a drop.'

The bird on the wardrobe puffed out its chest.

'And that was twenty years ago,' said Mr Kidd. 'It's never eaten a bite or sung a note. Never even dropped a feather. That bird, my friend, is over a hundred and fifty years old.'

He slapped his knees and shook his head; these were gestures of such pride and pleasure, and they suggested such cheerful submission to the surprises of life, such joy at having been wrong, that Christopher was tempted, for a moment, to believe Mr Kidd, to believe the bird as it twitched on the wardrobe, to walk through the lobby and out into the unknown city looking at everyone he passed, to believe in them, to find some steadfast one to love and trust, to burn with something – anything – in the bright, blank holiday afternoon.

The bird flew down from the wardrobe and onto Mr Kidd's shoulder. It beaked his beard. It ticked and trembled.

Christopher wanted to touch it.

'What's it made of?' he asked.

'You're the expert,' said Mr Kidd. 'You tell me.'

Christopher stood and stepped close. He held out a finger; the bird, quizzical, looked at it. He touched the bird's back and felt ridged softness.

'Feathers,' he said.

Mr Kidd nodded. 'I figured as much,' he said. 'But how're they fixed in?'

'If I could look —' said Christopher, but Mr Kidd jumped and the bird, too, jumped, and flew back into its cage, because the pile of magazines on which Christopher had been sitting had collapsed from the chair and slid onto the floor, and over them skated his photocopied pages of waxwork women, disembowelled.

'Funny sort of line you're in, Chris,' said Mr Kidd, but he seemed unfazed; he had followed the bird to its cage and closed the door.

'You get used to it,' said Christopher, gathering the magazines.

'Leave it, leave it,' said Mr Kidd, and when Christopher looked up he saw the cage swinging before his face. 'Now, I've never been game, but you're a professional. How's this: I give you the bird for a day or two and you take it apart, you figure out how it works and you put it back together exactly as it was. You can write it all up for your thesis – fair's fair.'

Mr Kidd held the cage at arm's length from his body. His hand shook, and the cage, and the bird inside it. The cage was clean, except for scattered seed. A small bell rang beneath the tiny mirror. Mr Kidd shone above his offering. The bird said, 'Violet! Violet!' and Mr Kidd closed his eyes for a moment; his face when he opened them was both happy and grave.

'You want me to . . . open this bird?' asked Christopher.

'You've got the experience,' said Mr Kidd, nodding at the photocopies in Christopher's hand.

It occurred to Christopher that he could accept the cage, as Mr Kidd suggested, keep it for a night or two, and return it with a theory of a thousand moving parts. He could, in this time, watch the bird shit in the crumbs of its shucked seeds. This would be the kind, the generous thing to do. He took the cage from Mr Kidd, who dusted his hands as if free of a beloved burden.

'This is nice of you,' said Christopher.

'I've waited a lifetime,' said Mr Kidd, and Christopher nodded, said goodbye, entered his own room – vacuumed, apparently – and placed the cage on the writing desk.

He spent the afternoon reading at the desk; the bird stood on its perch and appeared to watch him. It neither ate nor drank, and it didn't speak, although Christopher looked up from his work at intervals and said, 'Hello? Hello?' The pigeons vibrated in the eaves.

When Christopher went out to buy a kebab for dinner, he saw the people of the city drinking and walking and eating together. Even those alone in the streets had some purpose: they hurried toward a beloved, an appointment; they were on their way to a house, an intimate room, they would enter the room and be unfastened. The lounge of the St George Hotel flickered at the corner of his eye as he crossed the lobby. He climbed the stairs to his floor. Fifth floor. He pulled some chicken from the kebab and offered it to the bird, which inspected and refused it. For hours he sat by the cage composing an anatomy for the bird – rubber hoses, bellows, wires, tiny gears and springs, silk feathers – he was absorbed in this work as he no longer was in his thesis. Mr Kidd, from next door, contributed his serial cough.

If it would just unleash a torrent of shit, thought Christopher. If it would just sing. It was so imperfectly a bird without the shit and the song. He covered the cage with a towel before going to bed, where he lay for some time, tucked into scrawny sheets, listening to passing feet in the corridor for evidence of drunkenness or injury. He slept until he was startled awake by the sound of buses as they took their nocturnal route through that part of the city. His mind had continued to work during sleep; he now saw a diagram of the inner bird, polished and bronze, and the bird itself opened out like a doll's house. The economy of the design delighted him. To have fitted all that inside such a tiny object! To create such a masterpiece in order to conceal it!

He went to the desk and began to draw; this drawing came so easily, and each minute part of it was the source of such serious pleasure for Christopher, that he grew anxious. A suspicion rose each time he heard Mr Kidd's cough through the flimsy walls: that all this, the bird, Mr Kidd's request, this beautiful, careful task, was a kind of joke, played upon him because he had slighted Mr Kidd in the hotel lounge that morning. It became clearer, as the night persisted and he continued to draw, that Christopher had been arranged, somehow, for sacrifice, and the bird along with him, so that Mr Kidd might walk freely through the lobby and into the lounge; might remain on first-name terms with Lori, the maid; might still be permitted to approach newcomers and startle them with his friendliness; might do all this under the watchful eye of the other men of the St George Hotel.

The bird rustled under its towel; Christopher uncovered it. It moved the waxen fingernail of its beak without producing any noise, and the lamplight lit its glassy eye.

'Hello, hello,' said Christopher, opening the cage.

The bird jumped down to the desk and onto Christopher's arm. It throbbed there, motionless.

'Hello, hello,' said Christopher, rubbing its tidy head, feeling the spidery weight of its claws. It was so living, there on his arm, so compact, so close: the strangest thing he had ever seen, blue and yellow and white and black; a sidling, a sitting, a lifting of the wing.

The bird remained on Christopher's arm as he gathered his slippers and papers, his third of a wardrobe's worth of clothes, and packed them into his suitcase. To perform these tasks one-handed gave them a steady grace. In order to change into his daytime clothes, he placed the bird on the end of the bed where the sheets were tucked so tightly his feet hadn't creased them. When he was dressed, he took the bird and wrapped it in the folds of his pyjama shirt. He placed this bundle of bird and shirt in the suitcase, which he closed and locked.

The hallways of the St George Hotel were quiet; there was no one to see Christopher slide his diagram beneath Mr Kidd's door. The stairwell was empty. The clerk at Reception seemed used to the furtive departure of paying guests. The St George, as Christopher left it, felt collegial to him, and he loved its tender, threadbare enterprise. Outside, the streets lived their constant life, but the men of the hotel were safe within, with their lukewarm lounge and their curtain-lit rooms. Mr Kidd would stir into this morning just beginning, and the pigeons at his window would lull and soothe him. The sky to the east was lightening into colour. 'Violet, Violet,' said Christopher, and he stepped with purpose into the street. He became, then, any traveller on his intimate way through the early city, groomed for the street and taking care not to bump his suitcase.

The Movie People

When the movie people left, the town grew sad. An air of disaster lingered in the stunned streets – of cuckoldry, or grief. There was something shameful to it, like defeated virtue, and also something confidential, because people were so in need of consolation they turned to each other with all their private burdens of ecstasy and despair. There was at that time a run of extraordinary weather – as if the blank blue sky, the unshaded sun, and the minor, pleasurable breeze had all been arranged by the movie people. The weather lasted for the duration of filming and then began to turn, so that within a few weeks of the close of production a stiff, mineral wind had swept television aerials from roofs and disorganised the fragile root systems of more recently imported shrubbery.

My main sense of this time is of a collective mourning in which the townspeople began to wear the clothes they had adopted as extras and meet on street corners to re-enact their past happiness. I didn't participate. I was happy the movie people had left. I was overjoyed, in fact, to see no more trucks in the streets, no more catering vans in the supermarket car park, no more boom lights standing in frail forests outside the town hall. The main street had been closed to traffic for filming and now the residents were reluctant to open it again. It's a broad street, lined with trees and old-fashioned gaslights (subtly electrified) and those slim, prudish Victorian shopfronts that huddle graciously together like people in church, and as I rode my scooter down it on those windy days after the movie people left, it looked more than ever like the picturesque period street, frozen in the nineteenth century, that brought the movie to us in the first place.

I rode my scooter to the disgust of women in crinolines with their hair braided and looped, men in waistcoats and top hats: citizens of some elderly republic that had been given an unexpected opportunity to sun itself in the wan light of the twenty-first century. I knew these people as butchers, plumbers, city commuters, waterers of thirsty lawns, walkers of imbecile dogs, washers of cars, postmen, and all the women who ever taught me at school. They stayed in the street all day. They eddied and flocked. Up the street, and down again, as if they were following the same deep and certain instinct that drives herring through the North Sea. They consulted fob watches and pressed handkerchiefs to their sorrowful breasts. The wind blew out their hooped skirts. It rolled the last of the plastic recycling bins down the street and out into the countryside, where they nestled lifelessly together in the scrub.

I rode my scooter to the home of my wife's parents. She was sheltering there, my wife – Alice – because the movie people had left. She loved them, you see. Not her parents – that tranquil couple of bleached invertebrates – but the director, the key grip, the costume ladies, the hairdressers, the boom operators, most particularly the star. The whole town loved the star. Even I succumbed, just a little – to the unpredictable feeling we all had in the weeks he was among us that he might at any moment emerge from a dimly bulbed doorway or unfold his long legs from a rooftop. We'd never seen anyone so beautiful. He shone with a strange, interior, asexual light, and his head seemed to hang in midair as if it required nothing so substantial as a body. Looking at him was like entering a familiar room in which you see everything at once, and at the same time, nothing.

I rode to my wife and said, 'Alice, darling, he's left now, they've all left, so can you please come home and love me forever, entangle your limbs in mine on the sofa while watching television, pluck your eyebrows in the bathroom mirror while I'm trying to shave, go running with me in the gorgeous mornings, and dance to bad disco music in your underwear?'

But Alice, who now wore the costume of a sexy, spinsterly librarian, was trim with repressed desire and lit, at her throat, by Edwardian lace; she only sat on her parents' chaise longue embroidering silken roses with inconsolable fingers. Her parents sat nearby: her father, that placid old sinner, was dressed as a country parson with a monocle in his crooked eye, and her mother peered out at me from the battered piano, which until recently had been nothing but a prop for picture frames. Now she played it with a watchful plink and plunk, with maternal suspicion tinkling over the expanse of her oatmeal-coloured face, a frill of veil in her ornamental hair.

Other times I visited, the door was opened by a sour maid who informed me that my wife was not at home.

'Is she not at home?' I asked. 'Or is she not *at home*?'

The maid, with a grim, polite smile, shut the door in my face.

The mood of the town improved with the success of the movie. A special preview was held just for us, in the town hall; we sat in the municipal pews and called out the names of everyone who appeared on screen in a long and lustful litany. We laughed and teased in order to conceal our bashful pride; it felt as if finally the world had reached a solicitous hand into our innermost beings and, liking what it found there, held us up for emulation and respect. We were so distracted that, afterward, nobody was sure what had actually happened in the movie. A forbidden love, generally – something greenish and unrequited – one of those glacial *fin-de-siècle* stories in which the tiniest gestures provoke terrible consequences about which no one in polite company speaks.

At the premiere party, the townspeople danced the gavotte

and the quadrille, they waltzed among potted palms with a slow, bucolic concentration, and they feasted on tremulous dishes of jellies and aspic. All throughout that strange, orchidaceous, combustible room, women fainted into arms and onto sofas, and a tiny orchestra of men with Dickensian whiskers played endlessly into the night as Alice – my Alice – danced time and double time and time and again with the star, who appeared to have flown in especially for the occasion. Her parents nodded and smiled and accepted the nods and smiles of other doting gentry, and Alice flew over the carpets, her face alight.

I demanded of everyone I met, 'Who does he think he is? Just because he's famous, he can dance all night with another man's wife?'

Unlike that decorous crowd, I was insensible of my own dignity. Finally, the man who used to service my scooter (dressed now in the handsome uniform of an English corporal, which made of his red belly a regimental drum) drew me aside to tell me that the man Alice was dancing with wasn't famous at all; was, in fact, Edward Smith-Jones, a man of the law, and selected from among the townspeople as the star's stand-in. Apparently it was obvious to everyone that the entire scene in the stables featured this man and not the star, who was nervous around horses, especially during thunderstorms. So there he danced, lordly Eddie, with another man's haircut and another man's wife; but as my kind corporal pointed out, Alice wore white in the film and her hair on her shoulders, was unwed, available, and Edward's hand rested on Alice's supple back, and my heart was filled with hatred for the movie people.

When I asked Alice for a waltz she told me, with a demure shake of her head, that her card was full.

I lost my job when the graphic design firm I worked for was asked to move elsewhere. Certain other sectors of the citizenry were also politely dissuaded: the Greek fruit shop became a dapper greengrocer's, manned by a portly ex-IT consultant with Irish cheeks and a handlebar moustache. He measured out damsons and quinces on gleaming bronze scales. Unless they were willing to wear their hair in long plaits, the Chinese people of the town were encouraged to stay off the main street between the hours of eight-thirty and six, and preferably to remain invisible on weekends. The gym was forced to close for lack of customers, and the Video Ezy. The tourists came in excitable herds, transported from the nearest town in traps and buggies. They mistook me for another tourist, and I was comfortable walking amongst them, watching as my wife strolled in the botanical gardens, her face in parasol twilight, a brass band playing in the rotunda, a British flag afloat above the trumpets, nannies sitting with their neat ankles crossed on benches as children toddled near duck ponds. Alice walked with her Edward, and her parents followed close behind. She tilted her head this way and that. In the movie she had been one of those extras who almost have a speaking part, the kind the camera focuses on to gauge the reaction of a comely crowd.

When I heard they were engaged, Alice and Mr Smith-Jones, I retired my scooter. I took a job at a printer's, and the finicky hours of setting type gave me time to think things over. On the day of their wedding I dressed in costume. In the movie I play the role of a man about town; you can see me in the lower right at 20:16, loafing with friends on a street corner while gauzy women flutter behind us, in and out of seedy cottages. Yes, right there – I'm the one watching the dog. I walked to the church among applecarts and small sooty boys, and there was a yellow quality to the air, a residual loveliness, as if the sun had gone down hours before but stayed just below the horizon. The church doors swung open before me, revealing soft pale heads among bridal flowers. The parson – my father-in-law – trembled in the moment when I should speak or forever hold my peace. I spoke. Eddie and I met in the aisle; he swung and I dodged and I swung. Alice shook in her slim white dress, and roses fell from her hands. I floored Eddie; he pulled me down. We rolled on that ecclesiastical carpet, up and over and around and down, while flustered ushers danced at the edges of our combat. Ed would be on the verge of springing up, a lawyerly Lazarus, but I clawed him back down; I, on my knees, would be making my way altar-ward, only to find him wedded to my foot. The organ began to play. The congregation piped in alarm. An elderly woman keened among her millinery. Finally we exhausted ourselves, and it was me – me! – Alice came to comfort. Edward loped away into the high noon of heartbreak. Her counterfeit father had been ready to join them in mock matrimony, but with a merry shake of his worldly head he rejoined us instead. The sun set, and the moon rose. We ate ices at the reception, and great silver fish surrounded by lemons, and that night my wife gave a virginal shudder as she withdrew her slender foot from her slender slipper.

There followed a happy time of croquet and boating expeditions; then Alice went through her suffragette period, of which I pretended to disapprove. Things are more settled now. We read Darwin together, without telling her parents, and she's discovered Marx. We take walks in the country, where my naturalist wife sends me scrambling into trees for birds' nests. Things aren't what they used to be, but there are consolations: a certain elegance to the way she stands at open windows, and longer, darker nights now that the town has switched from electricity to gas. But I've noticed in her lately a strange inability to see the resemblances between things: a tennis ball (she plays modestly, in white dresses) is nothing like the sun; a glass of water, she says, has no relation to the ocean; she scowls if I comment on the similarity between her neck and a swan's. In fact she dislikes the similarity of things even without recognising their likeness, and can't bear, for example, to see a brown short-haired dog on brown short-haired grass. The rest of the town is like this too. They have a horror of seeing photographs of themselves, even the hoary daguerreotypes they love so much. They've removed all the mirrors from their houses, and the paintings of jaded horses on hillsides, and the china that depicts, in blue and white, the far-flung tale of luckless lovers. It's as if they're allergic to the very idea of reproduction; or, at the very least, don't wish to be reminded of it. What a singular world they live in, in which no thing has any relation to another! They no longer mention the movie. They no longer watch movies. They've taken up laudanum. They expect to live forever. They seem happy, however – timeless and happy. I watch them all, a little wistfully, in my fraudulent frockcoat. Meanwhile, the trees shake out their leaves in the wind, and in the evenings my wife walks through the spent garden. Her face is like a flag that says *Surrender*.

Cara Mia

Cara's mother was at her best on Saturday nights. On Saturday nights she lit long white strings of Christmas lights and little candles in tins. She took the rubber bands off the wind chimes, which otherwise kept her awake at night, and hung paper lanterns from the clothesline. The back screen door opened and shut as the children ran in and out of the garden, to see the lanterns and bat at the wind chimes; the door snapped and thundered and let in gusts of mosquitoes until Cara told them to stop it, and Cara was the eldest, so they did. But their mother, Rachel, didn't care how much noise they made, because it was Saturday night. She was black-haired and red-mouthed, she wore a sharp scent and a floating white dress, and now she produced her purse from somewhere (she always hid her purse, with so many children and so many boyfriends, though for the moment there was only one boyfriend, only Adam). She sent Adam out for fish and chips. Now that he lived with them, he could be sent on errands. Cassidy went with him, because Cass was the oldest boy.

Cara set the long dining table while they were gone. First she bundled away last week's dirty tablecloth. The younger children bumped and ran and offered their help, and Cara had to calm them – she let them straighten the new tablecloth, carry knives and forks, salt and pepper, and, in a confident mood, the cool pink bottles of sweet chilli sauce. But only Cara was allowed to open the cabinet in the corner and choose the platters for the middle of the table, the special glasses in blue and green and purple, and the vases in milky silver. The children trailed Cara into the garden and watched as she cut flowers (she had little shining scissors expressly for this task, they used to be her grandmother's, and they hung in the kitchen from a piece of velvet ribbon); depending on the season, she cut freesias or ferns or squat yellow daisies, swags of Christmas bush or oleander, and whatever she chose Rachel accepted and turned into bouquets, perfect, without even trying.

The guests began to arrive: friends of Adam's, friends of Rachel's, people Rachel worked with and people Cara had never heard of before, not always young and pretty but always with some distinguishing feature – an electric-blue hat, a foreign accent, a vast cosy beard – and they brought bottles of wine or beer and sometimes sweet-smelling dishes covered with tea towels, and baskets of bread. The children were introduced: Cara, Wallis, Marcus, Elsa; Cassidy is out with Adam getting dinner, said Rachel, don't worry about remembering their names, nobody does. The younger children looked at their mother, anxious. They were shy for a minute and wanted jobs to do.

Cara turned ice cubes out into glasses. She found bags of nuts in the cupboards and poured them into smooth wooden bowls; the kids could pass them around. Elsa was naked and it didn't matter. Marcus had unearthed two old Christmas crackers; they snapped, people shouted and laughed, Marcus and Wally wore tissue-paper crowns for the rest of the night. Cass and Adam returned, laughing in the steam of their hot parcels, Cass self-important because he had been allowed to burrow into his for salty chips on the way home. Into the dishes on the table: piles of battered fish, potato scallops, chips, and lemons cut in wedges. Coleslaw out of a plastic container. Then the long meal, the arms crowded onto the table, everybody swinging plates and lifting drinks, using their fingers, kicking each other without meaning to. Apologies, jokes, music to which no one listened. Elsa spilled her drink; Cara mopped it. Cara found more lemons. Stains bloomed on the white tablecloth, the ice all melted. Send Adam for more! Adam went for more ice; Cara offered to go with him. Out into the dark streets, the running traffic, people walking to the pubs or walking their dogs or walking arm in arm and who knows where. The service station was only two

streets away, and Adam smoked as he walked; he said very little, sang one time, turned his head from Cara to blow smoke.
Cara hung back as he bought the ice. She watched as girls came
into the service station swinging the keys to their little cars; she
watched as they spotted Adam, looked again – some of them
knew him and approached with cries and squeezes. Sometimes
he would introduce her as 'my Cara mia', and these girls would
smile and squeeze her, too. Once, some girls from Cara's school
were there; they asked who he was and Cara said, 'He's Mum's
boyfriend,' but she would have preferred to say 'I'm his Cara
mia.' And the girls from school gaped and said, 'I thought he
might be your brother,' which was a compliment, because he
was so good-looking, but it also meant he was too young to be
any mother's boyfriend. The best part was coming home: the
house lit up behind the trees, all the windows wide, and everyone inside quiet for a moment as the man with the beard told
a story or the woman with the accent sang a song; then, just
as Cara and Adam passed through the front gate, all the voices
started up, sometimes applause or laughter, and the people
walking on the street would see and hear and wish they could
go into the house and be welcomed there; and Cara could.

With the help of the children, Cara carried the dishes to
the kitchen. The greasy fishy paper curled in fantastic shapes
on the floor beside the rubbish bin and flower cuttings littered
the table. Cara washed and Cass dried. The other children wan-
dered in and out – into the lounge room, where the adults drank
and talked, and Rachel leaned into Adam on the couch; into
the kitchen, where Cara clattered in the sink, where Cass might

snap them with a tea towel; out into the garden, where the snails crawled on silver paths, until Cara told them *again* to stop banging the door. The adults made drowsy, wistful talk. Rachel lifted her arms to push the hair out of her face and her children heard the jangle of gold bracelets. The younger ones tiptoed in and volunteered for goodnight kisses, which they received from Adam and the woman in the electric-blue hat – Rachel blew kisses from the palm of her hand. Cara made the children brush their teeth before bed. She closed their bedroom doors herself. The candles were slugs of light curled in the bottom of the tins and the tablecloth was sticky wherever the chilli sauce had touched it. The guests called: Leave the table, Cara. Come and sit down, said the woman in the blue hat. Her hair was tightly curled, she wore yellow stockings. How old are you, Cara? she asked. Only fourteen? She looks older, don't you agree? Adam agreed, and Rachel smiled with a yawn. Someone had brought a tray of pastries from the Greek café. Cara spilled icing sugar on the carpet, it didn't matter. The children slept. Adam moved his thumb over Rachel's forearm, up and down and slowly. The Christmas lights above his head were a crown of stars. Cara, shy, laughed when the adults did. One of them wanted to smoke. You don't mind, Cara, do you? It isn't cigarettes. Cara shook her head. Nobody told her to leave, but she went to bed. Now that Adam had moved in, Cara was the only person in the house to have her own bedroom. Outside, the palm trees shrugged and struggled in the wind. That was Saturday night.

They lived in a low wide white weatherboard house in a Greek part of Sydney, right next to an Orthodox church. On Sunday mornings the noise of chanting men rolled out over the ripe garden. Under the sound of it, Cara lifted a blue shirt against the clothesline and pegged it in place: now there were five Adam shirts floating on the line. She lay in the grass beneath them. It was November; the fierce magpie mothers were nesting in the gums and an ibis stood sentry in every palm. Cara thought Rachel looked like an ibis: long-legged, with a black curve of hair along the neck. Rachel and Adam were in bed. Every Sunday morning: in bed. All the children had shooed themselves from the house. The yellow bedroom curtains remained shut; the house was sweet, white, forbidding. Marcus and Elsa hunted lizards, Wallis stripped bark from a tree, Cass kicked at a ball. Cara lay curled in the sun with an arm across her face. She was too tall, with a rushed vertical look and no chest or hips to speak of. And black hair like her mother's. She curled to hide her height.

The children began to complain, as they did every week. 'We're hungry,' they said, not so much to Cara as to each other.

'Cass, go in, get us something to eat,' said Wallis. Wally knew she was named for a king's girlfriend and liked to issue commands.

'Shit no,' said Cass, pleasant and slow, kicking his ball.

Cara lifted her arms above her head. A high laugh came from the house, which was worse than silence. Wallis sat on Cara's legs; Elsa came through the garden and collapsed over Cara's flat front. Cara could summon the girls like that, only by lifting her arms. Not the boys – but who cared? They only yelled all day and had a weird kicking way of walking. She used to love them blindly, with a vicious loyalty, but when Adam came she saw him size them up, laugh, and shake his head; then she knew their deficiencies. Sometimes she copied Adam's way of reaching out to mess their hair – a soft skating cuff to the rough backs of their heads that made them duck and grin when he did it. With her they only scowled.

'Cara,' said Wally, and Elsa said it too. 'Cara Cara Cara,' they chanted, and slapped their small hands against her feet and legs.

'How long will it be?' asked Wallis. 'It's hot out here. Is it hot?'

Cara wanted only to lie still and feel the sun and think about the church, which was white with a dome and a blue cross, and palm trees and ibises, so that it might be somewhere in the Mediterranean, and if that were true then Cara might be, also, somewhere on a foreign sea, maybe older, maybe beautiful, Cara mia. If Adam was out here, she thought, he would put Elsa in the laundry basket, or Marcus, and lift them high over his head. They would shriek and laugh and tumble into the grass. Then Adam would go away from them, from the garden and the house, to walk around the block and smoke. Rachel had told him never to smoke in front of the children. Cara thought of Adam smoking, the way his forearm looked as he lifted the cigarette to his mouth, the particular tense muscle that clenched in his golden jaw. She shivered in the grass. Wallis caught Cara's shiver and hugged herself.

The singing quietened down next door. The doorbell was

ringing – on a Sunday? And who ever rang the doorbell? The postman with a special package, Cara's teacher the time she visited, men in suits who wanted to save everybody from hell. Didn't they all know: don't make noise on a Sunday, not on a Sunday morning, and not with the doorbell, a real brass bell (brought back from India, from the neck of a sacred cow dripping with flowers, or from Switzerland maybe, a healthy Swiss cow in a high mountain pasture), so loud it could wake the dead. Cara lunged up from the grass so that Wally and Elsa slid and tumbled. She hurried around the side of the house where weeks ago Cass had drawn a penis in blue chalk. The children followed. Who was at the front door, waking the dead? A girl with brown hair, a small, wheeled suitcase and an enormous belly. A pregnant girl. Cara pulled at the hem of her short blue dress. The other children pressed behind her, except for Cassidy, who was eleven. He slouched against the fence, pretending indifference. The church opened up behind him and people milled about.

'Hi,' said the girl, and Cara said, 'Can I help you?'

Oh, the girl didn't seem to know. She let go of her suitcase and began to cry. The crying made her red face redder, her hair damper, and there were rings of sweat under her arms and on the yellow T-shirt that stretched so far over her stomach; the rainbow on the T-shirt was twisted and wide.

'Is this where Adam lives?' asked the girl, and because she said his name – this was how it seemed to Cara – Adam opened the front door. He stood there for a moment wearing only a pair of shorts, his hair in all directions. Then he stepped outside and held the girl – his arms were long enough to reach around her, despite her belly, and she pressed her face into his chest with her hands knotted under her chin, crying, crying, until all the children ran away and only Cara saw him kiss the stringy top of the girl's damp head.

Adam smiled at Cara after giving the kiss.

'This is my sister,' he said, and the girl lifted her swollen face. 'This is Danny. And Danny, this is Cara.'

Cara could see in Danny's soggy smile that she was more happy than sad; or that her sadness, now that she had been held in Adam's arms, was complicated by joy. So Cara felt savage and said, 'Does Mum know?'

Adam only laughed and stepped back from Danny, which made him disappear into the house. Danny followed. Cara pulled the suitcase behind them as quietly as she could. She eased the front door closed. The door to Rachel's room was still shut, sealed by Sunday; Danny seemed to know to lower her voice. Adam didn't, but his voice was never loud, although it carried. In the night and on Sunday mornings it carried and carried.

He looked at swollen Danny. 'Johnno?' he asked, and she nodded. In a shy way she seemed pleased with herself. Her face looked rubbed and sore but pleased. 'And why'd you leave?'

'Dad.'

Adam stood with his hands on his hips the way he did at barbecues and the beach.

'Ah,' he said, and Cara, standing beside the suitcase, felt all the tolerant history of that 'Ah' and hated it and found it lovely.

Adam rocked back onto his heels. 'You should sit down.'

Danny sank onto the couch in exactly the place Rachel had sat last night in her shining dress.

'Well, here you are,' said Adam.

'I'm sorry,' said Danny, crying again, and at this Adam knelt before her, he held her hands over her knees and kissed them, he said, 'Hey, Dan Dan, Dannygirl, you've done the right thing, it's good, I'm glad you're here, it's fucking amazing to see you, Dan. Hey, it's beautiful.'

He pressed his face into Danny's knees. She looked at Cara over the top of his head; her face was so naked with relief and self-pity Cara turned away.

'Want to tell me about Dad?' asked Adam, raising himself as if to join her on the couch, but he paused before sitting. 'Wait,' he said. 'We need coffee. Coffee?'

Danny shook her head.

'I'll just duck out and grab one for me, yeah? I'll be five minutes. Less.'

He went to Rachel's door and opened it; the light swimming out of the room was green and murky, and Cara noticed the way he entered without hesitation. He said something and returned with a T-shirt and thongs. He took his cigarettes from where he hid them behind the piano, winked at Cara and said, 'Back in a mo.' And left, shaking the coins in the pocket of his shorts. The house collapsed a little, emptier. The younger children crept to the doorway and peered at Danny, who peered back.

Now that she wasn't crying, Danny looked like Adam, but wasn't pretty: her mouth was too large, her eyes too small, and instead of his burning gold she was only an ordinary pinkish-brown. It was hard to think of her buckling under some loving man. She didn't touch her belly the way some women do; she only looked at it as if someone had put a cushion in her lap without telling her why. She would endure the cushion for the sake of politeness.

'Are you hungry?' asked Cara, because she was hungry, and the girl said no.

'Do you live near here?' asked Cara, and the girl said no.

'How old are you?'

Danny placed one hand on her stomach. 'Sixteen,' she said.

'Mum was sixteen when she had me.'

'I'll be seventeen when it's born,' said Danny, which meant her birthday must be soon, because she was big: as big as Rachel had been right before she had Marcus and Elsa. Then Danny said, 'Your house is nice.'

The house was messy from last night: the cushions crushed, the carpet dusty with sugar, the finished candles now just blackened tins. The big wooden windows poured with light that revealed the age of the furniture and the stains on the walls. Someone had braided half the fringe on the tall pink lampshade.

'It's my grandmother's house. It was,' said Cara. 'Before she died.'

Rachel's door opened and she came out in her red kimono: it had a bird of paradise embroidered on the back in blue, yellow and white. Her hair was caught in her hooped earrings. She might have been beautiful once, Cara conceded; maybe even last night.

Rachel pulled her kimono around her waist and said, 'Come into the kitchen.'

The children fled the kitchen when their mother appeared. They pushed past Danny and Cara into the lounge room, wanting to be invisible, but near. Rachel didn't seem to notice. She stood by the sink drinking water from a green glass. Cara and Danny watched as she drank one cup and then another.

'Have you fed the kids?' Rachel asked, and Danny started a little as if she might be expected to do the feeding. Cara prised bread from the freezer. Rachel sat at the kitchen table, sighing as she sat and pulling her hair out of her earrings. Danny sat too.

'Adam's gone for coffee,' said Rachel, as if this were news. She stabbed one finger into the top of the table and picked at the formica while Cara rattled the toaster.

'I'm sorry to just show up like this,' said Danny.

Rachel only sighed in a hushing, regretful way, pressing down on the formica she had picked. 'Adam will be back soon,' she said.

A tear oozed from Danny's left eye. Cara saw it. Ah, then Danny knew Adam might not be back soon. He was out on the road somewhere, walking away, not thinking of any of them. Cara knew he didn't think of them when he was gone. He had a smooth, untroubled mind, he liked ease and cheerful noise, and small things caught his attention: a woman walking away from church in a pair of very high heels, the line of people waiting for tables outside the Chinese restaurant, the body of a baby ibis beneath a palm tree, a man on his tiny balcony, three floors up, pouring coffee from a Turkish pot. And that would remind Adam he wanted coffee. So he would keep walking, looking for coffee, happy to be out of the house and on the move; he accepted every errand, he went cheerfully to buy fish and bags of ice, and he would take Cara or Cassidy with him if they wanted to come, he would take anyone who asked, but he didn't care if he was alone or not. He might introduce Cara as 'Cara mia' or, when she met his sister, only as Cara. He wasn't afraid of Rachel. He never hurried. He would take his time.

Occasionally a child would lift the heavy lid of the piano in the lounge room, consider the keys, and make an attempt at middle C; if Rachel heard, she'd cry out, 'Who's that? Who?' It was only to hear her call that any of them ever played. 'Who's that? Who? Who?' – like an owl. Today when middle C played Rachel only closed her eyes.

'It was Marcus-Sparkus,' announced Wallis.

There was a soft, upholstered punching sound, then a crying out. Wallis ran in on spinning feet.

'What are you savages doing in there?' said Rachel, wearily, as if somehow obliged, maybe because of Danny; Cara didn't know. Danny sent a fuzzy smile in Wally's direction. Proud, savage Wallis leaned against her mother.

'Marcus hit me,' she said.

Marcus sang, 'Dip dip dog shit! Up your arse with a piece of glass!' from the lounge room, wild with the strange visitor on a Sunday morning, brave and wild. Rachel stood and went in to him. Cara didn't call out a warning; he deserved it. You had to know Rachel might be ready for anger and equipped, this morning, with her hard, low, violent voice. You had to know you might be punished, even with a guest in the house – if weepy Danny counted as a guest. Still, Cara's chest ached when she heard Marcus crying, when he was banished to the garden and all the children with him, and no breakfast.

But Marcus, once outside, didn't care; or pretended not to. Wally and the others cared for only a little longer. They were hungry, but Adam might come home with a bag of bread rolls, the way he sometimes did on Sundays, and maybe a barbecue chicken or a cardboard tray of baklava. That would be breakfast. Cara ate buttery toast at the kitchen window and watched the young ones roll in the grass. Cass was pressed to the back fence, where the Jouberts lived; they were South African and Cass liked their daughter, who sunbathed on the back deck in a bikini. Cara rolled her sickened eyes. Look what happened when you liked someone's daughter: look at Danny, puffed at the table.

Having exiled the children, Rachel didn't return to the kitchen; she went into her room, closing the door behind her. Danny seemed surprised by this and looked to Cara for assistance, so Cara fussed with a little silver toast rack that had belonged to her grandmother. Her grandmother had been a sensible woman who liked objects designed for specific purposes. There were those little silver scissors on their velvet ribbon, designed for nothing but cutting flowers. Cara's grandmother must have stood in the garden with her scissors and observed the neighbourhood and noticed the Greeks moving in (Rachel said her mother was never happy about the Greeks moving in). But she liked furniture with multiple functions. You could lift the needlepoint lid of the piano seat and find sheet music: on top, *The Well-Tempered Clavier*. Cara thought of her grandmother as being well tempered. She died when Cara was seven. There had been a grandfather too, who lasted longer, but he only sat in the garden reading the paper and smoking; there was something wrong with his right leg and he couldn't speak without wheezing. All he cooked were blackened chops and baked beans from a tin, and he didn't count as an adult in the house at night – if Rachel was out you were scared lying in bed, even as he coughed in the lounge room. He died after Marcus was born. Then the house belonged to Rachel, and that meant Rachel had to live there all the time; no more India, no more Switzerland, no more going in and out at night. So she invited her friends home instead, nearly every night at first, and then, as she got older, as she 'settled down' (Cara used this phrase with her schoolfriends), only on Saturdays. There were plenty of rooms in the house, but the children filled them. When friends stayed over they slept on couches or the floor.

'You'll have to sleep on the couch,' Cara told Danny. She was protective of her private room.

'Will your mum let me stay?' Danny was braver now that Rachel wasn't there.

Cara shrugged, which meant yes. Why not? There were plenty of plates. There were already extra chairs at the table. Cara looked at Danny's stomach and knew she would give up her room. Just until the baby came.

'I have some money,' said Danny. 'For rent.'

And she began to cry again, so that Cara had no choice but to squat beside her chair, to hold her red hands and say, 'You sure you don't want some toast?'

Danny shook her head. 'It's just my mum,' she said. 'Should I tell her I'm safe?'

'Maybe,' said Cara. She was so exasperated by pink, dripping, pregnant Danny. 'The phone's on the piano.'

Danny, with some trouble, pulled herself out of the chair. She gave a little smile when this manoeuvre succeeded; then her face collapsed into tears and she said, 'I can't call while I'm like this.'

Cara shrugged. 'We'll be outside,' she said. She took a half-eaten bag of salt-and-vinegar chips into the garden.

The children – even Cass – crowded around her. Their salty hands plunged in and out of the bag. Cara held it higher than their heads and distributed the remaining chips more slowly; the children accepted this ceremony and waited with their hands outstretched. When they dispersed Cass took the empty bag, turned it inside out and licked it all over.

Cara lay in the grass. She noticed a fantastic, bell-like lift to the sky, a pealing quality to the light, and she peered into this high, rising brightness hoping she might burn her retinas, just a little – just enough to see something different when she looked out at the world. She drummed her heels into the ground. If I sleep here, she thought, the day will pass by, and no one will notice. It'll be like a fairytale. And like a fairytale, her belly swelled the way Danny's had; she felt it rise, a fat loaf, and she rubbed at it as if she were pregnant. Then she let out her breath and flattened again. She felt the way she did in bed at night with no one looking or asking questions or needing her. She lifted her arms over her head and expected Wally or Elsa to fall onto her legs, but they were waiting by the door for Danny to come out.

When Danny came, she was no longer crying. She was prettier. There was a gravity about her, a sense of permission, and she shone with some other thing, some sweet sadness. It was sticky, and the children stuck. She knelt down to them. She let them take her hand and lead her through the garden, and she knew how to part a curtain of leaves so that the space on the other side became important. Cara was scornful of this indulgence. She never played with the children. She was for climbing on, for comforting, for giving orders, for hiding behind; but Danny knew how to play.

Cara closed her eyes. She was in the Mediterranean. Adam was there with her in some hazy form. He wasn't a body, a lover, or even a ghost, but she could touch him and he belonged to her. There was something frightening about this belonging; it took on strange geometric shapes, so that she and Adam were only lines on a bell-shaped sea. But these lines fitted together. They were double, the two of them; they were like a solution written on clean paper. Cara's eyes had been closed for hours, she thought. Perhaps, if she opened them now, there would be nothing there. There would just be nothing.

She opened her eyes. The garden was there, and the washing on the line, and Danny with the children. Also Rachel, unexpectedly, lying on her kimono in the middle of the lawn.

She wore a green bikini and her stomach was flat and pale with little pleats of shiny pink. Her black hair funnelled into the grass. She was so white and red in the midday sun, and indestructible.

Cara made sure to raise her voice. 'I didn't know he had a sister,' she said.

Rachel said, 'He has three.' She shifted her hips. 'Three little sisters in a pretty little town.'

But none of this could be right – the sisters, the mother, the little town. Rachel formed Adam when she brought him to the house. She found him and formed him at the same time. The sisters and mother and the father who made him say 'Ah' didn't exist when he was with Cara and Rachel and the children, just as Cara and Rachel and the children didn't exist when he was with other people.

'She doesn't look like someone who'd run away from home. Or get pregnant,' said Cara.

'Anyone can get pregnant.'

'I can't.'

'Don't be so sure.'

'I don't have my period yet.'

'Lucky you,' said Rachel.

Cara closed her eyes again.

'What do you think they look like?' asked Rachel. 'People who run away?'

'I don't know,' said Cara. 'Like you.'

Rachel laughed. She lay on the grass in the garden she grew up in, surrounded by the children she had made, and raised one hand to her forehead to block the sun. Cara saw black stubble in the armpit and was disgusted and this disgust felt righteous; she pulled a handful of shiny grass and scattered it in the hope it would fly across to annoy her mother, and when it didn't she went inside and walked with purpose into Rachel's room. She stood for some time looking at the messed bed, as if it might relate in some way to what she had seen earlier: the clean white paper and she and Adam, solved. And it might have, in a minute, except that the doorbell rang again, not so insistently this time; Cara thought they might not have heard it in the garden.

Two men stood outside, fuzzed a little by the flyscreen. They had earnest expressions, they stood with their shoulders pushed back, and they seemed surprised to see her. Cara thought this must be some kind of church door-knocking thing. It was Sunday, after all: a day on which people might actually expect to be saved.

'Excuse me,' said the man closest to the door. He had the hopeful look of a visiting teacher. His lips were very wet in his brown beard. 'I'm looking for my daughter – Danielle.'

The word 'Danielle' prompted the man behind him to take a step forward. He was revealed, then, as a sweet-faced tattooed boy, red-haired, with a reef of acne scars on his lower jaw. His expression wasn't so much hopeful as pleading.

'Danny,' said the boy.

'Come in,' said Cara, and she even smiled, because they would take Danny away.

Both men wiped their feet before stepping through the door. They shuffled into the lounge room; the boy in particular looked

bereft, as if he were used to carrying large objects and was startled to find his hands empty. The father didn't seem the kind of
man to make you run away from home, though Cara recognised
in herself a tendency to be fooled by the kindliness of beards.
She wondered what would happen if she offered herself instead
of Danny. What would her life be like in the little town, with
the fairytale sisters?

'This way,' she said. She led them through the kitchen and
out into the garden, which she presented with a flourish: long
Rachel on the long grass, Adam's five shirts buoyant on the line,
Elsa naked as usual, Cass furtive at the Jouberts' fence, Wallis
running, Marcus clambering over Danny whose abdomen
seemed larger, more obscene among the passionfruit vine and
the rusted wheelbarrow and lidless washing machine, and all the
small grassy nests of cans and chocolate wrappers and junk mail
that gathered and grew. Everything in the garden was moving,
except for Rachel; but when Cara and the men came out onto
the grass all that movement stilled. Danny held Marcus tight
against one leg and touched her belly. She looked at the top of
Marcus's head but the way she looked at it was for the sad, red,
tattooed boy.

'Mum,' said Cara.

'Yes,' said Rachel, without opening her eyes.

'Mum.'

Rachel propped herself on her elbows, glorious in green,
almost naked. Marcus disentangled himself from Danny and
went to join the other children, who watched from the rim of
the garden with shut faces.

The man stepped forward. His shadow fell across Rachel's legs and she moved them.

'Sorry to bother you,' he said, but this seemed not to have been the way he wanted to begin, and he shook his head a little, as if clearing it. 'Greg Armstrong,' he said. 'And this is Jonathan.'

'Johnno,' said the boy.

Cara felt that more might be required. 'Danny's – you know – Johnno,' she said.

Johnno wiped his feet on the lawn and Rachel's head fell back as if in exhaustion. Her narrow neck seemed to spring out sunless from the grass.

'Adam's not here,' she said.

'I've come for my daughter,' said the man, his hands spread like a salesman. He looked at Danny and said, 'Danny,' and she kicked at the grass with one foot and didn't raise her eyes. 'Danielle,' he said. His voice was louder this time.

Rachel sighed and turned onto her stomach. Cara thought for a moment she might undo her bikini top and make them all endure her loose white breasts.

The man now gave off a beleaguered air. He was winding himself into complaint. He was lost in the garden, and frightened of Rachel; he might be the kind who felt most aggrieved when outmatched. Possibly he loved Danny and would be persistent in that love, although he had done something to make her leave home.

'Danny, come on now,' he said. 'You don't belong here.'

Danny moved closer to Rachel, as if for safety, and Cara saw that this was wise. Probably there was no safety at all in the garden, but if there were any, it would come from Rachel; she was its only possible source. In order to win, the man must make himself calm and purposeful, show no fear of Rachel's nakedness, take his daughter and run from the garden. Cara wanted to push him in the small of his back. She wanted to counsel him. She wanted to help Johnno too, because she liked the way the holes in his earlobes meant she could see through them to the other side.

But now Rachel was moving. She was pulling the kimono up from the grass. This seemed to give Danny courage. 'I'm staying here, Dad,' she said. 'With Adam.'

'Adam!' said the man. He spat it – *Adam*. Cara had never heard an 'Adam' like this. She stepped away from the man to further study his face, but it was hidden by beard and age and seemed ordinary enough, just a father's face. He wore pale jeans, loose at the knee, belted, with a tucked-in short-sleeved shirt. His back pocket bulged with wallet. He was the father of brown Adam, who went down the front path with his coins ringing loose. The man's ordinariness now seemed a great failure.

'I've had just about enough of this,' said Adam's father.

Rachel stood, wrapped in red.

'This is my house,' she said, with her most precise smile.

'No one's denying that.'

'And Danny is welcome here.'

'She belongs with her family.'

'Adam is her family,' said Rachel, so reasonably, thought Cara, with such settled purpose in her pale face. She wasn't arguing with the man, didn't care if he spoke again; she had made her decision and would now enforce it.

'Get the children inside,' said Rachel to Cara. Cara didn't move, but the children, even Cassidy, went into the house, where they let out a shout or two, and one high-pitched whistle.

'Danny,' said Rachel, and held out her hand. Danny took it.

'She's eight months pregnant,' said the man.

'Exactly,' said Rachel. She moved over the grass in her gold sandals, taking Danny with her. They were going to the house – inside – they were going to disappear inside the house, and Cara would go with them and leave the man and Johnno in the garden to huff and puff. But Johnno, with his tattoos and freckles, looked as if he would cry.

'You stupid bloody selfish child,' said the man, and Cara checked to see who he might be talking to. But he was looking at the sky, in the direction of the church's cross. It was hard to see in the daytime, but at night it lit up in neon blue. Cara drew a line between the top of the cross and Adam's father's face.

'Do you have any idea what you're doing to your mother?' he said. 'Tell her, Johnno.'

Johnno folded his arms over the top of his head. His body was inclined almost tidally toward the house. 'Sorry,' he said, and ran over the grass to Danny, who accepted him: she pressed her face, briefly, into his shoulder. Rachel opened the door to admit Danny and Johnno, and finally she turned to Cara. Cara stood too long, not moving, and Rachel closed the door.

The man dropped his head as Cara approached.

'She can sleep in my room,' she said.

The man swayed a little.

'And she won't like it here,' Cara said. 'She won't want to stay. Come around the side way.'

She led him past the faint blue penis and into the front garden. He knocked on one of the windows with his fist as he passed, but nothing happened.

'It's her funeral,' he said into his beard.

'She won't want to stay once she's had the baby.'

'The baby,' said the man – he spat it, the way he had *Adam*.

'And she's got Adam here.'

This made the man laugh. 'You know, he just went out one night. He said to his mother, "See you tomorrow." Next thing we know he's in Sydney. Not a word to us. Never came back.'

Cara nodded. She watched as the man got into a small grey car with awkward movements, as if he were dismantling himself in order to fit, and she watched as he drove away. Then she walked to the front door, rang the bell, and waited to be let in.

Adam wasn't home by dinnertime. He had never been gone this long before. Cara changed the sheets on her bed and took her school uniform and pyjamas out into the lounge room. She heated up meat pies and Johnno helped her by mashing potato. He was a serious boy who hardly spoke. He was the kind of boy who might go from door to door asking if he could clean people's gutters or mow their lawns, and when they said no he would thank them and walk away with his hands in his pockets. Rachel ate in her room, watching television. The children were in love with Danny, but she was less attentive to them now. She watched Johnno and held onto her belly. He liked to pull at her earlobes as he walked past her, and they went to bed early.

Cara had homework to do. She sat at the kitchen table while the children watched something on the lounge-room TV. Sunday nights always felt this way: subdued, companionless. But this evening was worse, with Adam gone all day. Nobody spoke to Rachel when she came out of her room. She went into the bathroom, ran a bath, and stayed there so long the children had to use the toilet in the laundry before they went to bed. Cara read in her history textbook about a foolish English king. She thought she heard Adam return, but it was someone else opening doors and walking the wooden floors of the house. Probably Rachel, finally finished in the bath.

Cara realised she had left her toothbrush in her bedroom. She kept it there because if left in the bathroom someone else would use it. She knocked quietly on the door, and when there was no answer, stepped with care into the room. Danny and Johnno were asleep on Cara's bed. Johnno was bent around Danny's belly with an arm under hers as if it might be the only thing keeping him from rolling off. The bed had never been so full. The quilts twisted at their feet. They were close to naked: Johnno wore underpants, and Danny wore a long thin singlet that rose above her bump. They were both asleep with their mouths open, with formless faces and loose hands, so pink in the blue streetlight, so bundled, that Cara was embarrassed for them, but also fascinated by the ease of their limbs, by the damp fan of Danny's hair across the boy's shoulder, by all the ways their soft, sweet bodies rose and fell and fitted together. It was as if a curtain had been pulled away, some heavy velvet churchy curtain, and behind it were these two humans, who suddenly seemed so young to Cara – younger than she was, children really, sleeping around the child they had made. The curtain should be allowed to fall again. Cara looked and breathed and felt that she knew nothing at all about love, or fright, or whatever it was that held them there, tangled on the bed; she was meek and deferential before them, and aware for the first time of the shapelessness of her longing, how wide and open it was, how enormous in her body and in the world.

Cara found her toothbrush. Neither lover stirred.

She opened the bathroom door onto a hot puff of steam. Rachel rose up out of the bath, out of all that thick greenish water. Her kimono lay just out of reach, draped over the toilet; the bird of paradise was trailing on the hairy floor. The hair on her head wasn't fully wet, but it pressed to her cheeks in damp curls, and hair erupted, too, from between her legs. Her thighs were brown and ribbed, and at the very top of her arms there was an unexpected slackening.

'Sorry, Mum, sorry,' Cara said, trying to pull the door closed, but it stuck on the tiles and would leave the smudge Rachel hated. All this time, while Cara tugged the door and the steam came out, exploratory, into the hallway, Rachel stood and stared. She squinted. She wasn't wearing her contact lenses.

'Leave it,' she said, and Cara backed away as Rachel stepped from the bath; there was that particular pour of water back into the bulk of itself, all the amplified tides of a bathtub. 'Come in.'

Cara came in and shut the door behind her. It swung easily when the tiles released it.

Rachel lifted the kimono, flashing red and yellow, and wrapped herself in it. The wet showed through in places. She had been in the bath so long her feet were baby-white. Cara began to brush her teeth.

'Is it midnight yet?' asked Rachel. She blew on the mirror to clear the steam and rubbed it with her towel.

'Nearly.' Cara's pyjamas were too thick for the heated room. Sweat prickled in the roots of her hair.

'Gone all day,' said Rachel, with a funny laugh, and she turned to Cara with her hands spread out, with a smile on her face, and said, 'What would you do, Cara? What would Cara do?' She couldn't say 'Help me' but she could smile like that, she could spread her hands, she could stand in the dripping bath-room and look the way a plaster saint looks, asking God for something.

Cara, rinsing her minty mouth, shrugged. She knew what she would do: lock and bolt the doors. Turn out the lights and plant thick trees. She would booby-trap the front gate and line the path with knives. Oh, but who would watch him when he smoked and that little muscle tightened in his jaw? Someone else would watch him. Some other girl.

But Rachel was waiting for an answer.

Cara spat into the sink. 'He's your boyfriend,' she said, and went to the lounge room to set up her bed. She closed her eyes tight when her mother passed through the room. She thought, I'll stay awake until I hear him. I'll sit up in bed – I'll call out his name, so he isn't frightened – and tell him everything that's happened. That way he'll be prepared to face her. She heard footsteps in the street she knew weren't his. Cara slept.

She woke to the noise of a person in the lounge room. It was Rachel, standing long and white above the makeshift bed.

'Come and sleep in with me,' she said.

Cara obeyed at once. She was half asleep, she was dreaming, she would remember every minute of this night. She followed her mother into the bedroom, where the yellow curtains were open and a bluish light fell onto the floor. Cara knew it was a streetlight, but chose to think of it as the light from the neon cross on top of the church. Rachel wrapped herself in all the blankets, so Cara lay down on top of the sheets on Adam's side of the bed. She slept again, and when she woke it was because her mother was sitting up and squinting at the time on her phone.

'Three twenty-four,' she said; evidently she knew Cara was awake.

Cara was cold. He'd told his mother he'd be back in the morning.

Rachel laughed, her low, sophisticated laugh, which was mirthless. 'And now I can't sleep with you in the bed.'

'I'll go back out,' said Cara, but soggily.

'No, sweetie,' said Rachel. 'I'll go out. I can't sleep anyway. I'll read or something.'

Cara could have reached out one arm – she almost did – and held fast to her mother's hair or her T-shirt. She could have kept her there, in the bed; she could have talked her to sleep, or brought her tea, or said she didn't mind a light on. But she had never been more leaden with sleep. *Sweetie.* That was an unfamiliar lullaby word. Cara tucked her knees to her chest. Then Rachel went, she was a gleam in the door and a shuffle in the lounge room, and Cara, guilty, rolled onto the other side of the bed, which smelt of her mother: that salty smoky perfume she wore, and a deeper note which Cara always thought of as a kind of fuzz, like the fuzz on a peach. She slept again, but woke as soon as Adam came. He came in the blue light from the window; he came in the solitary creak of a floorboard by the door. He blundered, but quietly. He pulled off his shirt and loomed up over the bed. His eyes were white, and his long loving throat, and his hands reached across the sheets to find her. To find Rachel. He buried his head in Cara's middle.

'I'm sorry,' he said with his boozy breath, 'I'm sorry, I love you, I'm sorry,' and Cara held his brittle hair, she let him kiss her stomach, she breathed up and down as he kissed her. 'I love you, I'm sorry. Please don't be angry, please, please,' he begged, and Cara felt for a moment the great holy fury of her mother, the height she stood upon, how easily she was disappointed, how much she was called to forgive, and how she must be spared the noise of life, and left alone, and how she must be loved. The blue light buzzed at the window. Cara felt how still she was compared to all the living heat of Adam, his warm head and hands at her waist. His face was wet; he was crying, but as if he didn't know it. He was also falling away into sleep, or a version of it in which he might lie forever with his heavy head on her stomach. She could let him do that. She could also wake him. She knew where to touch and what to say. It was dark enough, and he was drunk enough, and the morning was very far away.

In the bed, in the streetlight, Adam's golden skin was blue. He looked like Krishna. There was a picture of Krishna in the bathroom; he looked like that.

Cara breathed deeply to feel his head rise up, then pushed it off. She rolled out of bed and went to the lounge room, where her mother lay sleeping. Rachel wasn't a messy sleeper like Danny and the boy. She was laid out, white and black, with her red mouth shut. Cara had to touch her twice before she woke.

'He's back,' said Cara.

Rachel rose from the couch without speaking, went into the bedroom and closed the door. Cara listened, but could hear only the recycling truck, three streets away, lifting and pouring quantities of glass. Greek glass, she thought. It was nearly morning.

At breakfast, the children fussed and shouted when they heard Adam was home. They had to be reminded there were guests still sleeping. They dressed reluctantly for school. Cara bossed them into their uniforms, combed their hair, folded sandwiches into their schoolbags and into her own. They were ready to leave in a little flock when Rachel came out of her bedroom in her working clothes. She wore her hair up so her neck showed long and white and she smiled and laughed. She touched the children's heads and straightened their collars. Starting with Cara, she kissed each child in turn, and their kisses came like wicks from their dry lips.

Buttony

The children wanted to play Buttony.

'All right,' said Miss Lewis, and she clapped her hands five times in the rhythm that meant they must be quiet and copy her. They were quiet and copied her.

'All right,' she said with that smile she reserved for the sleepy, silly midafternoon. 'We'll play. Joseph, get the Button.'

The children approved the justice of this appointment; that was apparent from the small, satisfied sigh they made together. They watched Joseph walk to Miss Lewis's desk. Joseph was a compact, deliberate boy, and his straight black hair fell to his

shoulders. He wore his uniform in a way that seemed gen-
tlemanly, but at the same time casual. He was both kind and
beautiful, and they loved him.

The Button lay in a special tin in the right-hand corner of
Miss Lewis's top drawer. The children listened for the sound
this drawer made as Joseph opened it. They knew the shifting sound of that opening drawer meant largesse – gold stars
or stamps or, in exceptional cases, jelly frogs – and that Miss
Lewis's bounty was capable of falling upon them all, but perhaps more often on Joseph. Alternatively, the opening drawer
meant Buttony.

All the children handled the Button with reverence, but
none more so than Joseph. He was gifted in solemnity. He had
a processional walk and moved his head slowly when his name
was called – and it was regularly called. His attention was made
more valuable by its purposeful quality. He never leant in confi-
dentially to hear a secret; the other children came to his ear and
whispered there. Miss Lewis liked to call on him in class just to
see his measured face rise up out of that extraordinary hair. His
beauty startled her, until she met both parents – Vietnamese
mother, Polish father. Then he made lovely sense. When he held
the yellow Button out before him in the dish of his hands, Miss
Lewis was capable of forgetting the mustard-coloured cardi-
gan it had fallen off one winter's day. The Button was no longer
limited by its cheap yellow plastic; it seemed to pulse with life.
The children looked at it, and at Joseph, without appearing to
breathe. Miss Lewis wanted her children to live in a heightened
way, and she encouraged this sort of ceremony.

'Close the drawer, Joseph,' she said, because she found she liked nothing better, after admiring him, after giving him the opportunity to be admired, than to gently suggest a mundane task. Miss Lewis could close that drawer with her hip. Joseph used a shoulder. The sound of the closing drawer released the children. Now they hurried to line up at the door.

They always played Buttony outside.

'Quietly, quietly!' Miss Lewis scolded, brushing the tops of their heads as they filed past her into the corridor, led by Joseph and the Button. She followed them out. In the next-door classroom, 3A recited times tables under the priestly monotone of Mr Graham. One side of the corridor shone with 5B's scaled depiction of the solar system. The children claimed to like blue Saturn best, with its luminous rings, but Miss Lewis was fond of Neptune. She always put out a finger to touch its smooth crayon as she passed.

They gathered under the jacaranda tree. The day was sweet and green. Miss Lewis leant against the tree and crossed one ankle over the other. Her ankles were still slim; she wasn't so very old. The children formed a circle around Joseph, and there was something very natural about this, about Joseph being in the middle of a circle. Grave Joseph. He stood with the Button as if at some kind of memorial service. Then he raised it to his lips and kissed it. No one had ever kissed the Button before, and some of the children raised their own fingers to their lips. Miss Lewis pursed her mouth. One boy – she didn't see who – let out a brief scoff, but was ignored.

'Put out your hands,' said Miss Lewis, and the children

lifted their cupped hands.

'Close your eyes,' said Miss Lewis, closing her own eyes. She was often so tired, in the midafternoon, that this handful of seconds in which to close her eyes seemed the true blessing of Buttony. To stand under the jacaranda tree in the bright day and make darkness fall, and then to hear Joseph's voice. His eyes were open, of course. He made his way around the circle, and as he touched each set of hands he said, 'Buttony.'

Buttony, Buttony, twenty-one times. Miss Lewis counted them out, and when he was finished – all twenty-one pairs of hands, because none of her children were absent that day, no one was sick or pretending to be – she opened her eyes. The children stood motionless in the circle, and now their hands were closed, each set folded over themselves, possibly holding the Button. Joseph returned to the middle of the circle. He looked up at Miss Lewis and she looked at him and it was as if, from inside that hair, he were acknowledging sorrow and solitude and fatigue; also routine and expectation and quietness. And, because he was only a boy, trust. Miss Lewis nodded her head, and Joseph nodded back.

'Open your eyes,' said Miss Lewis. She loved to see her children open their eyes all at once. They always smiled, as if relieved to see the sun on the other side of their eyelids. They giggled and pressed their hands together, and looked at each other's hands, and looked at Joseph, and wondered who now had the Button. Oh, that beautiful Button: mustard-coloured, Joseph-kissed. Round as a planet on one side, sharp as a kiss on the other. Joseph stood with his hands behind his back. His hair hung over his eyes. It was hard to puzzle Joseph out in Buttony. The children delayed for a fond moment, as if wanting to leave him alone with his secret a little longer. Miss Lewis surveyed the circle to see who was blushing, who was still smiling, whose head was raised higher than usual, just because Joseph had favoured them with the Button. And she also looked for the disconsolate signs of a child who was clearly buttonless.

'You start, Miranda,' said Miss Lewis.

Miranda rubbed her right ear against her right shoulder. She swayed on one leg.

'Xin,' she said. Xin produced a goofy smile. Then she opened out her hands: there was no Button there.

'Blake,' said Xin. Blake grinned and threw his empty hands over his head.

Blake said Miranda. Miranda said Josie. Josie said Osea. Osea said Ramon. Miss Lewis closed her eyes. She opened them again and thought, Jyoti. It took eleven more children to guess Jyoti. She was one of those girls you didn't suspect. Her socks slipped. She had a mole on her left cheek. It was like Joseph to have picked Jyoti. It was like Jyoti to stand burning invisibly in the circle, hardly able to believe her luck. Her hands unfolded and there was the Button. The other children craned to look. For a moment they loved her. For a moment she held Joseph's kiss in her hands. She stepped into the middle of the circle and Joseph took her place. She raised the Button to her lips, but didn't kiss it.

'Hands out, eyes closed,' said Miss Lewis, and darkness fell. 'Don't forget, Jyoti, no giving the Button to the person who was just It. Don't give the Button to Joseph.'

It was necessary to remind the children of this rule at the beginning of every game; otherwise they were capable of handing the Button over to Joseph at any opportunity. As it was, Jyoti picked Archie and Archie picked Joseph. Joseph picked Mimi who picked Miranda who picked Joseph. The afternoon grew brighter. Planes flew overhead in all directions. The jacaranda dropped its spring flowers. Every now and then Miss Lewis saw faces at the windows of classrooms, as other children looked out to see them playing Buttony. How long had they been playing now? These children could spend the whole afternoon hoping to be chosen by Joseph. They would never tire of it.

Joseph picked Ruby picked Ramon picked Joseph picked Liam S picked Liam M picked Joseph. Joseph said, Buttony, Buttony, Buttony, twenty-one times. Miss Lewis closed her eyes and kept them closed when she said, 'Open your eyes.' The children, in turn, said, Buttony, Buttony, Buttony. She uncrossed her ankles and crossed them again and thought, Every day could pass like this, quite easily. Every day could be sweet and green with the jacaranda and the children and the sun and the planes. And then at the end of them all, the sweet days and the children, Would you open your eyes? Would your hands fall open? Would they be empty?

Miss Lewis looked. Joseph stood in the circle.

'Hands out, close your eyes,' she said, and the children obeyed. They bent their heads as if praying. She was moved by the tenderness she saw fall on each of them. They were like children in a fairytale, under a spell. She looked at Joseph and he was watching her, so she nodded at him. His face was impassive. He made her think of a Swiss guard at the Vatican. He received her nod by beginning to walk around the circle, and each hand he touched trembled, and every child lowered their head still further as he passed them. Their hands closed like sea anemones. Joseph hadn't yet given away the Button. Fifteen, nineteen, twenty-one times he said Buttony. Then he raised his neutral face and looked at Miss Lewis and opened his mouth and placed the Button inside it. The Button made no indentation in his cheek. Miss Lewis crossed her arms. You will solve this, she thought, and suffer for it. Joseph blinked inside his hair.

'Open your eyes,' said Miss Lewis. The children lifted their heads into the burden of their love for Joseph. They smiled and squirmed and began to guess: Phoebe, Ruby, Usha, Archie, Blake. Joseph turned toward every name as it was called, as if waiting to see who might produce the Button. Liam S, Bella, Jackson, Xin. Twenty names, and twenty hands falling open. Only Jyoti remained. She stood with her rigid hands, with her desperate smile, with her socks slipping. No one wanted to say her name. They wanted her to give herself up. Miss Lewis, too, wanted Jyoti to give herself up. Eventually Ramon said, 'Jyoti.'

Jyoti opened her empty hands.

The circle laughed. Miss Lewis had found that children, as a rule, didn't like practical jokes. There was a certain kind of laughter that, in children, was a howl. Ramon took Jyoti's wrists and inspected her hands. No one looked at Joseph but they all saw Jyoti: the mole on her cheek, the dusty mark where she'd rubbed her shin with the heel of her shoe, the crookedness of her teeth. Jyoti might have been crying. Ramon threw her wrists down as if discarding them. Then every child save Joseph and Jyoti began to cry out, just as they'd done when they wanted to play Buttony. They stamped their feet and kicked at the grass. They shook their uniforms and looked up into the branches of the jacaranda tree, as if they might find the Button in these places. Their circle broke open as they shook and kicked and shouted, and faces appeared again in classroom windows.

Miss Lewis watched Joseph stand there with his mouth closed and his hands behind his back. Although the circle had broken, he still seemed to be in the middle of it. He was only a boy and he was alone and proud and terrible. Miss Lewis stepped away from the tree. She would order him to open his mouth and spit out the Button. She would make him say what he had done, how he had stood and watched the children guess; she would shame him, and the faces in the windows would see it.

But first she should settle the children. She clapped her hands five times in the rhythm that meant they must be quiet and copy her. They were quiet, but they didn't copy her. She saw the way they looked at her; she saw their fury. Ramon came first, to pull at her pockets. Then Josie, who had lost a tooth that morning; her mouth was open as she searched the grass at Miss Lewis's feet. Osea and Mimi scratched at the scabbed bark of the tree. Miss Lewis swatted and slapped, but the children still came. They opened her hands and dug in her elbows. Liam S squatted to peer up her skirt, and when she crouched to stop him it was Jyoti who pulled the pins from her hair, as if the Button might be hidden in its roots. Now Miss Lewis cried out. She lifted her head and saw Mr Graham running from the 3A classroom. And Joseph was behind him, not quite running, not altogether, but like a shadow, long and blank and beautiful.

Good News for
Modern Man

When I began my study of the colossal squid, I still believed in
God. The squid seemed to me then, in those God days, to be
the secretly swimming proof of a vast maker who had bestowed
intelligence – surprisingly, here and there – on both man and
mollusc. I've discussed this with Charles Darwin, who visits me
most days, always a little out of breath. His cheeks are red, his
hair white. He looks nothing like a ghost. He puts his feet up
on the rocks and gazes out over this small corner of the Pacific,
calm at sundown and partially obscured by a mosquito haze.
We sit above the tree line and consider the movements of the

colossal squid in her bay below. She moves this way and that; she floats and billows in the tide. She reminds me of my mother's underwear soaking in a holiday basin. Her official name, her name in polite company, is *Mesonychoteuthis hamiltoni*. We've named her Mabel and together we plan to free her.

It's no easy thing, this freeing of a colossal squid. It was difficult enough to imprison her in the first place. There is the issue of her size.

'A colossal squid,' I tell Darwin, 'makes a giant squid look like a bath toy.'

He agrees with me, although as far as I know he has never seen either a bath toy or a giant squid. He remains surprisingly unexcited by my account of Mabel's capture: the months-long hunt with smaller squid for bait, the boredom and fussy seasickness, Mabel emerging from the sea with her hood pink in the sudden sun. She flailed at the surface, she swam and sounded, smelling as much like the sea as anything I have ever smelled. But we hooked her, and we panicked her, and she raced ahead of us, right into this bay, through a narrow channel that we were able to block. And now she spends her days here, rotating among her many arms, and I spend my days watching her. They're going to build her a facility, but first there's money to raise and laws to change. For now it's just the two of us – and Darwin.

Darwin first appeared on my 402nd day on the island. We often argue, but in a neutral, brotherly sort of way, and I appreciate his company. The sun sinks into the sea, but we also see it rise from the sea. This makes the world seem very small, even though we're two hours from any town. There's a Catholic school higher up the mountain and we see the girls walk down to the water and back up again. I hear their singing in the early morning and it surprises me; at sundown it makes me sad. Late in the afternoons they swim in the white sea – far out into the lagoon, where I often see bullet-shaped sharks. Darwin and I take turns peering through my binoculars. It's an innocent and companionable lechery. Although he's a ghost, he leaves sweat around the eyepieces.

I've been thinking for some time of taking one of the monthly supply boats back to New Zealand, then a plane home. At home the rain will be cold, pigeons will grow fat, there will be supermarkets. I've refused replacements and talked up the malarial solitude and now no one will come, not even over-eager graduate students with an itching for the Pacific. But this is my 498th day on the island, and lately I'm troubled by headaches and abrupt changes in temperature. There's something fever-ish about this air. It's not only the headaches, although they're bad enough; my major symptom is a kind of vertigo, a frequent and sudden awareness that the universe is expanding out from me. This feeling begins with my feet, as if the ground – the planet – the galaxy – has suddenly dropped away from them and I'm floating untethered in space, only space doesn't exist, and neither does my body. I can only describe the sensation as the suspension of nothing in nothing. But I look down and there are my feet, dirt-brown, and there are Darwin's, sensibly shod. Below our feet swims Mabel. It's only while watching Mabel that I feel tied to the earth once more and a sense of order is restored. Still, that moment of vertigo is briefly and terrifyingly glorious. It reminds me of the way, when I was younger, I used to feel my body respond to the singing of hymns: an interior fire, a constriction of the heart that I took for a visitation of the Holy Spirit. I never mentioned this sensation to anyone. Maybe other people feel it. Perhaps the schoolgirls on the mountain feel it, singing in their concrete church: the large feeling of singing toward something that sings back. I often wondered if sex felt that way, undernourished adolescent that I was. And now – the quiet sky, the patient waiting, the tick of time in the bones, until the world rushes out and the vanishing of the cosmos presents itself again, magnificent.

I've told Darwin of my troubles (he suspects malaria, which is possible; I stopped taking my meds on day 300, partly because of the dreams they gave me, bright crystal dreams of exhausting flight). Sitting here, atop our hot rock, we might be the last two survivors of the flood, chosen by Noah: a pair of scientists, two by two. But the ark broke up somewhere along the Line and left us stranded with a squid for company. Darwin regards me sadly when I say this, stroking his diluvian chin.

'Geology,' he says, 'disproves you.'

'I know,' I tell him. 'It's a joke.'

I live in an astronomical observation station owned and, until recently, forgotten by the New Zealand government. It's part way up the mountain, and I can walk down to the sea in thirteen minutes. Paths have been cut into the rock, as if this were a holiday beach frequented by sure-footed children, but it's still a relief to step out onto the sand from the mountain path, to see the sea spread wide and to my left the smaller inlet that is Mabel's temporary home. The clear water is deeper than it looks from above. When I say the water in Mabel's bay is clear, I don't mean it's transparent, but that it's see-throughable, and Mabel is see-able there at the bottom. I feed her fish thawed from a deep freeze, or freshly caught if I'm in the mood, and these she grasps at the end of her tentacles and rolls up toward her beaked mouth. The coral sand is sharp and clean and my feet never feel dirty. When Darwin accompanies me (which he usually does on those days I'm feeling my worst) he only removes his shoes to wade into the shallows, and then his feet are the delicate brown and blue and yellow of Galápagos finches.

The view of Mabel from the shore is more intimate than the bird's-eye view from my station fifteen metres above. It's impossible to take in her vastness or the pattern of her tentacles and arms, so it's her eyes that fascinate me. They interest Darwin as well. They're hard to avoid. Mabel has the largest eye in creation, and it looks like ours, although its structure is entirely different. This humanoid appearance far out on the lone branch of invertebrate evolution gave scientists pause, at one time; they paused over Darwin and his theory of natural selection. The eye of the squid once gave my friend a great deal of trouble. Now he and I stand on the shore and consider the vertebrate appearance of Mabel's canny eye. It looks so very God-given. Difficult to assume that such an eye doesn't think, or ponder, or dream.

I think about squid too much, Darwin cautions me.

'A squid is not a human,' he says.

'A human is just another animal,' I say.

'Oh no,' says Darwin. 'The highest of the animals.'

'Careful,' I tell him.

We argue about this – the concept of progress, the tricky politics of supposing one thing higher than another. He's impatient with the twentieth century on this point. He doesn't seem to have noticed the twenty-first has begun, and I don't tell him. I do tell him that whenever I spend an extended length of time with Mabel, peering into her large eye from the rocks on the shore, I find myself shaking off the feeling that there's a person inside her, watching me. Darwin mocks this as sentimental. He says this sensation is so typical as to be 'fatally unfresh'. I suppose my desire to free Mabel is similarly unfresh. But there are no fresh desires.

Today I feel very well. I feel an immense good health. Today I feel with great certainty my precise location upon the earth, the latitude and longitude, the position of the sun. This is important, because today we free Mabel. The date is September 23rd, but that's elsewhere. Here on this island we've dropped out of time, although once, I believe, the island was within time: when it was first created, it was a definite volcanic event. Then the rock subsided, the sea settled, the coral multiplied, and the powerful boats of the islanders came. Whalers and traders, adventurers, missionaries, and gentleman naturalists endlessly agog at the taxonomic world. Mabel's arrival might qualify as an occasion, a specific point on a timeline, except that the strangest of sea creatures must come butting up against this place in secret, yesterday and today and tomorrow, and usually there's no one here to care or notice. No, the real things of the world take place elsewhere. And yet today will be an eventful day, and yesterday was too. So these are the end times.

Yesterday I visited the Catholic school. I have an arrangement with the school: I go there once a month and am driven into town by the school's driver. We travel in a primordial jeep. In town, I pick up the supplies shipped in by my research group and send my month's data home; then we drive back to the school. It's a suitable arrangement for everyone, worked out in the distant days in which I was apparently capable of dreaming up such things: the school, which seems to exist in a state of immaculate fundlessness, gets some of my grant money, and I don't have to go to the trouble of maintaining a vehicle. I order in treats for the schoolgirls: lollies and biscuits, novelty erasers, books. These I pass on to the head of the school, Father Anthony, who always wants me to come to his office for a chat; I always refuse him. Every month I anticipate these trips with an obscure dread.

For the past few months, Father Anthony has been inviting me to address his students on the subject of marine life. I declined at first. It felt false to arrive at the school and pose as an expert when a) I no longer believe in God, and b) to this date my most significant contribution to the science of the squid is the observation that male colossal squid probably do have a penis. I discussed my qualms with Darwin and he rejected them immediately. First of all, he said, I am a scientist, and these priests and nuns and children are not. They don't know how many papers I haven't had in *Nature*. Second, I've been invited to speak on marine, not heavenly, life, so my lack of faith shouldn't interfere. And third, I have a problem that I need help with: namely, freeing Mabel. It was Darwin's suggestion that the school may be able to provide this help. He has a tactical mind.

I delivered my talk yesterday, after my usual visit to town in the jeep. The driver of the jeep, Eric, is a sinewy man of tremendous energy. I understand that he does various kinds of physical work for the school: gardening and maintenance as well as driving. When he talks, which is rarely, it's mostly about the branch of his family who moved to America long ago and are thriving there as if having discovered a taproot from which they were once dramatically severed. Eric speaks of America with an ancient nostalgia, but refuses to go because he was born on this island and his elderly father lives here. His energy is badly placed behind the wheel of a car. He sits in tense nearsightedness, coiled, attentive, as if he's offended by the stillness required in order to travel so far so quickly. The roads are covered at all times in blotchy fruits that, when crushed, spill out slippery seeds. Apparently, the animal that would once have eaten them – a large bird with a frighteningly hooked claw – is so near extinction it now trembles with evolutionary neurosis in the quietest corners of the forest, eating less perilous fruits. These are the roads we take – viscous, birdless – into town. Town: one store and five drinking establishments. When the supply ship docks, the entire place seems to double in size. I like arriving with Eric. He knows everyone, and with him I'm greeted like a brother. Without him I appear to go unnoticed, which I know is not the case.

Yesterday, everything was quite normal – my crates were

stacked on the dock, already clear of 'Customs' – except for the presence of five white women, all young and dressed in T-shirts and baseball caps. They sat together on benches by the dock, fanning themselves with the necks of their shirts and glowing with satisfaction at their evident discomfort. The girls rested their heads on each other's shoulders and took self-portraits with their mobile phones, and no one paid them any attention. They looked to have been sitting there for some time.

'Who are they?' I asked Eric.

'Students,' he said.

'Students? Where from?'

'Who knows?'

'Someone must know!' I said. 'What are they doing here?'

'They're waiting for someone to drive them.'

'To drive them where?'

'Around.'

After our errands we went to a bar, where we found the young men who clearly accompanied the girls outside. They were discussing this question of a driver with the patrons. Their American voices and emphatic gestures lacked economy in the midmorning heat. Eric expressed no interest in interacting with the visitors, so I lost interest in them too. All kinds of people come through this place, just as I've done. They're none of my business. We drank, we drove the slippery roads, and Eric delivered me back to the school in time for my presentation.

This is how I prefer to remember all my contacts with civilisation: as briefly as possible.

Fans revolved idly in the school's lobby. A row of African

violets butted up against each window, brown in the heat, and a small table was stacked with copies of a pamphlet called 'Good News for Modern Man'. I read it while I waited for Father Anthony, and it reminded me of the Church I grew up in: the primary colours and cheerful messages, the merry Heaven and blotty, yellow Hell. 'For God so loved the world,' it told me in a bright, responsible voice. I felt a small nostalgia. I had one of my headaches and all the angles of the world seemed wrong.

'Dr Birch!' cried Father Anthony, arriving. Father Anthony seems always to be arriving: there is a perpetual commotion about him. I've also never met a pinker man in all my life. His face is rose and his ears are salmon. His neck folds into itself like certain kinds of coral. His hands sprout from the ends of his arms anemone-like and gloved in pink.

'Dr Birch!' he cried again.

'Call me Bill.'

'Bill, Bill,' he said with delight, shaking my brown hand with his pink one. His was smooth and cool; mine was damp. Father Anthony has a gift for the comfortable use of names. He dispenses them like small gifts, as if they've been prepared lovingly in advance. I can imagine it – this small recognition – feeling large enough to turn a soul back to God. I believe that Father Anthony's God is an old friend to him, gracious and prudent, with a priest's sympathy, a compassionate memory, and a steady heart for his flock's misgivings and undoings and hurts.

'This way, Bill, this way,' said Father Anthony, ushering me along with his hands. I wonder if, like certain corals, they glow all the pinker in the dark. 'We're proud to welcome you. The sisters are very excited, as are our students. This is quite a treat. What a treat. We have so few visitors. The bishop once – what an occasion. This is in my lifetime. Well, my tenure here – a life-time in itself. Ha, ha! This way, this way.'

He escorted me into a small, overcrowded hall in which nuns quieted students and drew blinds over windows. They went about their tasks with a sensible bustle I found intimidating.

Father Anthony introduced me as Dr William Birch, emi-nent marine biologist. I introduced myself as Bill Birch, malacologist.

'A malacologist,' I explained, 'is a scientist who studies molluscs.'

It occurred to me for the first time that this title of mine is extremely ominous, belonging as it does to the list of dis-tasteful words beginning with 'mal': malcontent, maladjusted, malformed, malicious. I wanted to explain that until my passion for the colossal squid blotted out my love for all other marine organisms I was a conchologist, which sounds much safer. More avuncular, sort of bumbling. Instead I loomed above them, mal-acologist, and ordered the lights out.

The students watched my slideshow presentation raptur-ously in the semi-dark. Their crowded bodies gave out a smell of warmed fruit about to spoil. It seemed to me as if their hair were filling up the room and muffling my voice, and when I felt prickles of fever up my legs and sweat behind my knees, I couldn't be sure of the cause – sickness, or girls?

A tiger shark swam across the screen. The girls all breathed together, softly, 'Shark.' An anemone appeared, and they sang

together, 'Anemone.' 'Starfish,' they sighed, and 'Seahorse,' 'Eel.'
I showed them a beach camouflaged by thousands of newly
hatched turtles and they inhaled collectively (we slow-breeding
humans are always astonished by the extravagance with which
sea creatures, seasonally awash in salt and sperm, reproduce
themselves). I showed a photograph of myself in the observation station, taken by my departing colleagues. I paused on this
photograph for too long because I was struck by the plump
health of my former self, with his light tan and professional-
ism (he stands in the station doorway in prudent boots and his
posture is in no way diminished by the tropical mountain rising above him). Then I showed pictures of Mabel in her bay and
the students giggled. They know Mabel, although we have taken
care not to publicise her. They know I'm the man who watches
Mabel in the long afternoons and then watches them with his
long binoculars. They laughed at her, friendly, and they laughed
at me.

'Thanks to the wonders of technology,' said Father Anthony,
'you have shown us the goodness of creation.'

The students can walk for minutes through the goodness of
creation to see firsthand, in the blood-temperature sea, the same
wonders I had just displayed. Since leaving the school I've found
myself repeating the girls' breathless catalogue: shark, anemone,
starfish, seahorse, eel. A children's book of the sea. And I think
of the waste involved, the sea full of death and the dying: all
of creation's necessary hunters fanning out among the reefs and
rocks and sunken ships, all of them hungry and if not hungry,
dead. What if I'd discussed this in my talk? A Lecture on the

Origin of Species? But Father Anthony seems a sensible man. Perhaps the students are taught evolution. I suspect we think similarly, all of us who were trapped yesterday in that hot room: we're worried, daily, by the vast number of unredeemed things in the world.

Father Anthony took me to his study after my presentation. A white room with a view of jungle trees, and above the window, an ivory Christ on an ebony cross. Sun-faded copies of 'Good News for Modern Man' filled a low bookshelf. The sun ages everything so quickly that they might have come in on last month's supply ship. Even Darwin looks a little more worn around the edges than when he arrived a few months ago, glumly agnostic. Only the thirsty trees seem to resist the sun, growing greener by the day, sweating out a greenness that hurts my eyes and forces me to keep them trained on the sea. The mosquitoes, also, seem unaffected, but I suppose they hide from the sun in the daytime.

'May I ask you a question?' said Father Anthony.

'Of course,' I said.

'Are you a man of faith, Bill?'

'That seems like the kind of thing you'd ask before letting me get up there in front of your girls.'

'Our students are not necessarily young women of faith, Bill. And we would never keep you away from them on the basis of your beliefs.'

This implied – I was sure of it – that Father Anthony had considered keeping me away from them on some other basis.

'Well, I'm not a man of faith,' I said. 'No, I'm not.'

And because this seemed so definitive – because this was the first time I had said anything like it aloud to a living man – I wanted to qualify it. I said, 'I used to believe, you know. God, the maker of Heaven and Earth, Jesus Christ, conceived by the Holy Spirit. The third day he rose again from the dead. You know, all that. The Church of England.'

'But not any more?'

'Not any more,' I said. 'So I suppose that means I'm going to hell.'

And I regretted this immediately; it was such an amateur thing to say. But my head was bad and I was worried I might have an attack – a vertigo attack – right there in his office.

'God knows your heart better than I do,' said Father Anthony. 'I thought you might be a believer because in your lecture you said the way a squid eats is like a camel passing through the eye of a needle. Ha, ha! I found that very funny. It's rare these days to come across a good biblical joke. Can I order you some tea?'

Father Anthony is a kind and good-natured man, one of those beaming, healthful men who truly believe drinking a hot liquid in insufferable heat will cool you down, and my heart went out to him – broke for him, really – and I loved my fellow men and wanted to sail home to them instantly. I wanted to have sailed already. And why hadn't I? Mabel, I suppose, whom only I could save. I was also embarrassed at having said so much. I was talkative in my guilt and sorrow, and would admit to anything.

'No tea, no thanks,' I said. 'Sorry.'

'If you don't mind, I'll have some. 'A "spot of tea", yes? I'll ring the bell. Something cool for you, perhaps, Bill?'

His hand was poised in midair, holding a small silver bell. Did I mention we were both sitting, him behind his desk, and me in front of it? It was like being at school again.

'Yes please, something cool,' I said.

I pressed my hand against my forehead, and when the something cool came, I pressed the glass against my forehead too. Father Anthony looked concerned. He looked on the point of ringing his little bell again.

'When you agreed to give this presentation today,' said Father Anthony, 'you asked for a favour in return. You said there was a scientific matter we could help you with. Is it to do with your squid?'

'With Mabel, yes,' I said. 'Strictly speaking, of course, she's not *my* squid. She's not anybody's – not even God's. Do you see? I want to free her. That's what I want your help with.'

'You agree, then, with those activists in town?' said Father Anthony. I realised he was referring to the young people I'd seen at the port; I understood that Mabel was no longer a secret and they were here to protest her captivity. This explained why Eric had been so unforthcoming with me.

'I don't know who they are or what they believe,' I said.

'They want the very same thing you do – to release the squid. You could ask for *their* help.'

I thought of the boys in the bar and the girls on the dock, of their sincerity, their photogenic martyrdom, and the primary colours of their T-shirts, and I said, 'Tomorrow, Father

Anthony, it has to be tomorrow. Before they find her and turn her into something she isn't.'

'Turn her into what?' he asked.

'Do you know very much about colossal squid, Father Anthony?'

'Only the information you presented in your lecture today,' he said. 'Their brains are round with holes in them, like donuts. They have eight arms and two long tentacles.'

'The most important thing I said about colossal squid today, Father Anthony, was that we don't know anything about them. And even though I've been watching Mabel for over a year now, I still know nothing. It's even possible that Mabel is still immature, that she could get bigger. How can we be sure of the true size of the colossal squid? Who knows what we'll fish up some day – the gargantuan squid? We might have gone a step too far, calling this one colossal. Soon we'll run out of superlatives. Wouldn't it be better just to leave things be? They've recorded a mysterious bloop, you know, coming from somewhere underwater, which could only have been made by an animal of unthinkable size. I hope we never find it.'

Father Anthony waved his hand in the direction of his tree-crowded window as if mysterious bloops were none of his business.

'The squid an infant – interesting,' he said. 'But wouldn't it look different if it were so young? Forgive me, but you must know that at least? You scientists?'

'No!' I cried. 'It's impossible to tell. Darwin talks about it in *Origin*: "there is no metamorphosis; the cephalopodic character is established long before the parts of the embryo are completed". A squid is always a squid, right from birth – so we talk of mature or immature squid, but never of infants. The squid has no infancy, which means no nostalgia. It has no Romantic period. Squid think Wordsworth is full of horseshit. They have no childhood! None at all! They're born adult, and the only change they undertake is death. There is no metamorphosis!'

At the end of this speech I felt as pink as Father Anthony looked. There was a ticking in the room; I thought it came from the ivory Jesus crucified on the wall.

Father Anthony drew a long breath. 'Do you like it here on our island?' he asked.

'Actually I'm thinking of leaving.'

'Do you crave human company? That's only natural.'

'I want to be surrounded by people again, but I don't have much desire to talk to them.'

'But you have so many ideas to share,' said Father Anthony. 'If you'll excuse my asking, do you feel quite well? Not everyone can withstand this climate. I myself, many years ago, spent an entire year supine on my bed. The heat, you see, and it led to a sort of spiritual crisis, a lack of faith, you might say, in the sustaining hand of God. I thought I may have dreamed winter. It was only prayer that gave me strength, Bill – the strength of God against the burden of His creation.'

'Prayer!' I said. 'Can I ask you a question? Doesn't faith feel to you like a deep-down knowing, something you've discovered rather than made? And what do you do when you've lost that *knowing*? Hope that praying to something you no longer *know* will get it back for you?'

'Would you like me to pray for you, Bill?'

'I'm not well,' I said. 'I have headaches.'

'I understand,' said Father Anthony, reaching out a hand, and I was able, then, to imagine him laid out on a bed, dreaming winter. 'Why not leave?'

'Mabel.'

'Mabel is the squid, yes?'

'She belongs in the sea.'

'And what do you propose?'

I explained that the net with which we'd plugged Mabel's bay was impossible to move with only two men. I corrected myself – one man. Of course he didn't know about Darwin. Could a priest see the ghost of Darwin? Unlikely. But if all the students were to come down to the bay and we worked together, we could unfasten the net and, very swiftly, move it from one side of the bay to the other, so that Mabel, on escaping, wouldn't tangle herself in it. (Confession: when I imagine this, I have in mind a delirious scene from the Marlon Brando version of *Mutiny on the Bounty* where the girls of Tahiti, bare-breasted, hold an enormous net in the water, into which the native men drive schools of fish.) Father Anthony seemed concerned about this plan. He asked if there would be any danger. I told him no, there would be no danger – unlike octopi, squid are not dangerous to human beings. All those old etchings of whaleboats embraced by monstrous tentacled creatures are completely false. I said this, but we don't really know. No one has ever swum with a colossal squid. But just to be on the safe side, it's my plan to feed Mabel all the fish I have while the girls move the net. I'll get into the water to distract her if I have to. I'll get so close I'll fill her clever eyes.

'Select your strongest swimmers,' I said to Father Anthony. 'Those girls will take the end of the net farthest from the beach. They'll be the ones to swim across the entrance to the bay.'

'I see you've thought this through. Would you excuse me for a minute? I must consult a colleague.'

I let him go with regret. It had begun to grow cool in the room, if it's possible here to have any sense of what cool truly is, and I fancied that this relief emanated in some way from Father Anthony. His pink skin suggested not clammy heat but the smooth, cool skin of a baby. I was content, sitting there in that office. My presentation had gone well. I was acting on my belief that Mabel should be free. It was good to talk to another man again. And, as if offended by this betrayal, Darwin – who was he, if not another man? – appeared at the window with the air of someone casually strolling by. He peered in.

'It's safe,' I said in a loud whisper. Then I gave him the victory sign, at which he looked puzzled.

'Where is he?' asked Darwin.

'Gone for help.'

'Help for whom?'

Darwin ambled away from the window and out into the trees, but I could see the bright camel colour of his naturalist's coat among the greenery; he hadn't gone far. Sitting comfortably in that cooling office, I considered the ways in which Darwin had never been particularly helpful to me, despite the initial promise of his appearance. After all, to a man – a scientist, no less – who has recently lost his faith, the ghost of Darwin could be a rich resource. We might have sat and talked about God's sovereignty, and then about its dissolution: a little of God vanishing into the dodo, a little into the long-lost ichthyosaurus. But he seems impatient when I raise these topics, and I've come to avoid them. I used to think of Charles Darwin in the same way some people think of Jesus Christ: he was a real man who existed in a specific historical time and he taught some valuable lessons, many of which I could adopt with no sense of contradiction. In short, I was a sensible man. I was no Creationist. I was reconciled with Darwin. I weighed it all up, and with the same clever hands I held something else entirely: that joyful faith of mine, impregnable.

I was once quite certain that God so loved the world. How sudden it was, on day 282: God's absence upon my shoulders, like a heavy flightless bird that can still hop to a height. How sobering to pass from Dr William Birch, beloved of God, to Bill Birch, organism. Just to be there on my sticky cliff and feel this way for no specific reason – it was a kind of grief. And I saw Mabel differently after that. How could I help it? She has nothing to do with me. I can't eat or reproduce with her. She's without complication. I was sure of one thing, until I was no longer sure; now my conviction is that Mabel must be free. And not for her own sake, no; although I love her, I would have put her in a tank and watched her in it for the rest of her life, or mine. But now I think she should remain a mystery. There must be some things in the world that no one sees and no one knows. Some monsters.

I began to worry about Father Anthony. Why was he taking so long? I rang the silver bell and a girl appeared. She was about sixteen, neat and shy behind heavy hair, and I felt like a *Bounty* sailor encountering beauty for the first time. I thought of the one mutineer who had the date on which he first saw Tahiti tattooed on his quivering arm.

'Hello,' I said.

'Hello,' she answered. She was solemn, and so was I. The heat had returned.

'Who are you?'

'I'm Faith,' she said, and she was so allegorical, standing there, she may as well have been draped in white robes, placed on a plinth above a plaque that read 'Faith'. I laughed, which startled her.

'Is that really your name?' I asked. 'Or did Father Anthony ask you to come in here and tell me that?'

She was confused but pleased. I knew I wouldn't touch her – I'm not so mad as to have touched her – but I wanted to. I want to. Oh, Tahiti! Was Darwin ever there? No, I don't think so. He preferred dustier places, godforsaken places like the Galápagos, prehistoric with tortoises. This girl and girls like her would come to the beach with me and draw aside the net.

'Do you like to swim, Faith?' I asked.

'Yes,' she answered.

Father Anthony entered the office, and behind him was Eric, the driver.

'Faith!' Father Anthony cried, as if overjoyed to see her, and he ushered her merrily out. She looked back at me very quickly, the way she might look over one shoulder while swimming. Where had she appeared from and where would she go now? Father Anthony went behind his desk but didn't sit down. Eric leaned against the bookshelf.

'Now, Bill,' said Father Anthony. 'You mentioned headaches. The brain is a very delicate thing, which you as a scientist would know very well. The brain and the mind – two different things, yes? Both very delicate. If we're going to help you, I'd like you to do me a favour first.'

'I already gave the lecture,' I said. 'You owe *me* a favour.'

Father Anthony laughed.

'Very true, very true,' he said. 'You're right. But perhaps you'd consider doing this favour anyway. For my sake. Let me just tell you what I have in mind. I'd like you to see a doctor about these headaches of yours. Symptoms that seem harmless enough in other places become much more serious on an island like ours. When I first arrived, I was reluctant to see doctors. I thought I could cope with all the discomforts. But things escalated until I was in the grip of a brain fever.'

'You called it a spiritual crisis,' I pointed out.

'It was, Bill, it was,' he said, smiling, pinker than ever. 'I want you to travel back to town with Eric. There's a doctor on the supply ship, and he's willing to see you. It's either today or you'll have to wait another month. Why suffer needlessly?'

'And the squid?'

'You see the doctor,' said Father Anthony, 'and then we'll worry about the squid.'

'It has to be tomorrow,' I said.

'Tomorrow,' nodded Father Anthony.

Of course he was transparent; a man like Father Anthony always is. He was perched on the edge of his desk, becalmed in his own solicitude, hoping I would submit without fuss to his will. So I did. I allowed myself to be ushered out, I allowed him to assure me that my supplies had been refrigerated, I allowed myself to be seated comfortably in the jeep. Father Anthony followed the jeep as Eric reversed it onto the road, he waved us off as if with a valedictory handkerchief, and I turned my head at the first corner to see him walking toward the school with his arms behind his back, his head lowered, as if in prayer.

Around that first corner I offered to pay Eric to stop the jeep.

'No, no,' he said, intent on the road.

'Please, Eric. This is important. How can I make you understand?'

'Forget it,' he said. 'I'll lose my job. You know how hard it is to earn money here if you want to stay legal? I have a Bachelor of Commerce from the University of Auckland and this is the only work there is. I'll drive you into town. After that you do what you want, I don't care, and if anyone finds out, it's not because I've told them.'

We drove on. Soon afterward I noticed movement in the trees alongside the road. There was Darwin, running. I've never seen a man move so fast. He couldn't quite keep up with the jeep, although he managed it for stretches of a minute or two and at times seemed to extend his right arm out to reach the car door. Perhaps he was trying to warn me of what I already knew. Faithful Darwin sped beside us, the wings of his coat flying out behind him, his feet a blur and his face a study of determined strength. We lost him shortly before town when it was necessary to cross a river and he made the mistake of plunging into the water rather than waiting to follow us on the narrow bridge. I turned to look and saw him thrashing about with the incredulous fury of an Olympian who's just lost the final.

Eric and I parted in town. He made no reference to the doctor, but also no promise of a lift back to the school. I walked through the sandy streets to the end of the beach farthest from the dock, observing the population as I myself was no doubt observed, and I hoped that once I left the island I would never see a place like it again in my life. I longed for escape. The supply ship sat smugly in the harbour, equipped with its doctor, and I was tempted to board it waving a white flag. But who then would free Mabel? If she doesn't belong to God, she belongs nowhere. I must remember to write that into my grant report.

I thought I might find Darwin on the beach, but I found the protesters instead. They talked in groups in the extended shadows of the palm trees. I walked toward them with my hands in the pockets of my trousers, and when they saw me coming they stirred with hope and indignation. I stopped a few feet from them, and despite the failing light they peered up at me with their hands cupped over their eyes, as if the absurd sun of the island's midday had forced them into a permanent habit.

'Good evening,' I said.

'Hi,' they chorused.

A blond boy stood, handsome, a kind of voluntary Achilles. He advanced toward me. 'Maybe you can help us,' he said. He seemed to be wondering aloud. A ripple of assent went through the group: Yes, yes, they seemed to sigh, maybe he can help us.

'I hear you're looking for transportation,' I said.

'Do you have a car? Even better, a truck?' said the boy.

'A bus?' called one wag, and they laughed.

'Where is it that you'd like to go?'

'We need to get to the other side of the island,' said the boy. 'Do you know of a scientist, a Dr William Birch?'

'Bill Birch, yes. Sure I do.'

'And you're not him?'

'Me? I'm no scientist,' I answered, and for some reason they all laughed again, perhaps in relief. The boy began to explain to me that he – they – objected to the work Dr Birch was doing with a certain captive squid. He was guarded, but furious. They'd all been together on some kind of ecology project in the Cook Islands when news of Dr Birch's work broke, and had talked their way onto the supply ship.

'That was only three days ago,' the boy said, with pride. 'We're here before the media.'

'So you want to get to Dr Birch,' I said.

'No one seems to know where he is,' said the boy. 'It's like he's a hermit or something.'

It thrills me to know the locals protected me from that lovable, good-looking, deluded band.

'I know where he is,' I said, 'and I'll do what I can to get you to him.'

They rose up as one then, and surrounded me with their relief and zeal, shouting names at me and asking mine.

'Eric Anthony,' I said. 'Now tell me, what would you have said if I'd been Dr Birch?'

'We'd have said we were marine biology students,' said Todd, the Achilles. 'Who wouldn't want to see a colossal squid if they had the chance?'

And they asked me to take a photo of them, all together on the beach; it was a beautiful picture, sand-lit, and they pressed together inside its frame with such health and trust that I wanted to – I did – like them, very much. And I knew they would help me if I asked them to; they would swim out across the bay, they would remove the net, they would farewell Mabel with me, sending her seaward, and every second of her escape would be captured on their phones. Mabel would swim forever in a digital sea. She'd be free, but all the world would know her.

In town, I had more luck than they had finding transportation. I paid for the use of a utility truck owned by a friend of Eric's and the crusaders climbed into the tray with their knapsacks. I even bought them supplies and checked the batteries in their torches. The townspeople watched us. Again, it pleased me to think that the only person they would betray me to was myself. Todd rode in the front with me. He asked what I did on the island and I told him I taught in a Catholic school near Dr Birch's camp. I told him we would pass the school and that they should walk up to visit me there whenever they needed to get into town. He asked if I lived at the school, and I said yes. He asked if I was Catholic, and I said yes. This all came very easily.

Todd is an earnest and admirable young man. I'd be proud to have a son like him. But he plays no part in my vision of freeing Mabel, and my principal concern was to cause him as much inconvenience as possible. To accomplish this, I dropped him and his cheerful gang at the head of a trail leading to a beach a few bays east of my observation station and told them that Mabel, far from being trapped in a small inlet, was enclosed by the coral reef and had the whole lagoon to move around in.

'Don't go swimming,' I said. 'She's probably pretty angry by now.'

'Are colossal squid dangerous?' asked Todd.

'Deadly.'

I told them Bill Birch moved his camp from place to place in the jungle, so they might have trouble finding him at first. I said that he was essentially harmless, that the machete he carried was only for cutting paths; I warned them, too, that he was hard of hearing and jumpy when startled. I said I knew they were responsible kids and would act with appropriate caution. We unloaded their gear onto the road. I moved the truck so the headlights shone down along the trail. They remarked on the audible ocean and seemed much less nervous than they should have; they said goodbye, they expressed their gratitude, and then they plunged off into the humid trees. When they were far beyond the beam of my headlights, Darwin bounded onto the road like a stricken kangaroo.

'There you are,' I said.

He climbed into the truck and sat rigidly, like a boy waiting for a rollercoaster to descend its first hill.

'You've never been in a car before, have you?' I said.

He shook his head. I gave him quite a ride. There are some hairpin bends on this old volcano that can knot your intestines like a skilful sailor. By the time we got back to the observation station we were both giddy as schoolboys. We walked out onto the cliff and looked down at Mabel. It was dark, of course, and colossal squid are not, to my or anyone's knowledge, phosphorescent, but I would be willing to swear that I saw her outline glowing very faintly from the bottom of her bay.

That was last night. I slept late this morning, day 498, and spent the afternoon writing this account. Now Darwin is with me, and it's pleasant to see him in the fullest light of the day; he seems more definite and in this way more ordinary. The weather is clear, so we amuse ourselves by pretending we can see New Zealand. I don't know what's become of Eric; I don't know what report he's given Father Anthony. No one has come looking for me. I imagine the supply ship has left by now. I imagine I'll spend the next month in town living on this newly discovered goodwill of the locals, just another oddball wanderer. The protesters will find me, eventually, and we'll make friends; we'll laugh together when they hear what it is I've done, and one of the girls, less pretty, perhaps, but kind, will take pity on me. I'll resign my position, of course. I'll take the next ship; I'll go home. Darwin says he won't come with me. He's scornful of Australia and talks of England with the adoration of exile. This is all as it should be. Unless, unless, I get too close to Mabel, and she takes me with her.

In these last few minutes I've felt the swimmy brimming

that precedes an attack of vertigo. I feel it as a pressure in my feet. Soon, I know, the earth will fall away from them, and this too is as it should be. My head seems to press outward. To myself I say, Shark, anemone, starfish, seahorse, eel. My main concern was that if Eric raised the alarm, Father Anthony wouldn't permit the girls to take their daily swim. But here they come now, down the mountain. They're singing, of course, and Faith is among them. She's singing softly. She likes to swim. She'll wade out into the water and the other girls will follow her. What is it about being immersed in water that's so exciting, so vital to us? We all experience it – this thrill of feeling the medium we move in as something dangerous and contingent. It reminds us of the artifice of oxygen and gravity, the sheer unlikelihood of their provision. We feel the water close around our arms and legs and we make our way through it with difficulty and determination, singing and proclaiming and making promises, kneeling and rising and sitting and standing. It feels like the unbearable presence of God, His hands on our submarine chests. A blowfish might waft past, inflated, with a look of dumb surprise on its face. I have basketfuls of fish ready to feed to Mabel. The girls will take hold of the net; I'll watch as they rise through the sea with it into the air. The light will billow and flare around them in the bright wind, and their hands will reach out to Heaven as if strung on trapeze wires. I'll wade through the shallows, wet to my stupid waist, then I'll kick downward and swim. Darwin will observe from the shore in his nineteenth-century socks. And Mabel will fly seaward, holy and beautiful, a bony-beaked messenger bringing no news.

The High Places

In the fifth year of drought, Jack prayed for rain. His wife was always praying and had developed a pinched, devout look, which Jack found more and more distasteful as the drought years passed. He felt her praying in bed beside him, with her hands folded in the bony country of her ribs, and was irritated by her little offerings to Heaven. She went to church every Sunday and took the children, who were invariably difficult when they returned home. For a long time, Jack thought this was because of the drive: two hours there, two hours back, shuddering on the torn, hot seats of the truck. The girls on Sundays were skittish and rude, and they complained: about the heat, the flies, and the style of their church dresses. During the week they kept to themselves. They stayed in their bedroom – the Girls' Room – taking lessons by two-way radio. But on Sundays they were reminded of what it was like to be among people, and it was this, Jack concluded, that made them unruly. They teased him on Sundays, which he quite enjoyed, until one of them went too far. Then by certain gestures of his, and his tone of voice, they knew to stop.

The boy was harder to understand, not because he was wild but because he spent his Sundays vague and blushing. Jack disliked his son's solitary nature. There was no form to it. It had a feeble, dreamy quality, and he was always worse after church. Then he would take his bible and sit outside under the red gum to read. Grass had never grown under the red gum, even before the drought, but the ground was littered with the bark and leaves the tree shed. The messy ground sloped down to the dry waterhole, which was itself such a white, rocky pit in the afternoon heat that the boy, on the bright ground under the loose tree, appeared to be sitting and reading his bible in a lit haze, in a ring of fire. He was sixteen. He was old enough to know it was too hot to be outside, too fruitless to read the Bible, too dangerous to sit under the fragile limbs of a red gum, known with good reason as widowmakers. Watching his son beneath the tree, Jack felt a tightening of the inner organs. Every Sunday, the boy came to dinner only reluctantly, as if ashamed to need any sustenance beyond the word of God. And he kept his bible with him at the table, by his plate, where its blank burgundy face accused Jack of something he couldn't identify: some form of neglect, some deficiency, some failure of will or spirit.

There was a Sunday in the fifth year of the drought, before Jack had begun to pray for rain, on which the boy came to dinner willingly and, rather than just leaving the bible on the table, opened it and cleared his throat, preparing to read. The girls giggled. They were all younger than he was, with smoother skin and blonder hair; they considered their brother weird. Jack's wife turned her tired, ready face to her son. The kitchen buzzed under neon light and the moths of early evening battered the window screens. Jack took a lamb chop in his hands.

'Listen,' read the boy. 'I tell you a mystery: we will not all sleep, but we will all be changed – in a flash, in the twinkling of an eye, at the last trumpet. For the trumpet will sound, the dead will be raised imperishable, and we will be changed.'

Jack bit into his lamb chop.

'Amen,' said his wife.

'Can we eat now?' asked the oldest girl, and as if her question had been a form of permission, she and her sisters took up their knives and forks and began to scrape and chew.

'We will not all sleep,' said the boy. 'But we will all be changed.'

'All right, son,' said Jack, and the boy gave him a dim, unseeing look, put the bible down, and turned to his dinner. The family ate without speaking, and when they had finished it was night.

In bed, Jack felt the slight movement of his wife's hands as she prayed.

'Do you ever pray for rain?' he asked her.

'Not specifically,' she said. 'I pray for God's will to be done.' And she leaned over to kiss him on the cheek. Her body was like the thin run of a creek in the bed, a low creek that puts out the small noises of a comfort it can't deliver.

Jack's mind turned over his son's phrase: 'We will all be changed.' He liked the sound of it. It seemed generous to him. But the dead rising imperishable bothered Jack, who had killed and buried most of his sheep when he couldn't afford to feed them; he knew the rot and stink of a sheep left too long. He amused himself, anyway, with a vision: he heard the last trumpet, which sounded like the Reveille, and saw his sheep rise from the earth, whole and round and white, like silly clouds. He smiled in his dry bed, and slept.

The next day was one on which Jack always felt certain of himself. It was time, on Mondays, to create the world again. Jack and the boy drove out to the western edge of the property to repair fences. The shake of the truck over the ridged paddocks produced so much noise that whole thirsty flocks of birds flew out of the few trees. The boy, too, was different on Mondays: obedient, attentive, with a sort of waiting stillness his father took for concentration. They worked together all morning, although they both knew there was no need to repair these particular fences, which kept nothing in or out. The land was flat and grey. There was no wind, but the soil was so fine it flew up with every kick or shuffle of a boot, and that was like wind. The boy sang a little. They worked hard through the long, steady morning.

At midday the boy stopped to look at the sky. So Jack looked and saw, coming toward them, a long, light cloud, like a pillar laid sideways, like a plank of quality wood. The sky was otherwise empty. There was no rain in the cloud, Jack could tell, but it was moving so quickly and was such a strange colour, so golden-green, as if it were reflecting the steady burning of a diseased flame, that he became uneasy. The air was charged, the way it used to be before a storm. The boy dropped to his knees in a slack and yielding way. He took up fistfuls of dirt, which he rubbed in his hair.

'Christ almighty,' said Jack, as he might have said another day, at some other peculiarity of his son's, but today the boy made a strangled yell as if to smother the words. The cloud rushed toward them. It reminded Jack of the surf he'd seen on a coastal holiday: a long green running line. And there was that same ominous, swimming feeling.

'Cover your eyes!' called the boy, and pressed his face to the ground. The cloud was so close now that Jack thought he should be able to see through it to the sky beyond, but it was as if the sky behind the cloud were no longer there, and nothing had replaced it. He found himself hiding his face in terror as the cloud passed overhead. A brief, cold shadow crossed the ground. The boy sobbed and shook, lying there in the dirt, and Jack saw, to his surprise, that he too was crouched down and shaking. But the sky and the world were ordinary now, the smell of the dirt was ordinary, and there was no sign of the cloud. Jack wasn't afraid to look. He wondered why he'd been so frightened.

'Come on now,' he said to his son. 'Back at it.'

But the boy had lost his strength. He tried to stand and couldn't. His skin was an unusual shade of yellow-pink and a thick liquid ran from his nose. The joy of Monday and of work was lost for Jack, so he took the gear to the truck and stood over his son, nudged him in the back with a boot, and, when he didn't move, bent down and lifted him at the armpits. He dragged the boy to the truck and hoisted him in. A sixteen-year-old son is heavy. His feet are large and his limbs are long. Only closing the door of the truck very quickly could keep him from tumbling out of it.

Driving home, Jack said, 'Fix yourself up,' and, 'Jesus Christ,' and stopped the truck so the boy could lean out of the window to be sick. Afterward the boy slumped against the door, exhausted, but was able to manage the weight of his head.

They arrived at the house. 'No need to say anything much to your mother,' said Jack.

They walked together up the steps to the veranda and into the front hall; the boy leaned on Jack as he went, with one hand held out in front of him as if afraid he might fall. Dirt flickered from his hair.

The girls swarmed out of their bedroom with wide eyes.

'What's wrong with him?' said the oldest. 'Is he sick?' The radio spoke behind them: 'A verb,' it said, 'is a doing word.'

Jack's wife came from the kitchen. She ran to the boy and touched his filthy hair.

'Too much sun,' said Jack.

They were a solemn procession going down the hallway to the boy's bedroom: the boy leaning on his father, his mother behind them, the girls following until she shooed them.

'Does he need a doctor?' she asked.

Jack shook his head. He pressed the boy down onto the bed.

'Was there a voice?' asked the boy. 'Did you hear it?'

'Let him sleep it off,' said Jack.

'The whirlwind,' said the boy.

Jack led his wife from the room.

'What's this about a whirlwind?' she asked.

'A lot of rot,' said Jack.

He left the house, climbed into the truck, and drove over to look at the last of his sheep. They trembled under the pepper trees. They were loaded with flies. Jack went carefully to his knees and prayed for rain.

The boy stayed in his bedroom for a few days. The girls lost interest in him. His mother brought him food and news of the unchanging weather. Jack went out to work on the fences. He prayed as he worked, and, having begun to pray, grew more impatient with the passivity of his wife's prayers. He disliked the helpless, quiet way she made her approach and her lack of any particular request. His own prayers were more specific. *Almighty God*, he said, *make it rain. Create a weather pattern that means rain. Raise the air, God, faster and faster, until a cloud forms. Load the cloud until it has to rain. Fill the waterhole and the creek and the dams. Make the grass grow. And while it does, lower the price of hay.*

Protect my land from the banks. May the banks shrivel up and die, like my grass. May they be killed and buried, like my sheep. Bring my sheep back from the dead, imperishable. And look after my son, Lord, if he's crazy. May he not be crazy. May he be content with life, and strong. Amen.

Jack didn't tell his wife he had begun to pray because he didn't want to go to church with her. He also thought it would be unjust if she took any credit for his prayerfulness, which had more to do with the absence of the sky behind the cloud than her own scheduled devotion. The Sunday following his son's 'turn', Jack stayed in bed until long after he heard the truck driving away from the house. It had been easy to avoid his son while the boy slept and shuffled in his room, but the boy was up early that Sunday, calling his sisters out of bed, clattering up and down the hallway, telling his mother in a loud voice that he would drive. Jack couldn't stand to look at his rejuvenated son. He lay in bed until midday, which he hadn't done in decades, until he felt a sweat descend on him, and a buzzing in his legs. The sweat and buzzing got him out of bed.

There had been a time, when the children were small, when Jack wouldn't let his wife go to church because he didn't think small children should travel four hours in the old truck. He liked to see his wife on Sunday mornings, too; to keep her in bed. When she protested, he reminded her that she knew what she was getting into, marrying onto a sheep station in the middle of nowhere. But he'd bought the radio. It wasn't entirely a luxury, since they'd need one eventually for the children's education, but his wife thought of it that way. When it arrived and she saw the size of it, she held his hand. She listened to the city news and pretty songs and foreign languages, and on Sundays she tuned in to religious programmes. She sat in the Girls' Room, still a nursery, still not entirely filled with girls, and he heard her singing along with the hymns in a thin, fine voice, which seemed to lift up of its own accord and float above the house. He remembered hoping that the vastness of the sky over their property would not entirely dissolve the song. He'd been fanciful like that, in those days.

On the Sunday after the cloud, Jack went into the Girls' Room. The midday sun struck at the beds through the window. Each single bed was spread with a yellow coverlet; each little desk was clear of possessions. It was a room, Jack saw, to which no one was tied, and that no one would be sorry to leave. Against the far wall stood the high-frequency two-way radio transceiver through which his children learned, with growing confidence, of the existence of an outside world made up of things like tall buildings, speedboats, elephants and rain.

Jack tuned the radio in and out of pop songs and newsy chat until he found a promising voice: a deep, certain voice of painful energy and, behind it, the low hum of organ music.

'Have you noticed,' said the voice, 'how many significant biblical events take place on hilltops?'

Jack sat in one of his daughters' desk chairs.

'Let's think about it,' said the voice. 'The ark came to rest on Ararat. Abraham sacrificed Isaac on Mount Moriah. The bush burned on Mount Horeb, and the Law came to Moses on Sinai. Elijah tested the prophets of Baal on Mount Carmel,

David built his palace on Zion. Jesus preached from a mountain, and he died on Golgotha hill. He wept for Jerusalem on the Mount of Olives, and from the Mount of Olives he ascended to Heaven.'

Jack thought he recognised some of these stories.

'Listen, friend,' said the voice, which lulled and throbbed. 'God is in the high places.'

Jack thought about his property, which was flat to each horizon and lower than sea level. The whole plain on which his sheep had died and his wife had grown old had once been an inland sea. It had filled and sunk over millennia and was a long way from any mountain.

'The Israelites knew it,' said the voice, 'and before they built their Temple on the Mount, they sought out the high places to make sacrifices to Yahweh. They sought out the high places to make and fulfill vows. They went to the high places, friends, to worship God.'

Jack turned off the radio and left the Girls' Room. It angered him to think God listened harder to people standing on a hill; that those people might be given rain and healthy sons and living sheep. Even so, it seemed right that there might be particular places in which conversation with God would be more effective. He didn't think his wife, with her bedtime prayers, had found such a place.

Jack thought he would see what it felt like under the red gum. He walked out into the heat, which pressed at him from all sides; he felt the sweat gather in the small of his back, and he felt the sun dry it. The closer he got to the red gum, the more his inner organs suffered a kind of squeeze. He stood beneath the stifling tree, and the brightness of the light from the white waterhole was like a wall of fire, but if the boy could sit out here for hours every week then so could Jack. It didn't surprise him to learn that making requests of God might also involve suffering. He sat on the ground with his back against the trunk.

'Almighty God,' he said, 'make it rain.'

And the seriousness of what he was asking, the great size of it, was brought home to him by the noise of the gum as it cracked and strained, the hot light of the sun through the branches, and the sound of the largest, oldest, most rotten limb as it fell: the airborne rush of leaves, the snap of smaller sections, and finally the clatter of wood hitting the ground. The fallen branch was itself the size of a substantial tree, and it lay so close to him he could stretch out his foot to touch it; if he'd been sitting just a little farther to the left he would have been partially or wholly crushed. But he was unharmed. Jack moaned as the boy had done at the passing of the cloud. He gathered dirt in his hands. Unlike his son, he didn't rub the dirt in his hair. He only sat motionless beneath the tree, terrified by God.

When he heard the truck approaching the house, Jack found he was able to sit up and dust himself off. He watched the truck stop and the girls traipse inside. He watched their mother follow them with her handbag swinging, calling his name, and when he didn't answer, the girls began to call for him as well.

The boy turned away from the truck with his bible in his hand, heading for the tree. Jack stood. He felt composed enough to place one foot on the topmost part of the fallen branch, with his knee bent, as if he had planted a flag there and claimed it for his own.

The boy ran to him. 'It must be four metres long,' he said.

Jack kicked at the branch. 'What did I tell you? Widow-makers.'

His son looked up into the tree, lifting his bible to shield his eyes from the glare.

'Was it a wind?' the boy asked. 'Was it the cloud again?'

The girls and their mother came running from the house.

'Dad! Dad!' cried the girls, delighted by the catastrophe of the fallen branch. They inspected everything. Their mother stopped farther away. She wanted, Jack knew, to order them all out from under the tree. She wanted to gather and scold them, but had lost that habit.

Jack didn't tell them he'd been sitting under the tree when the limb fell. He said he'd heard it from the house. The boy stood with his bible shading his eyes, looking at the dirt on his father's back and under his fingernails.

Jack spent the afternoon cutting the branch into firewood. The boy paced on the veranda, where his sisters sat crowded over a borrowed magazine. The girls read with a solemnity unusual to them on a Sunday and kept looking up from the pages as if fascinated by their father's labour. Their mother stood at the kitchen window peeling vegetables in slow, even strokes. Jack felt them all keeping him in their sights. He felt it in his spine and his gut; it was a pleasant constriction. The girls talked in thrilled whispers about how lucky it was their brother hadn't been under the tree when the branch fell. There was a conspiracy among them, of longing and possibility and dread, and this glamorised their brother, so they endured his pacing and the strange way he cleared his throat at the sky.

The boy didn't bring his bible to dinner. He didn't speak as he had the previous week. He only stabbed a lamb chop with his fork and held it over his plate. The girls were more expectant than usual, bright around the eyes.

'Well, dig in,' said Jack, and the girls began to eat, their faces turned to their food. But they snuck looks at their brother, who finally lifted the chop with his fingers the way their father did and tore into it with his teeth.

Jack was revolted by the sound of the boy's teeth in the fibres of the lamb and the creaking of the bone as he dug out the marrow with his long finger. He couldn't eat with all this noise, and pushed away his plate. That was enough to stop his daughters, who held their knives and forks in the air. But the boy reached for another lamb chop with a slippery hand.

'The sermon was excellent this morning,' said his mother.

'Oh?' said Jack, careful to keep a casual, disdainful note in his voice.

'We learnt about sacrifice,' she said. She laid her cutlery down on the table. 'We learnt about making burnt offerings of our lives.'

'Burnt offerings!' scoffed her son, waving the lamb chop above his plate.

'Sounds uncomfortable,' said Jack. Still with that light tone in his voice, the one his daughters knew to be wary of.

'We have to be willing to give everything to God,' said the oldest girl in her proud and piping voice. Her sisters looked at her in awe. 'He demands it of us.'

'Oh, but we demand it of ourselves,' said her mother with a sigh, as if the effort of this demand were unbearably sweet.

The boy laughed again. 'Your descendants will be strangers in a country not their own,' he said. 'And we will all be changed.'

'You watch yourself,' said Jack, still light, but in a lower tone, with his face only partially turned toward his son. The girls shrank a little in their chairs. Their mother wore a plaintive face, her own burnt offering.

'I'm not afraid of you,' said the boy. He dropped the chop onto his plate, wiped his hands on the tablecloth, and said to his sisters, 'I'll tell you a great mystery. This man died today. He was crushed by a tree, but God raised him.'

Jack brought his fist down on the table and the plates and glasses jumped.

'He was raised, and he was changed. I'm not afraid of him.'

Jack leaned over and struck the back of his son's head. The boy cried out. Then he ducked his head and laughed.

'A burnt offering!' he said. His nose bubbled with snot. His sisters were silent; his mother lowered her face. Jack lifted his hand again. 'Fire from below,' said the boy, almost singing, 'and water from above.' He cringed as Jack's hand flew. 'That's what the voice said from the whirlwind. He heard it! This man!'

Jack's mouth was filled with a bitter fluid. He swallowed it down. He said, 'You make me sick.' Then he walked out of the house and climbed into the back seat of the truck. There was a blanket in there and he pulled it over him. He would spend the night in the truck, away from his family. He would stay out of the house so the roof couldn't fall on him. He pulled the blanket over his head so no part of the sky was visible. That way he might be hidden from God.

His sheep rose in the night. Jack felt them nudging at the truck, which rocked so that it seemed to him, lying in the back seat, as if he were in a boat. There was a sea sound, too – but it turned out to be the soft murmur of the sheep as they brushed against each other. They had risen from the dead, whole flocks of them, a wealth of sheep, imperishable after all: they were plump and perfectly shorn, not a nick on their bodies, not a curl of wool anywhere but on their heads, except they had the tails they were born with. Jack could see the sheep around the truck although he was still beneath the blanket. He was comforted by their perfection, their great number, their eternal life. He closed his eyes and slept.

When he woke, the truck was moving at some speed. He threw the blanket off and sat up. It was day and his son was driving. There *were* sheep – five or six dirty ewes in the bed of the truck. Jack's head thundered, and his throat was so dry he only wheezed when he opened his mouth to speak.

'Morning, Dad,' said the boy. 'Might want to wear your seatbelt.'

The truck flew over a ditch. Jack jumped in his seat and the sheep tumbled behind him.

'Slow down,' said Jack. His voice almost sounded like itself.

'Sorry,' said the boy.

Jack climbed between the seats into the front of the truck. The clock on the dashboard read 10:02, but they were already hours from the house and driving west: away from water, away from the last of the grass, and into that arid plain out of which the cloud had risen a week ago.

'You turn this truck around,' said Jack, without conviction.

His son grinned at him from behind the wheel. 'Nup,' he said.

'Where are we going?'

'Dunno,' the boy said.

'And the sheep?'

The boy laughed, but not the way he had the night before. This was a brief, ordinary, Monday laugh. It took in his father and the truck and the sheep and the sun as it rose over them, and it laughed at each of them in turn, and then at itself. It wasn't serious. 'Burnt offering,' he said.

Jack was in a state of steady calm. He felt as he once had when he sat down to a test at school and knew the answers.

'Then we go somewhere high,' he said. 'We find a hill.'

The boy nodded. 'All right then,' he said.

Jack felt a strange pulse in his side, the side closest to his son; he was aware of a tethering there, and he reached out his hand and put it on the boy's shoulder.

'Your mother will worry,' he said, and the sheep all cried out together as if in agreement. But it was the absence of his wife and her worry, and of his pretty daughters, that made Jack's calm possible. Without them he felt able to enter into a new arrangement with his son, which might turn out to be binding.

They drove all day to find a high place. There were a few mounds that sometimes looked like ancient burial sites and sometimes looked like piles of fossilised dung. But these mounds were high only in relation to the flatness of the land around them. By midafternoon, a ridge of hills became visible to the west, but they hung on the horizon as the truck continued to clamber over the plain and nothing ever grew nearer or farther away. The road was very rough now. It might not have been a road. There was spare petrol in a jerry can, but the boy had brought no food and only a small bottle of water. Their mouths were so dry they didn't speak unless it was absolutely necessary, and for hours it was never absolutely necessary. At one point they swapped seats and Jack drove. The boy opened the glove box and showed him the slaughter knife he had placed there. The truck pointed into the west.

They reached the hills in the early evening. The sun was low on the other side of the hills; the gum trees on their tops were lit gold, but the twilight on the eastern slopes seemed to Jack to be the shadow of the day of resurrection. It was there in the permanence of the rock, the perpetual grey-green of the eucalyptus trees, and the great flocks of white parrots that rose into the air like souls. Jack was so thirsty by this time he'd begun to think about licking his own eyeballs. The sheep had been silent for hours. His son, however, was animated and alert. Jack worried that night would fall before they reached the tallest hill. What if they chose a hill thinking it seemed the highest, but when they woke in the morning saw it was overshadowed by something higher? So he drove faster among the hills, finding the road and losing it again, driving along the gullies between the rises, while the sky dissolved.

Just before it was fully dark, the truck went skidding over a sandy patch of old river and tipped into the ditch of a dry waterhole.

It wasn't a deep hole. One good rain would soak it; one storm would fill it up. The truck hissed and the sheep scrambled onto the sloping ground. Jack and his son followed them up the rough sides of the hole. A hill rose above them, rounded in shape, and grass grew on it, which the sheep had seen or smelled. They butted against each other in their frenzy to eat, but Jack wouldn't let them stop. He ran at and around them, the way his dogs did; he clicked and yapped, and his son ran and yapped, too, the knife tucked into his belt. Jack's lungs tightened and burned as he struggled up the hill. The sheep scattered and were frightened by the smallest noise, but were too tired to disobey. Although it was dark by the time they reached the top, with only a small piece of moon rising in the east-northeast, Jack could feel the weight of the view all around him, and how much closer he was to the sky.

The sheep settled down to eat. The boy made a ring of stones around a bare patch of earth, and Jack stripped bark and branches from trees. One stray spark and the hills would catch and the fire would race over the waterless plain, all the way to the house and the girls and their mother. But they knew how to build a good, safe fire. Jack was careful about the length of the branches and the boy packed the stones tight. The cigarette lighter flicked in the dark as the boy sought out stones, and its flame sprang and kindled as it met the waiting wood. The fire was like liquid pouring up and out of the branches; Jack would have liked to drink it.

The boy hit the sheep on the back of the head with the handle of the knife, one by one until they all lay stunned on the ground. Then he gave the knife to his father, who slit their throats and severed their spinal cords. Jack angled the knife so the blood ran out in a tidy pool. The smell of it rose over the burning wood. His son helped him throw the sheep onto the fire. The flames dulled and grew waxy around the first carcass. By the fourth, they had to load on more wood and widen the stone circle. The final sheep took some effort to place: they heaved it onto the top of the fire, but it rolled down. It required three attempts. By then the fire was so high it lit the whole top of the hill. A breeze lifted and blew, but the fire stayed in its circle of stones.

Jack looked into the sky, which, being night, wasn't there.

'Almighty God,' he said. 'Make it rain.'

The boy turned to his father. 'That's all you want? Rain?'

Jack felt his intestines pull tight.

'When you could ask for anything?' said the boy. 'When God felled and raised you? When He spoke to you from the whirlwind? When you saw His hand?'

'I didn't see any hand,' said Jack. He held his own hands behind his back. The blood on them had dried. He wanted to lift them to the sky, or raise them to the fire. He wanted in some way to satisfy his son. 'What do you want, then?'

The boy turned back to the fire. 'To be changed,' he said.

They slept that night on the hill with the scratch of dirty grass and the smell of roasting sheep. There was a particular quality to Jack's second night of bedless sleep. It was leaden without being deep. It afforded no visions: he knew he was hungry and thirsty on top of a stinking hill, that his wife was alone in their wide bed, wondering and calling out to God, imagining disasters of every kind and bowing her head to accept them, and there was dignity in this, and it was hopeless. But no disasters came as he lay on the grass; no trees toppled, no stars fell, no fire spread. No snakes or spiders crawled across the ground. The world, in the morning, hadn't ended. So Jack expected, when he opened his eyes, to see the plain flooded with rain. Or if not that, then a clouded sky. Or at least to feel a barometric shift. He'd been obedient. He'd sought God. He had so few sheep to spare. But the early sky was empty.

Jack stood on the hilltop. It was so long since he'd seen an elevated view, and he was disgusted, standing there, by the terrible dry sloped world, the thinness he felt in the air around him, and the small distance between Heaven and Earth. He could look through one cloud and the sky was gone. He could look into the branches of a tree and watch Heaven's light fall beside him. He could stand on a hill and see the hand of God, laid out there over the plain: each knuckle and vein, and all the fingers.

The boy moaned. He lay covered in ash next to the fire. His hair and fingernails were ashy-white. The sheep were black but still whole. Flies and ants gathered at the blood. Jack wondered what his son had seen and heard in the night. Had a voice come? A cloud? Or some other thing that might visit a holy boy? But the boy only moaned in the ash. The moans were forced and slack. Jack stood above, looking down, as his son curled and wept. The change had come in the night, with the fire and the absence of voice and cloud. The boy was real now. He was abandoned and ready, again, to be loved. He turned his face into the ash; he breathed and coughed it. The sun was already heating the little dew.

Acknowledgements

The stories in this book were written over a period of ten years, and in that time many people offered me assistance, support, feedback, encouragement and love. I'm so thankful to all of them, and these ones in particular:

First, as always, my family: Ian, Lyn, Katrina, Evan, Bonita and Rowan McFarlane. In loving memory of Janice Jessop, my beautiful Aunty Jan. And welcome, little Anneka.

Everyone at the Gernert Company, but especially my wonderful, wise, patient agent, Stephanie Cabot, who has trusted and guided me since the time of angels. Particular thanks to Chris Parris-Lamb for his brilliant readings of the earlier stories.

Everyone at Penguin Books Australia, especially Ben Ball and Meredith Rose. At Sceptre, Carole Welch and Nikki Barrow. And at FSG, Mitzi Angel and Ileene Smith. Thank you for taking such care of my words, and for making them so much better.

All the editors who worked on the published versions of these stories, particularly Michael Ray at *Zoetrope: All-Story*, Deborah Treisman at the *New Yorker* and Evelyn Somers at the *Missouri Review*.

The writing of this book was supported by generous grants and fellowships from the Australia Council for the Arts; St John's College, Cambridge; the Fine Arts Work Center in Provincetown; Phillips Exeter Academy; and the Michener Center for Writers. Thank you for making these stories possible.

At Cambridge: the NCR – especially Andrew Goodwin, Jonathan Gledhill and Keiko Nowacka – and the AAAW. Also Sarah

Hall, Bharat Tandon and Jacob Polley, with thanks for their early encouragement.

At the Fine Arts Work Center: Salvatore Scibona, Roger Skillings and the glorious Fellows of 2006–7 and 2007–8 (especially the fiction writers). Members of Stuckshop: Mabel, unstuck, is for you, with eternal gratitude.

At the University of Texas: my beloved Michener class of 2012, all the other writers I shared classes and margaritas with, and all their partners and children who became my Texan family. My teachers, Elizabeth McCracken (again and again and again), Edward Carey, Pete La Salle, Tony Giardina, Joseph Skibell, Jim Crace and Brigit Pegeen Kelly. Jim Magnuson, Marla Akin, Debbie Dewees, Michael Adams and Elizabeth Cullingford, for all their wisdom, encouragement and kindness. The citizens of Porway. And my smart, funny, talented students.

Back in Sydney: Prue Axam, Ceridwen Dovey, Michelle de Kretser, Jack Ellis, Erin Gough, Liz Allen, Emma Kersey, Amelia Westlake, Cathryn Lee and the St George gang. You've made me love being home again.

Sophie Smith, Steve McClure and Cheri Johnson for taking such beautiful care of India and Charlotte.

India and Charlotte.

Special thanks and love to Virginia Reeves, Sally Smith, Sean Pryor, Nam Le, Luke Muszkiewicz, Hannah and Margot Muszkiewicz, Kate Finlinson and Mimi Chubb. Your friendship has been so important to this book and to me.

And to Emma Jones, who read every word first – thank you, for everything. This book is yours.

FIONA MCFARLANE

The Night Guest

In an isolated house on the New South Wales coast, Ruth, a widow whose sons have flown the nest, lives alone. Until one day a stranger bowls up, announcing that she's Frida, sent to be Ruth's carer.

At first, Ruth welcomes Frida's vigorous presence and her willingness to hear Ruth's tales of growing up in Fiji. She even helps reunite Ruth with a childhood sweetheart. But why does Ruth sense a tiger prowling through the house at night? Is she losing her wits? Can she trust the enigmatic Frida? And how far can she trust herself?

SCEPTRE